BILLIONAIRE SUICIDE CLUB

BILLIONAIRE SUICIDE CLUB

Inspired by Robert Louis Stevenson's *Suicide Club*

Guy Winter

ISBN: 9798644204908

"I am only a unit, but I am a unit in an army. I know Death's private door. I am one of his familiars, and can show you into eternity without ceremony and yet without scandal."

***The Story of the Young Man with the Cream Tarts,* Robert Louis Stevenson**

"The laws evolved by one particular species, for the convenience of that species, are, by their nature, concerned only with the capacities of that species - against a species with different capacities they simply become inapplicable."

***The Midwich Cuckoos,* John Wyndham**

"Hold up the light. Here is a small burnt patch of flooring; here is the tinder from a little bundle of burnt paper, but not so light as usual, seeming to be steeped in something; and here is—is it the cinder of a small charred and broken log of wood sprinkled with white ashes, or is it coal? Oh, horror, he IS here!"

***Bleak House,* Charles Dickens**

"Please don't confront me with my failures/

I had not forgotten them."

***These Days,* Nico**

CHAPTER 1

CASCO VIEJO, PANAMA CITY, REPUBLIC OF PANAMA

Laurence Pearce adjusted the acoustic tube earpiece one last time, then lit up a Camel to keep his fingers from fidgeting with it. It was like a mantra during his novitiate: the more you touch covert comms kit, the more likely the electronics are to fail. The dreaded technical fault that could leave you all alone in the field. And this was no time to be alone. He was way out in bandit country now, stranded on the bogey side of the metal detectors. He resisted the temptation to straighten his bow tie again. That could also come loose, if tampered with once too often. And a classic butterfly knot was one thing Pearce did pride himself on. This time the mission could depend on it. He watched his life flash by in freeze-frame, a series of reflections back from the black and white photos on the wall, as he strode along the corridor to Room 14. A portrait of the assassin as a young man. He smiled. His tailored dinner suit was elegant enough to convey the man of the world; well-worn enough to avoid the brashness of a rental.

"You're a sight for sore eyes, Mish Moneypenny…" he said.

Perhaps Father would have been proud of him after all. Proud of him for something, even if it was just the sheer exclusiveness of it. The élan- the isolation. Well, better late than never. He rapped on the lacquered hardwood. There was no Room 13, the brass door numbers went straight from 12 to 14. Latin Americans could be superstitious like that- just like Old Etonians. Haunting strains of *vallenato* music leaked out from Room 14. Subject likes local folk music, Laurence remembered. Prone to sentimentality. Don't cry for me, money-launderer. He knocked again.

"*¿Quién es?*" A man's voice through the door. Modulated- loud enough to carry to Pearce, soft enough not to ring out down the corridor.

"*Soy* Pearce," Laurence said, crushing the cigarette out into the mangled remains of a room-service crustacean, its fractured exoskeleton lolling on a plate outside the room. "Bloody prawns everywhere…" he whispered to himself. "They're taking over the world." In spite of everything, the tension, the misery, the proximity of the void, he almost laughed out loud.

"¿Señor Pearce? *¿El inglés?* The Englishman? They told you the words to give me? The password?"

"Bezique…" said Laurence. "Just Bezique."

There was a grinding of Ingersoll locks and then the door was pulled ajar. A gleaming round face stared out through the gap.

"Señor de la Peña?" Pearce said.

The fat man ushered him in. There was someone else in the room, Laurence saw. A woman in a discreet business suit, sat behind a laptop at an antique mahogany desk by the window. Subject has a personal assistant. Cifuentes, Caridad. Costa Rican national. She was very pretty, Laurence thought, with that exquisite *latina* perfection of eyebrow and cheekbone. All that was irrelevant now, of course. But she smiled at him, and he returned the greeting suavely enough.

"*Encantado…*"

"You have the code?" said de la Peña. Laurence nodded. "So give it to Miss Cifuentes over there, *señor*. Quickly! Time is money, *no*? For all of us!"

"You're sure you can move all the *plata*?" said Laurence. "The whole amount? We can't afford any mistakes with this one."

De la Peña took a step towards him and put a heavy hand on his shoulder.

"You really come from Bezique, Señor Pearce?" he said. "He knows what I do- my track record. We've worked together for a very long time."

"Yeah? Well, time's up..." said Laurence. "You know this is really Room 13?"

"*¿Qué quieres decir?*" said de la Peña, taking a step back, but Pearce was already pulling off his bow tie, straightening it between his hands and slipping it around de la Peña's sagging neck.

"There's no escaping your destiny," Laurence whispered. "Whatever room you try to lock it away in..."

"Stop!" croaked de la Peña. "You have no idea what you're doing! There's- there's no way out of here!"

"There's always one way out," said Laurence. "Death's private door."

De la Peña struggled hard, but the customised carbon-Kevlar of the tie was choking the life out of him, crushing his windpipe. The black hybrid fabric was strong, wiry- remorseless. And so was Laurence. This was it, this was what he had trained for. All those hours in the gym, all those hours of psych training. He had tasted failure too many times in his life to trifle with it now. He knew how it could stalk you, dog your footsteps, ooze through the tallest walls you built around it- creep back into your life and lie in wait for you. He knew that when you get your foot on failure's throat, you better stamp down as hard as you can.

"Despair is power!" he said, pulling the ends of the Kevlar together with one final effort, squeezing out the last drops of a life.

"*¡Por La Nueva Raza- todo!*" gasped de la Peña, and then slumped down into Pearce's arms.

"He's gone..." said Laurence.

He looked over at Caridad. He had expected her to be screaming the place down by now. Let her scream, he thought, it would be too late to save her obese boss anyway. But instead she was convulsing, a staccato, cracking sound ringing out from her chest. Click, click, click. Laurence watched in horrified fascination. Now he could see the bright flames flickering out from underneath her suit jacket. Acrid black smoke was pouring off her. Pearce stared at her, open-mouthed in shock, letting go of the bow tie. The money-launderer's body crashed down to the ground, unnoticed. Caridad was clutching her back now, fire raging through her slight body, her hair and clothes going up like a torch.

"*¡Estoy ardiendo de adentro! ¡Ayúdame!*" she screamed in agony. "*¡Señor Pearce!* Laurence! I'm burning! *¡Ayúdame, por favor!* Help me, Laurence! It is Aquiles… Aquiles has come!"

"Christ!" said Pearce. He threw a glass of water over her, then the whole bottle, but it just hissed up into steam as the fire devoured her body from within. He could feel the searing heat scorching his face. Then his earpiece hissed into life.

"Is it happening?"

"Something's happening!" Laurence shouted. "But what- what is it?"

"Evolution," said the voice.

"So what do I do now?"

"First, you turn up the music. You check your head. Then you burn it. Burn it all."

Pearce nodded, fighting hard to compose himself. He adjusted the volume dial on the old-fashioned radio, then slipped off his dinner jacket. Out of habit, he folded it neatly onto the bed. Under his snowy white dress shirt he wore a fabric bandolier, cross-belts filled with moulded plastique. He pulled the links out of the French cuffs of his shirt, twin coils of copper wire. He unwound them carefully, then pushed one end of each of them into a thin platinum cigarette case and the other into the high explosive.

"*Siento un gran cansancio en el corazón…*" mourned the radio, over Caridad's dying screams. I feel a great weariness in my heart.

Laurence picked up the cigarette case.

Now someone was knocking at the door.

"*¿Qué pasa adentro, señor?* What's going on in there?"

"That's Security. It's time, Brother," said the voice in his earpiece.

"We're coming in!" said the guard outside, turning the door handle.

"Death never misses his cue," said Bezique, in Laurence's ear. "Make sure you don't either."

Pearce looked across at the burning girl on the bed.

"No gods, no masters!" he said. "Together we greet the Reaper."

Then he pushed the ruby clasp of the cigarette case, the electronic detonator ignited and the front of the hotel disintegrated.

CHAPTER 2

EDINBURGH, UNITED KINGDOM

Strontian shook the black rain of the Cowgate off his brogues and cut up Scott's Close. Squirming rivulets of water ran down the stairs towards him, and he followed them up the dark alley to their source. Chambers Street. Stay on foot, stay out of the CCTV, break cover late. There could hardly be a better city in the world than Edinburgh for that. It was a covert operator's dream. All the spy satellites in the heavens couldn't track a man through the labyrinth of the Old Town. Not unless they could see through sooty slate and granite, swallowing up the light all around them. Strontian looked back down the close. No one tailing him. He stepped back up into the light. A hard right, and now there was a crowd to lose himself in. The others were in place. Strontian jostled his way through the picket of protesters outside the venue, pushing aside the leaflets and placards pressed into his face.

"You away to the Oil Barons' Ball there, mate?" said an earnest, twenty-something demonstrator. "Can I no' tell you a wee bit about renewable energy before you go in? Before it's too late?"

"It's already too late," said Strontian.

"Just think about it, eh?" said the protester. "Open your eyes, man, there's a better way! We've only the one planet to destroy, an' we cannae' drink oil! We need clean energy, and we need it now!"

"Waste of money, pal," said Strontian, pulling his invitation card out of his sporran. "You'll find that out yourself, if you ever start paying tax. Oil is what made Scotland rich. Black gold…"

"Right enough! I used tae' be on the offshore rigs myself, up there in Aberdeen," said a grey-haired security guard, scanning the bar-code on the invitation with a hand-held reader. "Brent Charlie, I was oot on. Welcome tae' the Club, Mr Sunart, sir!" He wrapped an adhesive band around Strontian's wrist. "Jist a security precaution, Mr Sunart. Ye'll see we've a few uninvited guests wi' us, the night…"

"Bloody students!" said Strontian. "Away with the fairies, the whole lot of them. What do they think's paying for their free university tuition, eh? Scotch mist?"

The guard laughed and waved him through.

Strontian paced up the ramp into the National Museum of Scotland and straight through the Kingdom of the Scots Gallery, pausing only to accept a glass of champagne on his way. The staircases and elevators up to the higher reaches of the Grand Gallery were all sealed off, the museum staff turning back any tipsy oil executives who strayed off the beaten track on their way to the dinner tables. The sound of bagpipes swirled through the corridors as the diners were piped to their seats. Strontian stood by the side of the stairwell up to Gallery 4, enjoying the music. He sipped his champagne. Then his watch vibrated. Right on cue, there was an eruption of sound from outside.

"Burn the rich, not the oil!" chanted the protesters. "Burn the rich, not the oil!"

Strontian leaned closer to the security guard behind the rope cordon on the staircase, eavesdropping on the stewards' channel over his walkie-talkie.

"All security staff to the Tower Entrance. Repeat, all security staff to the Tower Entrance! We have a serious fire hazard here, people. Some bloody idiots are lettin' flares off, man, it's like Celtic Park on Old Firm game day out here…"

"Shite!" muttered the guard, hurrying out through Hawthornden Court.

Strontian paused until he was out of sight and a straggling group of kilted diners had swayed past, then slipped past the cordon and up the stairs. Once you make your move, keep moving, don't stop for anything- or anyone. He smiled as he entered the second-floor gallery: 'The Animal Kingdom'.

"Home at last..." said Strontian.

"My Lords, Ladies and Gentlemen! Dinner is served!" cried the MC down below. "Please take your seats, without any further delay!"

Strontian was lying on the floor of the gallery now, peering down through the railings. The tumult seemed to have subsided outside on Chambers Street. Their part was done.

"Welcome to the twenty-seventh annual North Sea Oil Club Dinner!" boomed the Chairman. "We've had many dinners with the friends and supporters of the Scottish oil industry over the years- and even one or two with the Scottish Labour Party! But this is definitely our first tête-à-tête with the good folk of Anarchy Scotland Unincorporated! To paraphrase Robert Burns' famous comment on Ayr: 'Anarchy Scotland, whom ne'er a group surpasses, for honest men, and bonny lasses'..." He paused as the diners guffawed. But Strontian wasn't laughing. He was measuring distances in his mind, for the thousandth time. Sometimes you only get one shot. "And for those of you who'd like to get to know them better, I'm informed that some of their leading lights are currently chained to the exhibits in the Kingdom of the Scots Gallery. They chained themselves, mind you- this is Edinburgh, not Texas!" The diners turned to banter with their American colleagues, dispersed around the tables of tartan-clad oilmen. "And I'm sure you'd all like to join me in raising a glass to some real honest men and bonny lasses, for looking after us so diligently this evening- Police Scotland!" Those who could still stand up lurched to their feet and hoisted their glasses high.

"Police Scotland!"

"But we have another Club first for you, too..." continued the Chairman. "We're not as old-fashioned in this Club as Swampy and his little friends out there would have you think! You might say that we're more than an oil club.

And so I'm delighted to announce as our keynote speaker this evening a very new kind of Energy academic. Professor Malcolm Carmichael of Edinburgh University has forged an international reputation as one of the leading experts in Energy Market Disruption, and it's our good fortune that he's chosen this evening to launch his new paper: 'Large-Scale Ambient Energy Harvesting'." Strontian watched the professor glance around the room, nose twitching like a nervous prey animal breaking cover. "So without further ado- and with thanks to our main sponsor, Intercontinental Petroleum- Professor Carmichael, the floor is yours!"

Strontian leaned over the banister and unhooked the huge stag's head hanging from the other side of it. The screws had already been loosened by the inside team, but he braced himself against the weight as he twisted the bolts off and lifted the mount up onto the edge of the railing.

"Mr Chairman, Ladies and Gentlemen, you don't need me to tell you that the hydrocarbon age has already reached the beginning of its end," said Professor Carmichael. "Or even that the end is nigh! What might surprise you is how it will be replaced. Not with the giant windmills and solar PV panels that our friends outside are so eager to tell us about…"

"Enjoy the Feast of Belshazzar while you can, Oil Barons!" came a shout from the gallery below Strontian. "The writing is on the wall…" A ring of activists had thrown off their waiters' uniforms and fanned out around the railings, unfurling banners and igniting shipping flares. The vast Grand Gallery was filling with smoke, light- and anarchy, thought Strontian. One of the protesters, face painted like an angry clown, brandished a megaphone. He pushed his way through the mob and leaned over the banister, hooking one arm through the guard-rail and swinging out above the diners, leering down the barrel of his loudspeaker.

"Are the police still here, Mr Chairman?" said Professor Carmichael. "Things are getting a little- out of hand…"

"The pigs can't save you now!" shouted the Clown. "No one can save you from Nature's justice… For the Strontium Dog is here! The Strontium

Dog has numbered the days of your dark reign, and he has brought it to an end! Burn the rich, not the oil!" He tossed a glowing flare over the side of the gallery, scattering the terrified guests below. "Burn the rich!"

"It's the Strontium Dog!" shouted a steward. "Get him down from there!"

The Clown laughed through the megaphone, an eerie cackle that echoed around the galleries of Scottish history.

"I am not him! I am not the Light!" he screamed. "I have come for a witness, to bear witness of the Light, that all men through me might believe! But I am not that Light."

"Everyone stay calm!" said the Chairman, retreating under the cover of the first-floor gallery. His voice was lost in the sound and fury, as Strontian swung his leg over the railings, still unseen in the confusion. "Everyone stay calm! Stay calm, I urge you! The police are already on the premises. They'll have the situation under control in just a few minutes!"

"Control?" screamed the Clown. "Don't you know anarchy when you see it? The End of Days? *Viva* the Dog!"

"Strontium Dog! Strontium Dog! Strontium Dog!" chanted the demonstrators, as the ushers tried to haul them back from the edge of the gallery.

"Strontium?" said Professor Carmichael. "Good God! They don't mean Strontian the nihilist? Strontian the eco-terrorist? The terror of the North Sea! He's occupied three oil platforms this month alone…"

Strontian lifted the stag's head high up above his own. The protesters bayed support, reaching their hands up towards him, palms outstretched.

"Now it's four!" cried the Clown. "Enter the Strontium Dog! My work is done here…"

He tossed his megaphone down into the crowd. The diners at the table below him screamed as it sent wine bottles flying like skittles. Now all eyes were on Strontian.

"Enough!" shouted Strontian. "Your time is up. You stole this land from Nature, but now we're stealing it back! You cornered us like wild beasts, and now we will rip you apart! No gods, no masters!"

Professor Carmichael stared at him in fascination. He was still gazing upwards when Strontian launched himself straight off the second-floor gallery, holding the stag's head out before him, clutching its base to his chest. The antlers speared right through the academic's slight torso, pinning him to the table. Strontian's own limbs were horribly contorted, bones splintered by the impact. His shattered body lolled on top of the professor's, blood drenching the white table-cloth, lip pulled back from his canine teeth in a savage smile.

"Suicide Station?" murmured the Chairman, approaching the wreckage of the table as the other diners shrank away from it. "The Dog's day is over."

CHAPTER 3

ISLEWORTH CROWN COURT, LONDON, UNITED KINGDOM

Mason made his way through the cordon of photographers and into the public gallery of Court 12. The armed policemen touched their caps to him as he passed. They knew an officer when they saw one. Desertion, divorce and disillusion had taken a lot from David Mason, but they could never take that away from him. Mason looked up at the Crown's coat of arms, mounted on the wall behind the judge's bench. "*Dieu et mon droit*." The Crown knew all about protecting its own rights. But what about the people who risked their lives for it? Whatever they were to God, they seemed a good deal more disposable to Queen and country.

"Run silent, run deep..." Mason muttered to himself, touching the double dolphin badge on the lapel of his Gieves & Hawkes suit. The submariner's creed. He took his seat, just as the cross-examination resumed.

"Now, Mr Wright, I must ask you to address your answers very clearly to the members of the jury," said the prosecution barrister. "Not to me, or to my learned friend- however natural that may seem, when we are the ones putting the questions to you. This is a very large court, so please do project your voice as much as you can. Some of your answers yesterday were a little- indistinct…"

"Indistinct!" said the defendant. "You don't know how this has tortured me! What I see every night when my eyes close… If I dare to close them! I haven't been able to sleep, ever since it happened. Have some humanity, man! This has ruined my life…"

"Of course it has!" said the barrister. "And not just your life, either." Mason despised him for the arrogant detachment of his words. As if some smug lawyer had any idea what they could mean. He thought he had a pretty good idea himself. But as always, Mason ran silent. "Because you killed your friend, didn't you? And now it's eating you up inside! It's consuming you. The truth. The truth that we're here to uncover today…"

"No!" said the defendant. "I didn't do it! I couldn't have done it. How could I have?"

"Let's examine the facts though shall we, Mr Wright?" said the prosecutor. "He's dead now, isn't he? With no need for a cremation. Because you'd taken care of that already, hadn't you?"

"Really, Mr Smythe…" said the judge.

"My apologies, my Lady. Members of the jury," said the barrister. "But sadly Mr Harris was left burned beyond recognition at the end of his vigil with the defendant. As unpleasant as those facts may be, Mr Wright has to face up to the enormity of his actions."

The jury's faces looked hard, Mason thought. Conviction faces, ready to do their duty.

"Please…" said the defendant.

"And we've already established that the two of you were the only people in the room. In fact," said Smythe, turning to the jury. "What we've established from the extensive CCTV footage you've been shown is that the defendant and Mr Harris were the only people in the whole building. Isn't that right, Mr Wright?"

"I don't know about the building…" said the defendant. "Probably. There could have been contract cleaners. But in the room, definitely. Had to be. Like any night shift."

"And you do agree that no one else could possibly have entered without being caught on the CCTV cameras?" said Smythe. "That the whole facility is designed to ensure that? That's what you said in your statement to the police, isn't it?"

"Yeah, that's right," said the defendant.

"And why is that?"

"So no one can access the vaults without being recorded on at least seven different security cameras," said the defendant. "From all angles. Standard protocol, that was. You need it to be sure of facial recognition. The insurers require it, what with all the ice we was holding in the vaults that night."

"Ah yes- the vaults. And can you remind the court what type of vaults they were, Mr Wright?"

"They were diamond vaults, like I just said. You know that!"

"Please address your answers to the jury, Mr Wright," said Smythe. "So they were diamond vaults. And can you remind us of the approximate value of those diamonds?"

"It was about a billion pounds of ice on the night," said the defendant. "It varies from day to day. Depends what the buying's been like in that session. You never know what lots the traders will take. Not that it was any of our business, anyway. We was just looking after the stuff."

"Or not, in this case..." said the barrister. "There were £1.27 billion worth of uncut diamonds on the premises that night, to be precise. According to the official inventory for that day. Members of the jury will see that they have a copy of that inventory, in their folders with the indictment." The jurors rifled through their papers, eager for details of such opulent riches. Smythe held the inventory up to the court. "Is that correct, Mr Wright?"

"That must be it, then," said the defendant. "Like I said. About a bill. Ball-park."

"£1.27 billion. All those diamonds. And just two people. One of them lived, and one of them died. I think we're all starting to get the picture, aren't we?" said Smythe, turning to look at the jurors. Some of them nodded back. "And the rescue services had some difficulty telling which one of you was in distress, didn't they, Mr Wright? Now why was that?"

"It was the smoke…" said the defendant. "It was terrible in there. Horrible."

"And what effect did that smoke-screen- I beg your pardon, smoke- have on the security cameras, Mr Wright?"

"Control Centre couldn't make out the pictures," said the defendant. "The cameras themselves was working fine, but this was thick, black smoke- real acrid. You couldn't see a bloody thing. Pardon me, my Lady…"

"And these cameras- they were essential to the integrated security system that protected the facility?" said the barrister.

"Of course," said Wright. "That's the only way a facility like that could be staffed by two blokes on their own. You need continuous surveillance, so you can mobilise the back-up boys if anything goes down."

"And it went down that night, didn't it?" said the barrister.

"Not like that, it didn't…" said the defendant.

"No, exactly like that, Mr Wright!" said Smythe. "I put it to you that killed your colleague in cold blood; that you callously set fire to his body, to cover your own tracks; and that you would have stolen those diamonds too, if Control Centre hadn't decided to investigate before you could make off with them!"

"How could I have killed him? Why would I have burned him?" said Wright, close to tears.

"For the diamonds, of course!" said the barrister, holding his hands wide in supplication. He seemed to hold the jury in the palm of them now. "For the oldest motive of them all. It was always about the diamonds, wasn't it? About creating a distraction- a literal smoke-screen- to let you get your greedy hands on them. The precious 'ice' you had always hankered after, especially as your gambling debts started to mount up! Little by little, they began to seem like the only way out. You were desperate! It must have been a constant temptation to you. And only one person stood between you and financial security for the rest of your life. One innocent life…"

"No! He killed himself! I mean- he was killed…"

"Well, which one was it, Mr Wright?" interrupted the judge. "He killed himself, or he was killed? It had to be one or the other, didn't it? And you've already admitted that there could have been no mysterious 'Third Man' there, haven't you? So come, now- these are very serious offences you're charged with in this court! Murder- arson- armed robbery. I must ask you to answer counsel's questions as clearly as you can."

"Thank you, my Lady," said Smythe. "Quite so. So, Mr Wright. Did he kill himself, or was he killed?"

The jury leaned forward in their seats.

"Both…" whispered Wright. "It was both. I never laid a finger on him. It just… happened."

"What just happened?" said the barrister. "Again, I must ask you to address your answers clearly to the members of the jury, Mr Wright. Please project your voice as much as you can, right to the end of the sentence."

"Terry was doing the rounds, and I was on the monitors," said the defendant, clearing his throat. "We always took turns when we was on nights together. Break the monotony of it, like. So anyhow, when he moved from screen three to screen four, I noticed that he was bending over. Stooped. Kind of shaking. I radioed through to him. He- he couldn't speak…"

"That was convenient, wasn't it?" said the barrister. "Or the monitors would have captured it? Recorded it…"

"But then he started to cry out," said the defendant, ignoring him. "They caught that, alright. He was in pain! In agony. I could see him shuddering on screen four. So I got up myself, to go and help him."

"In blatant contravention of the official protocol?" said Smythe.

"Like I said, he was in pain! He was my mate! I thought he was having a heart attack. I couldn't just leave him there to suffer- to die in front of my eyes…"

"But you were supposed to call for help, weren't you?" said the prosecutor. "Not to leave your post? You knew that could jeopardise everyone's safety. That's precisely what the protocols are for, isn't it?"

Wright hung his head.

"Are you a doctor, Mr Wright?"

"You know I'm not!" said the defendant.

"The jury has heard perfectly clearly that the defendant was a security guard at all relevant times," said the judge. "Please don't toy with the witness, Mr Smythe."

"Very good, my Lady," said Smythe. "But in that case, Mr Wright, why would you think that your care would be more likely to help Mr Bolton than that of the trained paramedics at Control Centre? Or indeed of the much greater resources of the London Ambulance Service?"

"I know it looks bad, but I- I had to help him!" said the defendant. "To get to him. That came first…"

"No, Mr Wright- for you, stealing the diamonds came first!" said Smythe. "There were protocols to deal with illness- even with a stroke or heart attack! But you didn't follow those protocols when the fatal moment came, did you? Not one of them! Not when it didn't suit your purposes!"

"There were no protocols to deal with this!" said Wright. "How could there have been?" Mason leaned forward in his seat. "There are no protocols in the world that could've dealt with it! A man on fire! Harry was- he was burning up, my Lady!"

"The jury knows that, Mr Wright," said the barrister. "They've seen the pictures, in all their horror. And after this morning, now they know why he was burned too."

"But they don't know how it happened!" screamed Wright. "No one could imagine that! The horror of it! Of seeing your friend burst into flames like that…" The jurors stirred in their seats. It was impossible to ignore the raw anguish in front of them. Mason was already moving when the defendant spoke again, his hunter-killer instincts kicking in. Wait as long as you need to, wait forever if you have to- but when you break the surface, launch fast. "How quickly his body burned itself- from the inside! The heat... It came from the inside!"

The jurors were whispering to each other, questions breaking out like wild-fires.

"What?" said the barrister. "What did you say?"

But now Mason was vaulting over the gallery. He cleared the low wooden barrier and picked up the water-glass in front of the court usher in one movement. Mason never doubted for a second what was inside it. Everyone had their job to do. You build your team, and then you trust them to the end. Your weapons officer. That was the only way the system could work. He dowsed the defendant with the contents of the glass, then dashed it over the approaching court bailiff's head, before she could restrain him. The armed policemen were moving now, but they were crucial strides behind him. He was in the kill zone. Wright looked up into his eyes as Mason ignited the cigarette lighter.

"This is release, friend," said Mason. "Despair is power!"

"What do you mean?" whispered Wright.

"No one can judge you now. No gods, no masters!" said Mason, and wrapped his arms around him. Two broken strangers standing together. Wright closed his eyes as the dripping benzene from the glass roared into flame, kindling with the naptha infused in the fabric of Mason's suit, and then the chemical fire purged all the pain away.

CHAPTER 4

LIME STREET, CITY OF LONDON, UNITED KINGDOM

Ben Makepeace gazed out through the internal window of the Technical Performance Team meeting room, across the great atrium of the Lloyd's building. The escalators criss-crossed up to the top of the world's most famous insurance market, like a stairway to heaven. Like a crazy M.C. Escher optical illusion, Makepeace thought. Up and down are just relative values in this world. And in insurance. Only for him, there had been a hell of a lot more downs than ups.

"Surely we've got agents on the ground in Panama?" he said. "A Lloyd's agent in every port, isn't that how the sales pitch goes? And the Canal handles five per cent. of global trade. The great cross-roads of the Americas."

"Course we do!" said Braithwaite, sipping at an Evian bottle. "That's what the Empire was built on. Three firms, to be precise. United Steamship Agents, S.A., C. Palmer & Co. and Norfolk & Molino, S.A. All jolly pukka. But for the very reason you cite, young Benjamin, it's all Marine out there- bunkering disputes, busted container cranes, drunken stevedores, hull and machinery surveys. Even the agents with any game outside Marine don't have anything like your form- your finesse- in life assurance claims. And this is...

Well, it's rather a delicate case, I'm afraid."

"The local plods are treating it as homicide?" said Ben.

"Of course they are!" said Braithwaite, cracking his knuckles. "No one disputes that. The bleeding hotel was blown to smithereens! It wasn't a gas-leak, in case you were wondering. And wherever he was when he kicked the bucket, Laurence Pearce was a civilian. A very wealthy civilian to boot. Polo star, skier, rackets whiz, prominent London clubman. What the esteemed *Daily Mail* might call a millionaire playboy. Educated at Eton, Marlborough, Radley..."

"That's a lot of schools for one kid," said Ben.

"He was expelled from a lot of schools!" said Braithwaite. "His old man had to endow a lot of new sports halls, just to keep the admissions officers happy. Which, fortunately for Laurence, he was well able- if not exactly pleased- to do. Whilst he was still with us, that is." He pushed a ring-binder across the desk to Makepeace, who flipped it open and flicked through the pages. "You can't take it with you… So, like I said- a very well-heeled young fellow."

"With the best part of fifty million dollars in life insurance, freshly-inked with one of your most respectable syndicates," said Ben. "I'm starting to see the delicacy of the matter…"

"Quite," said Braithwaite. "Which is precisely why the TPT- why yours truly- is bringing you in."

"I should have known when I saw your fingerprints on this," said Ben. "We don't often see you in these parts, these days- not now you're in the big seat."

"I'm still Executive Chairman," said Braithwaite. "And I'm taking executive action on this. The chit is completed, a modest *per diem* is approved, and you're off to Panama on the milk train. KLM via Amsterdam, to be precise. You know the place?"

"I've been there," said Ben.

"I'll take that as a 'yes', then."

"It's not quite the same thing in Central America."

"You're a dark horse, old son!" said Braithwaite. "Whatever happened to you? You still look fit- lean and hungry. Like a soldier! What are you, thirty-five?"

"Thirty-two," said Makepeace.

"You were a 'Red Indian' back in the day, weren't you? 30 Commando?"

"IX," said Ben. "We attain by stealth. You've got the file, Mr Chairman. Maybe you should give it a read."

"Information Exploitation…" said Braithwaite. "Spooks, eh?"

"Data collection and analysis."

Braithwaite grunted.

"It takes different types of men to do our work. And different types of demons to drive them, I suppose. Listen, Makepeace," he said, gulping at his water-bottle, "I know you have history down there. Frankly, I don't care whether you choose to make your peace with it or not. For all I know, you may well be more useful as you are. A problem child. Just find out what on earth happened there, and make my life a bit easier for once, eh? And in the meantime, one for the road, sunshine? Can I tempt you with a mineral water?" He gestured towards a fridge full of soft drinks in the corner of the meeting room. "You can see that we're well-stocked with that, at least…"

"The hospitality's changed a bit around here," said Ben.

"You can't drink in here anymore, matey-boy," said Braithwaite. "You of all people. It's the new, professional face of Lloyd's. *Vorsprung durch Technik*! Perhaps old Nigel F is right- the glory days of the Proper Fucking Lunch really are over forever, and we'll all be healthier, wealthier and wiser on H2O..."

Ben laughed.

"Then why do you have Stolichnaya in yours?"

Braithwaite sniffed at his water bottle, his ruddy face flushing darker.

"It's supposed to have no scent! I even tested it on my secretary. Amy had no idea. I'm starting to remember why we put you in Special Projects in the first place. Keeps you out of my hair. What's left of it, that is…"

He rubbed his grizzled hair for effect.

"Alright, alright, I'm off," said Ben, ruffling his own sandy hair. "Take it easy on the Evian."

"Just out of interest," said Braithwaite. "What told you it was voddy? Asking for a friend, you understand."

"Water has a concave meniscus, Trevor."

"Ah…" said Braithwaite, peering at the bottle. "Is that up or down? Anyway, that's your thing, isn't it, fella? That's why we pay you the big bucks. Information Exploitation. You see things other people don't."

"And what do you want me to see in Panama?" said Ben.

"Oh, I think you know perfectly well, Benjamin," said Braithwaite, chuckling.

"All things considered, I'd imagine the syndicate has the criminal activity exclusion in mind," said Makepeace. "That would avoid an inconveniently large pay-out on the Pearce policy."

"Don't they always!" said Braithwaite. "Nonsense, of course. Nasty, suspicious minds that they have. But humour me on this one. Be a good man and see what you can dig up, eh? I don't care who you are, fifty mill is a chunk of change! Lloyd's has put its trust in you. It's time to make the donuts. For all of us."

Ben nodded and pulled the door shut behind him.

"Safe travels, old son!" called Braithwaite after him. "*Vaya con dios*, eh?"

CHAPTER 5

ST JAMES'S STREET, ST JAMES'S, LONDON, UNITED KINGDOM

"The ace of spades. The Death Card!" croaked Malthus, as applause rang around the dark oak panels of the *salle de jeux*. "He drew the ace of spades! By Jove, what a piece of luck! And only your twelfth night with us too, Newman. Twelfth Night… I count them, you see. I count them all- it's about the only thing that keeps the old mind active, at my age…"

His voice tailed off, lost in a bout of consumptive coughing.

"Champagne, Florizel!" called Bezique, clicking his fingers at the bow-tied club steward. Florizel placed a magnum of chilled Krug in a silver ice-bucket on the ivory-coloured stand by Bezique's right-hand side and bowed low from the waist.

"It is customary to stand the whole Club champagne on such occasions, Newman," said Bezique. "At a hundred thousand dollars a hand, the Game is not one for the parsimonious! Though some members do prefer a stiff brandy, when they turn up Old Frizzle- the ace of spades. Laurence Pearce drank off a whole pint of rum, which was appropriate enough, I suppose, given where he was going…"

"Latin America, eh?" said Malthus, reviving. "Bravo, Pearce! Nothing in ɔecame him like the leaving of it!"

ıere was another ripple of applause around the *salle de jeux.*

"Good old Lol!" shouted Kip Horrocks. "Trashing hotels like it's going out of style!"

Bezique nodded to Florizel.

"*Et maintenant- le sabrage...*" he said.

Florizel removed the cage and foil from the Krug and wrapped the base of the bottle in a white linen napkin. He held it out towards Bezique at arm's length. The president selected a sabre from the wall, balanced the weight of the sword in his hand and then unsheathed it.

"Would you care to do the honours yourself, Brother?" he asked, holding the hilt of the sword out towards Newman.

"Newman?" growled Malthus. "Come on, man, look lively!"

But Julian Newman hadn't heard a word any of them were saying. He just stared at the card, at that dreadful black hole in the middle of it. He felt as though it was sucking him straight down through it, into some new vortex of despair. His head was spinning, his stomach plummeting through the floor. He was falling off the face of the earth, and this time no one could catch him.

"I don't- this isn't..." he mouthed, but as usual no one was listening by then. He had always fluffed his bloody lines. The bigger the stage, the more complete the paralysis. The more humiliating the failure. And this time- this time he really had blown it. How fitting that a playing card had sealed his fate, he thought. It had taken one last ace to tell him he was finally out of aces.

Malthus sighed, and then the blade of the sword flashed towards Newman. The horrible wetness spread quickly across his shirt collar, burning his skin like acid. He screamed, and looked down at the bottle of champagne. It was foaming from its severed lip, the top sheered off completely by the sabre cut.

"A hit, a very palpable hit!" said Malthus, clapping Bezique on the back. "*Beau sabreur*, Bezique!"

"But I spilt some this time," said Bezique. "And over Mr Newman too.

Rather an ill omen…"

Florizel stepped forward and filled the champagne coupe in front of Newman to the brim, before letting the pale wine cascade into the pyramid of glasses on the baize table.

"Nonsense!" said Malthus, lifting the apex coupe from the pyramid in a toast. "To the Club!" He slurped at the champagne. "Drink up, Newman! You need it, by God- you're a nervous wreck, man. You're giving me the hee-bie-jeebies! Chin up in the *salle de jeux*, what? Club rules."

"He's right, Newman," said Bezique. "Whatever our problems may be, we leave them outside this room. For this is where we find our purpose. Where we draw the strength for our mission!"

Julian drew a queasy smile from some deep, un-Julian-like well of resistance. He held his glass up, forcing himself to look at the flushed faces around the table through the prism of the crystal.

"The Club!" he toasted.

The members applauded again, heavy hand-claps ringing through the swirling haze of exhilaration, relief and disappointment hanging over the room. An anthem for doomed youth, thought Newman. He'd never appreciated it until now- when it was nearly gone.

"*The only thing you see, you know it's gonna' be- the ace of spades*!" sang Kip Horrocks, getting up from the table, seizing a champagne coupe and rubbing the top of Newman's thinning hair in that way of his that Julian had always found so irritating. Horrocks looked more than ever like a schoolboy rugby player, with his shock of dark hair, gap-toothed grin and untucked shirt tails. "Only the bloody ace of spades! Not long now, old boy- for either of us…"

"Yes, good luck, Jules," whispered Rob Walker, folding an arm around Newman's narrow shoulders. "I hope it feels right for you when- when the time comes. We'll all be thinking of you. Hoping for the best, you know."

Walker always had been the compassionate one, thought Julian. So tall, slender and fair it seemed as though his delicate frame might just snap at any time. Too soft-hearted for the brutality of their school- for the freedom of

Oxford- for the free-for-all of the City. Now, it seemed, for this place too. This damned place! He'd never thought it would be so intense, so stifling. For so long, it had seemed like the answer to all of his problems. Now it only seemed like the end of them. He was all in.

"Take a walk with me, Julian," said Bezique, sheathing the sabre and hanging it back on the wall. "There are secrets that have not yet been revealed to you."

Newman was still gazing at the ace of spades. It had haunted his dreams for so long, and now here it was, vivid in black and white. He always had been more of a *rouge* or *noir* man. If he looked hard enough at it, his eyes lost focus and seemed to see right through it. Through to a future, he thought for a moment. A way out. But no, not quite that. The present always rushed up on him again too fast, a black dog at his throat that he could only hold off so long.

"You see the portrait hanging on the wall up there, Newman?" said Malthus, gripping Julian's elbow in his wrinkled hand. With a skeletal finger he pointed up to a gloomy oil painting, in pride of place above Bezique's chair in the *salle de jeux*. "Richard Harding was his name. The poor devil was hung, the day after that portrait was finished."

"What for?" Newman somehow managed to stutter.

"For forging the ace of spades!" said Malthus. "There was stamp duty to pay on playing cards back in 1805, you see. The Revenue stamped the 'Tax Card' against duty paid, and of course chancers like young Dick there would try to cheat them, by making their own. Forgery and uttering were capital offences, so they turned him off- he swung at the Old Bailey, at the ripe old age of 35! They say our patron Dickens' father was there as a young man- and Charles later based Ned Dennis on the duty hangman."

"I'm sorry?" said Julian.

"Ned Dennis- the hangman of Tyburn in *Barnaby Rudge*, man!" said Malthus. "And you an Etonian!"

"Sorry…" mumbled Julian.

He looked up at Harding's doleful face. The painter had known despair when he saw it.

"He looked at the cards much like you are now, when the evidence of his handiwork was shown to old Judge Heath," said Malthus. "The thousand yard stare. 'Hanging Heath' knew what to make of it, right enough! He always did. He put the black cap on like a bride donning her veil for her wedding day. So it's not surprising young Harding looks a bit glum in the picture, eh? They made this champagne stand from his thigh-bones and shin-bones. Longest bones in the human body! Rather a pretty curio, isn't it?"

Newman shuddered and shrank away from the macabre tripod. He would have given anything to get away from Malthus too. Would nothing stop this desiccated ghoul from harping on the horrors of the past?

"The Club had the portrait painted in the Old Bailey, when Harding was a dead man walking," continued the old man. "Paid him a guinea to sit for it. They should really have put the coin in the empty eye-socket of his skull to pay the Last Ferryman, like in ancient times!"

"But why?" breathed Julian. "Why record all this misery?"

"The President of the Club at the time had taken a shine to the story," said Malthus. "He even adopted the ace of spades as the trump card for the Game. And Harding's fate put the evil eye on Old Frizzle for ever after. That's why it's called the 'Death Card', to this day…"

"*Pushing up the ante, I know you gotta' see me…*" sung Horrocks. "*Read 'em and weep, the dead man's hand again! The ace of spades*!"

"It's not karaoke night in the Junior Common Room, Master Horrocks," said Bezique. "Show some decorum, man!" He handed the ace of spades to Horrocks. "Your ace has already turned up. You should be putting your affairs into order, before your flight. Malthus will tell you how the great brothers before you met their fates."

"There is no honour in meeting the Reaper like a lamb led to the slaughter," said Malthus. "This should be a dance, not a sacrifice. A Requiem."

Bezique took Newman by the arm and lifted him out of the chair.

"And now you will be wanting to discuss your own arrangements, Julian. You are in Death's antechamber now. You will find that the light is very different in the gaze of the Reaper. Everything is."

"Despair is power…" murmured Newman.

CHAPTER 6

ENTEBBE, UGANDA

The insects rose up in clouds in the Land Rover's headlamps, a million, billion Lake Victoria mosquitoes tripping the light fantastic over the Kampala Road. Kip Horrocks wondered which one of them carried the *plasmodium falciparum* parasite, the silent killer that spelled malaria. How many of them. But then what did that matter to him? He just turned up the music and gunned the Land Rover around the Sports Beach bend onto the Airport Road, electronic traction control keeping it clinging to the empty highway.

"Mr Hendrix plays Mr Dylan," said Horrocks aloud, as spangly shards of guitar ripped the inky night wide open. "And I'm so happy I could just- die."

For once he felt truly alive. As though he was driving without the handbrake on, pedal to the metal. It was what he had been waiting for his whole life. Just a bit more- head-space.

"*There must be some kind of way out of here/ Said the joker to the thief...*"

But this road wasn't completely empty either. It never fucking was, Kip thought. Not like him. Even here, he couldn't drive fast enough to escape the vacuum inside him. Black hole sun. That terrible emptiness he carried with him everywhere.

"Cargo 200 at two o'clock," said the voice in his earpiece.

So here came action at last, that same old release. It had taken Kip to some dark places in his life, but none so dark as this one. Or so vivid.

"You're sure it's him, Suicide Station?" said Horrocks.

"It's him."

Up ahead, the white Landcruiser was waved straight through the security checkpoint and off the international airport concourse.

"OK, so it's him. This is it. This is it!" said Kip.

"No loose ends, please, Horrocks," said Suicide Station.

"Who else is in the car?"

"The driver. Colonel Moussa. And two Moroccan Navy commandos. All travelling heavy. The General is in the front passenger's seat. One star on each epaulette."

"Good to know," said Kip. "If I get that close."

"You will get that close," said Bezique. "You'll have to."

"Roger that, Suicide Station."

Horrocks accelerated hard as the Landcruiser was swallowed up by the darkness on the Spennah bend.

"Now listen to me, I have something to say…" Kip said. He waited until he could see the huge letters 'UN' painted on the door, and then rammed the Land Rover straight into them as the driver cornered. "It's better to burn out than to fade away!"

Both vehicles exploded into a crazy mess of inflated airbags and shattered Perspex, the Landcruiser flipping right up onto its side. Horrocks dragged himself out of his wrecked car and grabbed the Heckler & Koch UMP and a canvas bag from the passenger seat. He flicked on the flash-light mounted on the barrel of the UMP and jogged up to the overturned Toyota.

"No witnesses. And no prisoners," said Suicide Station.

Horrocks dropped a stun grenade straight in through the broken window of the Landcruiser. He stepped back and waited a beat for the pyrotechnics to stupefy any survivors, then leaned forward and peered over the driver-side door, training the beam of the flash-light around the dark interior. The driver was hanging motionless in his seat-belt, but Horrocks put a single round through his head, just to make sure. In the back of the car two disoriented soldiers were stirring, trying to get up out of the wreckage, so he gave them a burst with the UMP.

"Status?"

"Three 200s," Kip said. "Repeat, three confirmed 200s inside the vehicle."

"They all have to be accounted for. Every last one."

In the front passenger seat, a burly man in an army uniform was slumped against the far door. His stars couldn't save him now. Not every star in the heavens, Kip thought.

"The General," he said. "Looks like he's gone too."

"So make sure," said Suicide Station.

Kip sprayed him with .45 AC rounds.

"That's another confirmed 200."

"And Moussa? What about Moussa?" said Suicide Station. "He's the one I want. Cold. He can never be allowed to make contact with the African cell. With his skillset, they would make him into a general- a warlord!"

There was a crackling sound from the depths of the Landcruiser. Horrocks aimed his flash-light towards it.

"Another 200," he said. "A smaller guy. He must have been knocked unconscious in the collision. He's coming to…"

"Get in there!" said Bezique. "He is more dangerous than you can possibly understand."

Kip climbed inside the wrecked car, choking on the acrid smoke. The slight man was writhing in his seat now, as though an electric current was running through his broken frame. Wisps of smoke were wafting through the buttons of his camouflage smock. Kip looked around him, but nothing else was on fire. The smell of burning was getting stronger and stronger, over-powering. Clothes, hair- flesh. Now the smoke was billowing, fumes stinging Horrocks' eyes in the confined space, blinding him. He was starting to panic.

"Is it Moussa?" said Suicide Station. "I need to know!"

Kip cursed and crawled further into the back of the Landcruiser.

"I can't see a fucking thing back here!" he said.

"Then improvise, man," said Bezique.

Horrocks smashed a window with the stock of the UMP, sending smoke spilling out into the night. The beam of his flash-light picked out some lettering on the wounded man's chest.

"Wait- there's a name tape…" he said.

He reached over to pull it into view, then cursed and pulled his hand away. It was hot. Burning hot.

"Shit! It's Moussa," said Kip. "Repeat, it is Moussa. But he's- he's…"

"Combusting?"

Kip stared at the burning man. Flames were reaching up from him now, blazing higher as they sucked in the oxygen all around his body. Colonel Moussa cried out with pain, and then blacked out again.

"Yeah," said Kip. "How did you know? And what the fuck do I do now?"

"You know exactly what to do," said the voice. "This is what you've trained for, soldier. Despair is power!"

Horrocks looked around him. He had finally run out of road. He could hardly see a thing now, but he pulled two Thermate-TH3 grenades out of his bag blind, just as he'd practised so many times before. Suddenly Moussa lurched upright, screaming. He lashed out, grabbing at Horrocks, hugging him towards him, as though to smother the flames against his body. For a moment the two condemned men wrestled in the cramped interior, fighting for their own way to die, and then the pain overwhelmed Moussa. His fingers lost their grip, and Kip managed to kick him away, lashing out against the dying man with all his strength. Kip was in agony, his own hair and skin scorched by the heat. Now he could hear sirens wailing, the emergency services racing out from Entebbe Airport towards the crash site.

"Do it!" said Bezique. "You can't be taken alive. None of you."

"I'm the only one left," said Horrocks. "I did it! Yeah! No gods, no masters. This is the greatest moment of my fucking life!" He held his fingers up in the sign of the horns, turned off the flash-light and then ripped the pins out of the thermate grenades. "Showtime, bitches… Together we greet the Reaper!"

The flaming Landcruiser lit the dark Entebbe night up as the powdered metal, sulphur and PBAN propellant ignited. The aluminothermic reaction melted through metal hillbilly armour and human flesh like candle wax. Then the fuel-tank kindled, and the blazing vehicle was ripped apart by the explosion, sending the police cars swerving across the highway to avoid careening shards of steel and aluminium.

"Yes, you did it, Kip," said Bezique. "He travels safest in the dark night who travels lightest."

CHAPTER 7

CROMWELL ROAD, LONDON, UNITED KINGDOM

The black cab rattled past stuccoed embassies and second-rate hotels, then ground to a halt at the traffic lights by the V&A. The museum was lit up in red, white and undulating blue: the 'Britannia Rules the Waves' exhibition. Julian Newman wilted under Victoria and Albert's stern gaze. London had never looked so beautiful to him- nor so disapprovingly back at him. And now he was leaving it forever. The great shipping line of Newman, Sime, Eldridge & Co. had ruled the waves too, forging red British maritime paths through Gibraltar, Marseilles, Port Said, Aden, Bombay and Calcutta- and vast Newman fortunes with them. Julian's grandfather had once taken him to see the bombastic gallery in the Museum that his forefathers had endowed. There was plenty of room in there, even for all the demons in Newman's head. He had still just been a boy, but he flushed as he remembered his grandad's words: one day you'll add your own chapter to the story. As he flicked through the stamped pages of the passport between his fingers, Newman could see the lanes his life had taken him down only too clearly- Atlantic City; Macau; Vegas; Sun City; Monte Carlo; Marina Bay. Losing those Newman fortunes all along the way. Old Newman, Sime and Eldridge wouldn't have minded him staking the ranch on a new *Titanic* or a deep-water terminal, Julian thought- just on *rouge* or *noir*. He felt their presence all the time, bewhiskered titans, frock-coated behemoths riding hard on his back. Why was Julian doomed to live in the Victorian age forever, saddled with values that the rest of the world had left behind generations ago? He was only thirty years old, for Christ's sake, despite his rapidly receding hairline. And why couldn't he just have been born poor, if that was his destiny? The pain was all in the journey down, the inexorable descent. Disappointing everyone at every step. And now- this. At least this would be someone else's problem. As little as he felt like speaking to anyone, it was still a relief when his battered iPhone started vibrating- even with no Caller ID. Maybe because there was no Caller ID. Then he remembered Bezique's words from his novitiate, and put it back in his pocket.

"You're off the grid now, Julian," he murmured to himself. "No one can reach you where you're going."

"Britain really was great back then, eh, Guv?" said the cabbie in broad cockney, gesturing out towards the National History Museum. It was literally glowing with Victorian smugness, Julian thought. Irradiated with racial arrogance. "They don't build 'em like the old 'Dead Zoo' there anymore!" He touched the brim of his flat cap in respect. "Standin' on the shoulders of giants, is what we are…"

When his phone vibrated again, Newman answered it, just to shut the voices out- his own most of all. He regretted it immediately. It was a familiar female voice.

"Jules! Thank God. Where are you? I've been trying to get hold of you for weeks! Have you even been back to the flat? Lenka says she hasn't seen you for days! And that you haven't touched any of the meals she's brought you. Or even slept in your bed…"

"Yeah, I've been really busy…" he said, already wondering how to get her off the phone. "Look, there's a terrible line here, and I'm just about to go into a tunnel. I'll call you later, alright?"

"Where are you?" she repeated. "Are you travelling? You know Dad doesn't want you going anywhere- anywhere there's a risk of you gambling like that again..."

"There are casinos everywhere!" Julian said, with a sudden snap of irritation. "There's a casino out there on the Cromwell Road! It might be a crumbling white town-house instead of Caesar's Palace, but it's still a bloody casino! I can lose Dad's precious money just as easily here as I can anywhere else, you know..."

"So you are here..." she said. "That's something. But heading west- to Heathrow, then? And then where?"

Julian laughed in spite of himself, as the cab bowled past Earl's Court and out over the Hammersmith flyover. If only he could fly over it all himself- lift off into a new life. Any life. For now, the darkness itself came as a relief, even as the mocking whisky bottles on the bill-boards loomed over him. Addictions love company, he thought.

"You always were the clever one, Laura," he said. "I can almost hear that big brain of yours whirring! Working out how to help me again- how to save me from myself. Hold the last broken fragments of our family together. You deserve it all- what's left of it, that is. I've ruined everything else for you..."

"You're really scaring me now, Julian," Laura said. "Just come back home, won't you? There's nothing that can't be sorted out. Money- debt- rehab, anything like that. We can talk it all through. Just come back, will you?"

"I can't!" said Newman. "I swore. Swore dreadful oaths- like you wouldn't believe. I have to go now..."

"But where, Jules? Where do you have to go?"

"Like you said- to the airport."

"Wait for me!" said Laura. "I'll come with you, wherever you're going! To the ends of the earth- I don't care. Just wait for me, and I'll buy the tickets. It'll be fun! Like old times, when we went back-packing. On gap years."

"I've had one fucking gap year too many," said Newman, holding his head in his hands. "You can't follow me now, Laura. Even you can't save me this time. This time Jules the fuck-up really has screwed it all up…"

"Is it something to do with that awful club of yours?" said Laura. "The Bohemian Sports Club? Is that where you've been all this time? Gambling? Jules, is someone there making you do this? Because we can deal with that too, if you'll just tell me what's going on!"

"Of course not," said Newman.

"Julian…"

"It's nothing to do with the bloody BSC!" said Newman. "It's just a club. Well, it's more than a club… That's what they're always drumming into our fucking heads, anyway. 'More than a club'. They have so many of these slogans, they repeat them over and over again like mantras, until you can't tell your own thoughts from the ones they've planted there… It's like *The Ipcress File* or something, I swear!"

"It sounds more like a cult," said Laura. "What exactly is the Club, Jules? What do they have over you? I'm sure it's nothing that can't be fixed. And Lenka says you've been spending all your time there lately- night after night. It doesn't sound healthy. What do you do there?"

"Lenka talks too much by half!" said Newman. "I don't pay her good money to spend her whole time blabbing my private business to anyone who'll listen. She's supposed to be my maid, my friend- not my keeper! The last thing I need right now is someone else to be disappointed in me. She can take a ticket and get in the fucking line!"

"Don't blame her- it's my fault," said Laura. "She's just worried about you. I am too. And you know what I'm like- I ask questions. I suppose I was quite persistent."

"Bloody nosy, more like it!" said Newman. "Like a dog with a bone…"

"Well then, we can agree on that at least!" said Laura. "So what have you been doing there? What are you looking for, Jules? What do you find at the Club that you can't find anywhere else?"

"I can't tell you!" said Newman. "They would… I mean, I swore!"

In a few minutes more the cab would lose itself in the oblivion of the M4.

If he could just make it out of London, away from the clutching tendrils of Laura's questions, then it would all be better. Or at least- over. Maybe that was the same thing. It would have to do for now, anyway.

"What would they do, Jules? What could they do? It's ridiculous to be afraid of them!" said Laura. "And all these oaths. It's not like you to be so secretive..."

"We gamblers are terrible liars, didn't you know?" said Julian. "Haven't you heard of a poker face?"

"But I thought you always lost at poker?" said Laura.

"That's not the bloody point!" said Newman. "Christ, I should've known there was something wrong when they didn't black-ball me, with my reputation in London... I mean, this place is like nowhere I've ever been. You feel part of something so exclusive, so- important. Before this, I couldn't even get into the RAC Club. I mean, the 'Chauffeurs' Club'- they'll take anyone!"

"Now you're starting to sound like Groucho Marx, Jules..."

"Nice one, sis," said Newman. Suddenly he felt exhausted. "God, it would be great to hang out for a while. Go on a trip together. Chill out a little and watch some old movies. But right now, I've really, really got to do this thing."

"You're a grown man, Julian!" said Laura. "No one can stop you from talking to your own sister. Or make you do anything you don't want to. It's a free country- they can't swear you to secrecy, and put the fear of God into you like this!"

"That's just it," said Newman. "I am a grown man. But they're- they're not like normal men at all. They're devils, Laura! Sucking my blood. The joining fee alone cost me a small fortune. And now they've even insured my life. Even my death isn't my own, anymore..."

And then the Perspex partition between the front and back of the cab slid open, a black-jack swung towards him and the iPhone was dashed from his hands onto the floor. The screen cracked immediately, the line cutting out.

"That's enough, Newman," hissed Malthus, pulling the cap off his head and turning back to the road. "Pull yourself together, man! You belong to the Club now. You have left behind your family- your friends- society! You stand at Death's private door, and that bell does not toll twice. You maggot of a man, you pathetic ingrate, think what the Club has done for you! We picked up the broken fragments of humanity that first crawled into my cab, drugged and drooling, lost forever in the Zombie Triangle. We brought them into our *salle de jeux*, begging for death at any price, rank with self-pity and self-hatred- and we moulded them back together. Forged something of a better, stronger metal. A tool for a noble task. Who else has ever done as much for you? Your school-mates? Your parents? Your sister? Hardly! What possible purpose has Miss Laura, have any of them, ever given you- to your so-called life? What need do any of them have of an empty shell like you? Don't you realise that they're all far better off with you dead- that they're secretly wishing it, even now? You can't go back now. You're in far, far too deep for that. That world is closed to you forever. Do you understand me? Do we understand each other at last?"

Julian nodded.

"And so how does that make you feel, Newman? Wretched? Humiliated? Broken? So very, very alone?"

Julian wiped at the hot tears that were sliding unchecked down his cheeks now.

"Good!" snarled Malthus. "That's just what you are! So use it! Bottle up the poison within you, and wait for it to bleed, to explode out of you. Throw the acid of your failure into the faces of your enemies! Of the Club's enemies. No gods, no masters!"

"No gods, no masters," muttered Newman. "No gods, no masters…"

"Now sit back and enjoy the ride, Guv'nor," said Malthus, putting his cap back on, a cockney once more. "We'll have you out at 'Fantasy Island' in a jiffy!"

Newman watched the London lights die away in the rear-view mirror, carried away in the stream of cars flooding west to Heathrow.

CHAPTER 8

ANCASH REGION, PERU

"The storms come in fast here," said the Peruvian, looking out of the panoramic window as freezing mist smothered the mountainside. "Like an avalanche on the Cordillera Blanca."

"They're gathering fast everywhere now," said the European. "That's why I'm here."

"After all these years! You come like a storm-cloud..."

"Like a storm-warning," said the European, getting up from his chair. His clipped hair was greying at the temples, clean-shaven face starting to blue with stubble.

"Is there a difference?" said the Peruvian.

"Perhaps not! But I don't ask you to welcome me- only to hear me out."

"Forgive my rudeness, *Señor Presidente*. I don't have many visitors up here."

"Really?"

The Peruvian smiled.

"The local people say that an ancient *pishtaco* stalks this mountainside," he said. "A damned spirit from colonial times. They believe it isn't safe to come up here without a priest..."

"And are they right?"

"Yes- and no." The Peruvian lit a cigarette. "A priest wouldn't help much. But a man like you needn't have brought a private army with you. If there is honour among thieves, can't there also be honour among- killers?"

The European laughed.

"I wasn't sure what reception I would get," he said. "After all these years." He gestured to the other side of the room, where a group of young men stood in a silent line against the wall, casting furtive glances over to their elders by the window. "And besides, these are my novices. I wanted them to meet you before I they go out into the field. To look a real assassin in the eyes- an elemental killer. To encounter a spirit from a different time. A time before men knew what pity was."

The Peruvian removed his shades and turned his gaze on him. His eyes were the vivid, mesmerising green of a Boyacá emerald. Only the deep crow's feet wrinkles around them gave any clue as to how old he must be.

"Few have done that and lived to speak of it, *Señor Presidente*."

"Indeed! Though I am one such. And I trust I do not presume too much on our old alliance now?"

Now it was the Peruvian's turn to laugh.

"There is nothing here to frighten an initiate, a high priest of death like you!" he said. "You are long past such things as fear and revenge. And it is right that your own journey has brought you up to our mountains once more. From the so-called Old World to the New. For even the greedy Spanish knew that something terrible had begun here. That something was changing deep inside men. That was why the first *pishtacos* started to take *la grasa-* the body fat- of the *indígenas* from us. Why they stole our children, and experimented on them. Why my people soon learned to fear the tall, fair men, with their long knives, always looking for the New Ones."

"They called them the 'New Ones'?" said the European. "Even then?"

"That's what the Quechua call them," said the Peruvian. "They always have. The foreigners did not fully understand what was happening. They do not even now! They always suspected that the truth lay in the composition of human fat. But the *pishtacos* did not take it for candle tallow or to grease their fire-spitting muskets, as idiot legend would have it. It was because they knew it must be the body fat that fuelled the strange fires. The terrifying fire that comes from within- the flames that can consume a man…"

"A certain type of man," said the European.

The Latin American nodded.

"The Spanish knew something of that- they were not completely blind," he said. "But then they were always so easily distracted by our gold and silver."

"What is it Cortés said?" said the European. "We Spaniards know a sickness of the heart that only gold can cure..."

"It is the white man's curse. The source of his corruption. And his power! The great Catholic king and queen across the water were not driving them here to pursue science, but *El Dorado.* And so they began to send the Indians down their silver mines, delving into our earth instead of our humanity. To exterminate our culture. The fools! As if gold could be more important than this struggle. As if anything could."

"Men find it easier to focus on the petty challenges of life than the great ones," said the European. "But that is not my way- nor yours."

The Peruvian shook his head.

"No, not us… We are doomed to look them in the eye. To fight horror with horror- extinction with annihilation. To be even more terrible than the terrors that we must face. To struggle in the shadows, and expect no thanks but death. And so I too became a *pishtaco*! But a Quechua *pishtaco*. A searcher for the truth, who did not scruple to look into the darkest places of all. Inside man himself. We all invent ourselves, and so I invented- a monster."

"And what are you now?"

"I am what I have always been, Bezique! One who fights for the old ways- for the ancient peoples of the world. For what is coming will sweep us all away in time, just like the Spanish swept the Quechua and Aymara away. And that is too fresh in our minds to suffer again. Memories linger long in the high country. We are very close to the other side here."

"To Pachamama?"

El Pishtaco smiled.

"I believe in crueller gods than the World Mother," he said.

"So do we," said Bezique. "It is our creed."

"I have heard it," said El Pishtaco. "Now it is time for your brothers to live up to their drunken boasts."

"And you?" said Bezique.

"I am ready," said El Pishtaco. "I have been waiting for you. This time, we must make a stand. There are no more places to retreat to. The lost cities are found, and all that remains to us is our humanity. We have to believe that it will be enough."

"Some call you the Inca Túpac Amaru," said Bezique. "The rebel king born again."

El Pishtaco gazed at the wild Andean landscape outside.

"Inca. Freedom fighter. Warlord. My ancestors had no written language. They knew that words do not capture us. That what is- is."

"But they are not!" said Bezique. "The Spanish blew them all away- like so much chaff in the wind…"

The Peruvian poured out two glasses of *pisco* and pushed one across to Bezique. They clinked glasses and then swigged down the raw brandy.

"Túpac had no chance of defeating Spain," said El Pishtaco. "The white man's grip was already too strong by then."

"And yet he picked up the battle axe."

"Too late!" said El Pishtaco. "Too late for anything but martyrdom."

"You don't want to be a martyr?" said Bezique. "Somehow I thought that might appeal to you."

"Martyrs are dead," said El Pishtaco, refilling the glasses. "And death is for other people. That is why we must act now. Before the darkness covers the mountains again. We are still the strong ones here. For now, at least."

"Once you fought with the MRTA- the *Movimiento Revolucionario Túpac Amaru…*" said Bezique.

"That name again!" said El Pishtaco. "Sometimes my enemy's enemy is my friend. But if I raised my hand to fight the *Sendero Luminoso*, believe that it was not to help the urban guerrillas- or the European elite in Lima! Nor to play the bounty hunter. It was because of what the Shining Path- what Abimael Guzmán himself- uncovered down there. Down there at the edges of human experience..."

"What did they find?" said Bezique, his voice hungry.

"What do you think?" said the Peruvian, with a smile. "What brings you to the high country again yourself, *Señor Presidente*? They found the great horror. They found humanity's final foe in those mountains. But they did not recognise it when they saw it."

CHAPTER 9

VIENTIANE, LAOS PEOPLE'S DEMOCRATIC REPUBLIC

Julian Newman cursed and hurled his earpiece out over the Mekong River. The swirling brown water swallowed it without a trace. So much for the spiritual balm of the East. It was hard enough just walking around Vientiane with the wet season coming on, without having to manage mercurial electronics. You raised a sweat turning a screw-driver. Julian had thought Mosquito Macau was bad in the monsoon time, but this was ridiculous. And he wasn't a techy person- he had never claimed to be. This bloody fiddly kit was built for Europe, not the relentless heat and humidity of Indochina. It got under your skin, inside your head, draining away your composure. Newman mopped his forehead for the millionth time, climbed back onto his motor-scooter and pulled out onto the Quai Fa Ngum. The scooter jolted over the gaping potholes and storm-drains, sending painful vibrations right through his skinny arms. Should have worn gloves, but then- the heat. The damn heat… He could feel his T-shirt clinging to his back, prickly sweat, the dirt streaking up his legs. And as always, the traffic out to Ban Na Son was murder. After three practice runs, he had got used to weaving his way through the cars, but the bikes and scooters seethed around him like the Mekong itself. Hell is other road-users, thought Julian. Somehow he managed to find his way, clutching his cracked mobile phone in slippery fingers as though his life depended on it. Google Maps was his only life-line now, and it had stress fractures snaking right through it. Maybe he had been too hasty, getting rid of the earpiece like that- literally hot-headed. Composure never had been his thing. But fuck it, this was on. The *Boun Bang Fai* procession was straggling on foot towards the park already, there was no time to waste in futile regret. He'd had a lifetime of that already. The jet black Health Ministry car was pulling up ahead of him now. It must have been the cleanest thing in Vientiane. It reminded him of that awful card- the ace of spades. Old Frizzle. He remembered Richard Harding's portrait at the Club, the fear in his eyes before he was hanged for forging the Tax Card. Yeah, well cry me a river, Rich- cry me a fucking Mekong Delta. Just obstructing an officer in the performance of his public duties carried a death penalty in Laos. Julian was already a dead man walking. He wouldn't get the pomp and circumstance of a trial at the Old Bailey to see him on his way. It would be straight out of a chicken hutch, and up against the prison wall for the firing squad. And now he would have to sleep-walk straight into the mission. Execute a cold op alone, without any preparation on the site, no recce around the temple site- the exact opposite of everything he'd been taught during his novitiate. But then maybe it was better that way. "Despair is power," he muttered to himself, for the hundredth time that day. Besides, Julian had always suffered from stage fright. 'Nervy Newman' they'd called him at school- that and other things he didn't care to dwell on, even now. And the Rocket Festival was nothing if not theatrical, it was the greatest show of the Laotian year. The huge wooden frames were set up like a stage, bamboo stairways to heaven, looming high above the lush green stalls of the park. Around them, men dressed up in wigs and outrageous drag were chanting and capering to entertain the crowd. One woman linked arms with a yellow-robed monk to perform an impromptu Laotian waltz. Pretty wild, but it had all been in the mission dossier. Subject never misses the *Boun Bang Fai*: think Bonfire Night, Mardi Gras and the Christmas Panto at the Palladium all rolled into one.

Somehow it seemed more meaningful than that to Julian though. It might have been a lot of superstitious nonsense to Bezique, perched up there in his technocratic Suicide Station. But when you walked the streets of Vientiane or Ban Na Son, it kind of made sense. Laos was at ease with its own spirituality, content to let harsh reality and superstition, office block and monastery, Communism and mysticism rub shoulders together in the melting-pot of its steaming streets. For a moment Newman was soothed by the conviction in the faces all around him, the child-like trust that this was the exact thing they wanted to be doing at that precise point in time. He had never felt that in his whole life, except for a few fleeting seconds as he placed the first bet of the night, wallet still plumped out with bank-notes. And even then, somewhere in his head there had always lurked the crushing realisation that he had failed again. That humiliation had stowed away in secret, and come along for the ride. But this was something different, this was a strange new peace inside himself. He even forgot how damn hot it was for once. God, he should have travelled here, Vietnam, Cambodia- while there was still time. Laurence Pearce had wanted to go to Vietnam with him, had even bought the Lonely Planet guide, but then Newman himself had persuaded the poor sod to go back to Macau with him. To lose some huge sum in games Julian couldn't even remember, in some gambling hell he couldn't picture. Had had to spend another fortune in booze and drugs to forget, as soon as possible afterwards. But now they would never do it- not together, nor alone. The Club had done for Laurence, had done for Kip Horrocks, and now Julian was waiting for Fifth Street in his own game. How long before it did for Rob Walker and Hugo Capstick too, and the full house was completed? The bloody Club… But then that reminded him.

"This is more than a club…" Julian whispered to himself. "It's a mission. Now where the fuck is the 200?"

The crowd opened to let through a chaotic reel of part-time drag queens, soft drink cans strung together in jangling chains around their waists, and now Newman could see Minister Keophothong clearly for the first time.

"We have visual contact..." he muttered, but there was no Suicide Station to hear it. That damn earpiece. He should never have left it behind. Bezique would be fuming. Well, screw him. What could he do it about it now? The end was nigh, and Julian was the one sweating it out on the ground here. Despair is power. "We have visual contact."

The Minister was wearing a light-weight Western suit and tie, but he applauded the bawdy *Boun Bang Fai* antics from his place of honour at the front, smiling and joking with his aides. Subject styles himself a man of the people. He was in the thick of it alright, pressing the flesh with the *hoi polloi*. Newman waded through the crowd, approaching the biggest rocket-frame. Two men, in jeans and T-shirts but with women's bras dangling outside their shirts, were tinkering with the bamboo-clad rocket. It was festooned with crumpled Laotian bank notes, blessed by monks- nearly ready for its mission up into the clouds. Another one-way mission, thought Newman. Ground control to Major Julian. He wondered why they felt the need to beg these gods for rain, when he could already feel it all around him.

The chanting intensified as the Minister himself stepped forward to ignite the first rocket. Truly this would be an auspicious *Boun Bang Fai*. The smoke started to swirl all around them as the fuse burned down, harsh chemical fumes catching Newman in the back of his throat. He couldn't breathe, couldn't think. Time was ticking away, and there was no Bezique to give him his cue. He was really starting to wish he hadn't lost that earpiece, but then he had to crowd that thought out of his mind too. This was taking forever. He couldn't hang around the Minister all day. Was that him turning to leave? If he got back into that bullet-proof car, it was game over. This was now or never, a one-time opportunity, it had to be. The aides were closing around the Minister, ushering him away.

"Suicide Station..." he whispered, but there was no one to hear. "Shit, shit, shit!"

"It doesn't matter what you do, as long as you do something," Kip

Horrocks would have said. And Horrocks had done alright, everyone knew that. So as the next battery of rockets was lit, Newman ignited the smoke bomb and dropped it onto the ground. Too soon. Far too bloody soon. Horrocks always was full of shit. The Minister wasn't close enough to him. Now people were screaming as the smoke billowed across the field, trapping the light of the exploding rockets inside it like sheet lightning. Suddenly the park was like a blitz, a war zone, a festival of chaos, with gasping, choking civilians staggering about in alternate blinding light and darkness. A teenager stumbled into him, and Newman screamed himself as he made out the image on his T-shirt: a Vietnam-era G.I.'s helmet, with a card tucked into the webbing. The ace of spades. Newman stared at it in horror. The boy just pushed him out of the way and blundered off into the smoke. But when he looked up again, Newman had lost the Minister. And the last shreds of his composure. He fumbled with his crack-screened iPhone, scrolling through his recent calls.

"Come on, Bezique, pick up, fucking pick up, man… I can't find him!" he shouted into the phone, panicking, raising his voice above the shouting all around him. "There's too much bloody smoke here! I've lost Cargo 200! Repeat, Cargo 200 is out of visual. I can't find Keophothong. I can't see a fucking thing out here!"

"Julian! Julian- just calm down and speak to me. What's going on there?"

"What?" screamed Newman. "I can't fucking hear you! Everyone's yelling all at once. It's all gone to shit, I tell you! I can't see him…"

Then the Minister loomed out of the smoke towards Newman, grabbing at him.

"It's the 200! Jesus Christ! He's… He's burning alive! Repeat, he's burning alive!" said Newman, shoving Keophothong away, sending him tumbling to the ground, black smoke still pouring off him. "But- but nothing touched him! I never touched him. He's just- burning…"

"What's happening, Julian? Who's burning? Who's that screaming? Just calm down a minute, and tell me. I can get help to you there, if you can just tell me where you are!"

"What?" yelled Newman. "I can't hear you!"

"Where are you, Julian? Who's burning? What is all this about?"

"The fucking Minister, of course!" screamed Julian, staring at Keophothong. The flames were devouring him now, consuming him from within. "Who do you think? He's dying right before my eyes! He's fucking burning! I- I've never seen anything like it…"

"Are you safe there, Julian? Tell me! Are you alright?"

"Who is this?" shouted Newman.

"It's me- Laura, of course!" she said, sobbing. "Your sister Laura! I couldn't trace your flight. I've failed you again… Where are you, Jules?"

"I can't fucking hear you! I can't wait any longer! I just want this to end… I'm initiating the end-game. Repeat, I'm initiating the end-game!"

"Don't do it!" cried Laura. "Whatever it is, don't do it, I'm begging you!"

"Tell everyone I'm sorry…" said Julian. "So very sorry. I've always been so sorry. But this has to end now. No gods, no masters!"

There was a volley of explosions, and then the line went dead.

"Julian!" screamed Laura. "Jules! My brother! My sweet brother…"

CHAPTER 10

ANCASH REGION, PERU

El Pishtaco waited for the last light to slide off the mountain-tops before he spoke again.

"The Shining Path held sway in Ayacucho, Apurímac and Huancavelica- in the old places," he said. "The high towers. For the first time Europeans had dared to leave their coastal city strongholds, to occupy the interior. And the *Senderistas* found strange things in those Southern Highlands. Things that had lain still through many silent Aymara centuries."

"And what did they do when they found them?" said Bezique.

"They didn't understand it all- not at first," said the Peruvian. "How could they, those book-taught sons of Europe? But soon they knew enough to speak to the *indígenas*. They were the first white men who had ever won the trust of the Indians. More fool you, *mi gente*!"

"And so they heard the tales about the New Ones?" said Bezique.

"In time," said El Pishtaco. "And soon they discovered for themselves that they were true. There was a burning. They say that Abimael Guzmán saw it with his own eyes- that he was fascinated by it. But whether that is true or not, he came to believe in it. Whatever else 'Chairman Gonzalo' may have been- vain peacock, monomaniac, mass-murderer- he was no fool."

"So what did they do?"

"They did what all white men do," said El Pishtaco. "They tried to turn it to their own advantage, of course! To steal it from us. They thought it could be their secret weapon, the indigenous *revolución* that would carry away the whole bourgeois establishment, like a great mud-slide running down from Ayacucho onto Lima. They didn't understand that no one could control it, once it took hold. That it would send their whole Shining Path up in flames, if they ever let it in. Even the so-called 'Fourth Sword of Communism' would not be strong enough to cut this down…"

"And that was why Guzmán had to die?" said Bezique.

El Pishtaco shrugged.

"He lives yet- in his own way. He is rotting in Callao Prison, locked away from the world. Without a voice. His vanity- his ambition- could have ruined everything. But now his half-life in the shadows prevents any successor from occupying his throne in Ayacucho. The whole business cost me a lot of trouble. That was why I had to leave these mountains. To pick up the gun again."

"And break the *Sendero Luminoso* in the old way?" said Bezique, raising his glass. "Here's to a simpler time! But perhaps it will be with us again soon…"

El Pishtaco drained his glass, then refilled both of them again.

"*Pisco*…The one good thing we gained from the European," said El Pishtaco. "And yet even that has poisoned our people."

"*Pisco*- and gunpowder?" said Bezique.

"The Spanish always kept the best guns for themselves," said El Pishtaco. "Just like you, Bezique."

"Perhaps you're right, my friend," said Bezique. "Perhaps it is time for us to pool our resources. So let's start with some information. What else did they know, these Maoist ideologues?"

El Pishtaco lit a cigarette.

"Stories started to reach Chairman Gonzalo's ears from his Communist brothers in Colombia," he said. "The FARC and ELN ruled the countryside during the days of *La Violencia*. And New Ones were appearing there too.

They were just whispers- ghosts. But then the rumours kept coming, trickles running down from the Cordillera Occidental and the Cauca Valley. Until they became torrents. Words travel without borders between the *indígenas.* They weave their way along the old Inca pathways. And from the other side too, from the *altiplano* in Bolivia. Where the Aymara are even older- even quieter. They brood on old wrongs, but eventually they come to speak too. And when they did, they told stories of unexplained burnings, and unimaginable power. Remote villages full of New Ones- a community of several towns. The Shining Path were starting to make connections. To see the invisible links between the New Ones. To see that the revolution here might not stop with the bourgeoisie- or even with Andean America."

"There is something special about the high places of the world- about the internal gas mix," said Bezique. "We have seen it happen at altitude in Asia and Africa too. Rapid pressure change exacerbates the effects. Any doctor can tell you that a decrease in atmospheric pressure, like a sudden ascent to altitude, causes inert gases to bubble out of the blood. In extreme cases, that leads to decompression sickness- the Bends. In the New Ones, the acceleration of bubble formation seems to increase the intensity of the combustion reaction, like the supercharger in an internal combustion engine. Each intake cycle of the reaction stimulates the formation of more gas plasma, increasing the sonoluminescent effect- and the probability of ignition."

El Pishtaco laughed.

"A lot of words for a simple concept," he said. "Fire!"

"A fire that is spreading," said Bezique. "The Firestarter genes are migrating from the poor highlands of the world to the rich lowlands. The cases are multiplying everywhere. There have been sixteen documented incidents, this month alone."

"Where?" said El Pishtaco.

"Europe. Africa. All over Asia," said Bezique. "Even with all our resources, all our technology- all our brothers- we just can't contain them anymore. We're chasing our tails. And so now there are loose ends. Stories are escaping.

Drawing them together…"

"Where?" repeated the Peruvian.

"On your side. Otherwise I would not have troubled you with this."

"Do not speak to me of trouble," said El Pishtaco. "Have I not pledged my life to this struggle? And have I ever walked away from a war before it ended? Just tell me what you have discovered, Bezique. Pool resources!"

"Listen to this…" said Bezique, opening an audio file on his cell phone.

"*¡Por La Nueva Raza- todo!*" came de la Peña's voice from the phone speaker.

"Play it again, *Señor Presidente*," said El Pishtaco.

Bezique held the phone up once more.

"*¡Por La Nueva Raza- todo!*"

"Everything for the New Race…" said El Pishtaco. For an instant he looked exhausted- ancient. Then his expression shifted, and he was ageless again. "Who said these words?"

"A money-launderer in Panama- just before my operative terminated him," said Bezique. "The Club puts business through all the major players there, to keep our ear close to the ground. This one was channelling dirty money to a secret community in Colombia, from an armed faction out in the jungle. Our sources say they're masquerading as a dissident wing of the *Fuerzas Armadas Revolucionarias de Colombia*."

"The FARC!" said El Pishtaco. "Now that name again. Clever. The broken shards of the revolution are still sharp enough to tear holes in the border between Panama and Colombia. Hundreds of them. And the drugs and the money still pour through them like water..."

"That's the problem," said Bezique. "We have tried to shut this one down. But someone is protecting them. Someone connected- someone we can't reach. Yet. And the Colombian Government isn't returning our calls."

"There is no one I can't reach on this side," said El Pishtaco. "Which *Frente* are they attached to?"

"We're still investigating," said Bezique. "All I have now is their street name: *El Clan de La Nueva Raza.*"

"The Clan of the New Race..." said El Pishtaco. "They are learning their own strength. And testing ours- our resolve. Our ruthlessness."

"That is as strong as ever, my friend," said Bezique. "It has to be. What worries me is that they are developing their own identity. Their own understanding of the genetic links and heat signatures that tie them together. And now even their own mythology. What does 'Achilles' mean to you? 'Aquiles', in Spanish?"

"It means nothing to me," said El Pishtaco. "That is a legend of Europe, is it not?"

"It was mentioned by the money-launderer's assistant," said Bezique. "A Costa Rican- one of *La Nueva Raza.* They must have adopted it for their own."

"It could be a person?" said El Pishtaco. "Spaniards have such names."

"Maybe," said Bezique. "But I fear that it is part of something deeper. History tells us that those who would take over the world must first find themselves- their culture, their purpose. Their unity."

El Pishtaco laughed.

"Perhaps your history, my friend. History written by victors... My history is about strength. And it tells me that when a new race invades your lands, a stronger race, it will not go away. You have one moment in time, to resist it with all your power."

"And if you don't?"

"Then you have many lifetimes to regret it. They are growing bold- and the great war is coming," said El Pishtaco. "Perhaps it is fitting that it should start in our own lands. Where the ancient peoples walked. We will see who are the true heirs to our Inca ancestors. For this time it must be a total war from the beginning! No mercy. They will show none to us- they can't. The jaguar does not lie down with the goat. Nor the New Ones with the old."

"So you'll go?" said Bezique. "You'll leave your mountain stronghold, and go and finish what you have started?"

"Did you ever doubt it?" said El Pishtaco. "Your journey has not been wasted, *Señor Presidente. Perro de buena raza, hasta la muerte caza*... I will never stop hunting them now."

CHAPTER 11

MIRAFLORES LOCKS, PANAMA CANAL, REPUBLIC OF PANAMA

"You came back then, Makepeace?" said Commissioner Herrera, sipping at the bitter Boquete coffee without looking round. "And to me. I suppose that shows a certain animal courage."

"You think I was unwise, *Señor Comisionado*?" said Ben.

"Panama is a free country, as you know," said Herrera. "But I don't think I would have returned here- if I was you."

Ben nodded.

"And yet here you are anyway," said the Commissioner of Police. "Loitering by my usual table, here in my favourite café. Don't you know that this is where I come to get away from people like you, Makepeace? People who have a gift for always asking the wrong questions. People who just don't know when to stop. I prefer to keep those kinds of people at Police Headquarters. The one place there is no danger at all of them stumbling upon the truth..."

"Maybe down the stairs though?" said Ben.

"There you go again, Makepeace," said Herrera. "Asking the wrong question. This is why Central America is not a happy place for you. This is not Europe. Here, people will shoot you in the face whilst they are still laughing at your joke. But then you know that already, *no*?"

"Yes, I know that, *Señor Comisionado*," said Ben. "That's why I came here first. To ask you what the right question is."

"Here, the right question is no question at all," said Herrera. "You should have learned that by now. After all your time in Panama! But that isn't your way, is it, Ben? So sit down, traveller, sit down."

"You haven't changed, Commissioner," said Makepeace. "Dapper as always! I thought that the head that wore the crown was heavy."

"Maybe the chief of police is not king in this town," said Herrera. "You look well too- perhaps a little thinner than before. Like you've come to fight- or to run. Either way, that worries me."

"I don't know yet," said Makepeace. "Maybe both. It depends what's at the end of this thread I'm pulling at."

"What's at the beginning?" said Herrera. "What have you found out so far?"

"What you always find in Panama," said Ben, pouring himself a cup of coffee from the silver pot in front of the Commissioner. They watched as the vast *NeoPanamax Century* container ship dropped fifty-four feet down into the depths of the Miraflores Locks, sinking from view before their eyes on its way to the Pacific Ocean on the other side. "Ghost ships disappearing in the night. More questions than answers. This is a city where everyone talks, and no one tells you anything."

"Of course!" said Herrera. "The worlds meet here on the Isthmus. You get to go home, Makepeace- to one or another of them. If anywhere is home for people like you… But some of us have to stay here. We must live with them both: East and West. Atlantic and Pacific. Black and white. So which one would you say the mysterious case of Señor Pearce is?"

"I'd say it's grey," said Ben.

"Grey!" said Herrera. "Well, I'm not so sure about that. Consider this hotel of Pearce's for a start- the *Joya del Istmo*. I know it very well. It's used- was used- as a safe house by the big money laundering operations. A Lloyd's market for dirty money, if you will. And the house rules were very strict- no guns, no knives, no weapons of any sort. You had to check your AK-47 or AR15 in at reception, pick up a receipt and then collect it when you left."

"Very civilised. So that's why you tolerated its existence this long?"

"Be careful what you say, Makepeace- even here," said Herrera. "No crime can be tolerated in Panama. But we cannot prosecute them all. Sometimes we have to keep our friends close, and our money-launderers closer. They do have their uses, you know."

"I'm sure there are millions of good reasons for keeping them around, *Comisionado*," said Ben.

"*Cállate la boca*, Makepeace," said Herrera. "I won't warn you again. I may be the Commissioner, but that doesn't make you Batman. Besides, the currency I'm interested in is not dollars. Here, we live or die by information. And the unofficial movement of cash through this country is the barometer for every upheaval in Panama- in all of Latin America."

"And where is the mercury now?"

"It's rising fast," said Herrera. "Can't you feel it?"

"Because a spoilt British kid was killed in a bad neighbourhood?"

"No, Makepeace," said Herrera, lighting a Dunhill and exhaling smoke through his nose. "Don't play the fool. Because it seems that this particular bomb was made of military-grade plastic explosive. Composition 4. That must have been how they got it through the security at the *Joya*. The guards were looking for fire-arms, not high energy compounds." He slid the pack of cigarettes across the table to Ben. "You keep looking at them! Just take one, it's annoying me."

"*¿Cómo no?*" said Makepeace. He picked up a book of matches from the bowl in the middle of the table. "So- C-4... Plasticised RDX. Not your average *sicario* hit, then. You'd need access to high explosives. And some det cord or a PETN detonator to trigger it." He struck a match and lit the cigarette. "No wonder it wrecked the place."

"It ripped the block apart like a corn *arepa*," said Herrera. "Hardly the way to kill one lost soul. It makes no sense. You don't need Carlos the Jackal to take out a *gringo* tourist, do you? But at the same time, the President lost some influential supporters in that explosion. People who thought they had- protection."

"They must be very important people if you're losing any sleep over them, *Señor Comisionado*," said Makepeace, putting the matches into his pocket. "Pearce was small fry."

"You're here, aren't you?" said Herrera. "And you had a very long way to come."

"Yeah, but that's my job," said Ben. "Life insurance."

"Ah yes…" said the Commissioner. "You're an insurance man now, Makepeace. I keep forgetting that! You seem more like a man who needs life insurance himself. You are always so ready to risk everything. But there's an English expression, isn't there: 'Poacher turned gamekeeper'?"

Makepeace laughed again.

"Sometimes there's a fine line. You should know about that."

"It's just because I know both sides of the line that I am so- uneasy- about recent developments," said Herrera. "There's a lot of dirty money moving through the back channels right now. Across the Darien border with Colombia. That border has a lot of history. But it can't be the Dirty War in Colombia this time. The guerrillas are on their knees there."

"Could the Americans be up to something in Venezuela again?" said Ben. "Regime change? They'd love to take out Maduro."

"It's always possible," said Herrera, grinding out his cigarette. "Maybe President Trump is just about crazy enough for a new Bay of Pigs affair. But I don't think so. Something new is coming in Colombia. Something more dramatic than the usual right wing, left wing see-saw. We will be drawn into it. And when Panama sneezes, South America catches a cold."

"Thanks for the tip," said Ben. "Is there anything else you can tell me?"

"You're not the only unexpected visitor to Panama right now, Makepeace," said Herrera, standing up. A waiter slipped his brocaded jacket back over his shoulders and proffered his peaked police hat. "So watch your back, insurance clerk. If I see more in this Pearce business than meets the eye, you can be sure that others will have too. And they may be less forgiving than I am."

"*Sí, señor…*" said Ben.

"And one more thing," said Herrera, putting his mirrored sun-glasses on. "You better make sure I find out what you've been doing here from your own lips first. Your Panama privileges are in the balance right now."

"And my life?" said Ben.

"Well, that's rather the same thing, isn't it?" said Herrera.

"I'll let you know what I find," said Ben.

Herrera nodded.

"So stop drinking my coffee and go crack the case, Makepeace," he said. "Where are you headed for now?"

"I'm going to ground zero," said Ben. "Where all this began."

"*Como usted mande.* We'll look out for you," said Herrera. "If we can. But remember that ground zero can be deeper than it looks- once you start digging. A man like you doesn't always know where to stop."

"Now I have to stop when the expenses run out," said Makepeace. "This is business."

"Is that a fact?" said Herrera. "Then you really have changed."

"One last thing, *Señor Comisionado,*" said Ben. "Is your family originally from Colombia?"

Herrera tilted his hat to Makepeace and then placed it on his perfect-ly-coiffured, dark head.

"The corn *arepa*?"

"It made me wonder," said Ben.

The Commissioner pulled his spotless white gloves on.

"Yes, my grandmother came here from Medellín," he said. "It's no secret. Keep thinking though, Makepeace. It might just keep you alive."

CHAPTER 12

TOCUMEN AIRPORT, PANAMA CITY, REPUBLIC OF PANAMA

El Pishtaco put his shades on and slipped out through the bustling humanity fringing the terminal. He was travelling light, no check-in baggage. A battered black, late '90s-model Jeep Cherokee pulled up next to him in the drop-off queue. The driver got out, looked around and then handed him the keys, before melting away into the crowd. El Pishtaco slid into the driver's seat and drove the car out of the airport, steering with one hand as he delved under the passenger seat with the other. There was a slim leather grip there, with a business card taped to the top of it. It only bore three letters: 'B.S.C.'

El Pishtaco opened the zip and glanced at the contents. It was all there. A pair of M9 Berettas with spare clips, an Ontario MK 3 Navy Knife, a machete in a leather sheath. And a bundle of used United States dollars, six inches thick.

"*Gracias,* Bohemian Sports Club," said El Pishtaco.

He rolled down the car window, reading the graffiti on the ragged clapboard walls of the liquor stores and *bodegas* outside as the rush-hour traffic crawled into down-town Panama City. The biggest slogan warned the president of the republic: "*A cada chancho, le llega su sábado*"- to every swine, his slaughter-day comes. El Pishtaco smiled to himself and lit a cigarette.

"And so even in poverty, there is defiance..."

A cell-phone rang out inside the car. El Pishtaco frowned, then rummaged deeper in the bag. Beneath a false bottom, a cheap disposable phone was taped to the leather.

"*¿Dígame?*" said the Peruvian.

"Our friends in Colombia. It was *Frente 57.*"

"57..." said El Pishtaco. "Yes, I know it- in Antioquia Province. They used to call them '*Muerte a Capitalistas*'. They wear MAC armbands in the field. Death to Capitalists..."

"Not any more," said Bezique. "Now they call them *El Clan de La Nueva Raza.*"

"That is the splinter cell?"

"Correct. Which will lead us to the South American social cell. That has its own name."

"Well?" said the Peruvian.

"They call it *Proyecto Luz.*"

"Only the darkness can purify Project Light..." murmured El Pishtaco.

He threw the cell-phone out of the window. It splashed into the swampy ditch by the side of the highway and sank like a stone. On the rickety billboard above the road, some unseen nihilist had changed the jaunty slogan '*Panama Positiva*' to 'Panama HIV Positive'.

El Pishtaco took a deep breath of damp air.

"*La costa*... It reeks of Spaniards- and corruption."

CHAPTER 13

MORTLAKE CREMATORIUM, RICHMOND, UNITED KINGDOM

Laura Newman wiped her eyes and looked out over the muddy swirl of river, onto the red-brick Victoriana of the University of Westminster Boathouse on the north bank of the River Thames.

"That's where the Boat Race finishes…" said Rob Walker. "And this is the finishing line for poor Jules too, I guess. Ironic, really- given that he fucking hated rowing."

"And Victorian architecture…" said Laura.

"So who chose this god-awful, depressing place anyway?" said Walker.

"Who do you think, Rob?" said Laura. "Dad wasn't exactly in thrall to Jules' preferences in life, was he?"

Walker laughed and lit up a cigarette.

"You don't mind, do you?" he said.

"Of course not," Laura said.

"Have one yourself?"

"I'll have two," she said.

He laughed again, and lit a cigarette for her. They watched the water flow under Chiswick Bridge in silence for a minute.

"The old boy certainly did have his foibles," said Walker. "But this is where he rests. The despair is all used up, and he's finally at peace."

"I suppose so," said Laura, blowing out smoke.

"And how about you, Laura?" said Walker. She looked at him. "Are you at peace?"

"You heard then?" she said.

Walker looked at his shoes.

"Yeah, of course I couldn't help hearing that there had been some kind of… unpleasantness. Then talk of legal action by the Club. But also that it had all blown over?"

"Maybe so far as Dad and his lawyers are concerned," said Laura.

"And so far as you're concerned?"

"I know what I heard, Rob," she said. "My brother watched the Laotian Minister of Health burn to death in front of his eyes. In a country he'd never been to before- where gambling is illegal. And now he's dead too. So if you know me at all- do you really think I'm done with this?"

"The Met have spoken to the local police though, haven't they?" said Walker. "The way I heard it, Minister Keophothong and Jules just happened to be killed in the same explosion. Absolutely tragic- but completely accidental. That damn Rocket Festival kills and maims dozens of people a year. I mean, basic breaches of Health and Safety practice are commonplace there."

"And Kip Horrocks?" said Laura. "Another tragic accident, I suppose?"

"Well, yeah," said Walker. "A car crash, you know. That could have happened anywhere. On the A4. Anywhere."

"You don't see it as a bit of a coincidence, Rob?" said Laura. "Kip and Julian both being killed like that, within the space of a few days? And the police in both countries treating them as accidental deaths, without any further investigation? It reeks of a cover-up!"

"Think where they were, though, Laura…" said Walker. "Panama and Laos! I mean, Third World countries. Everyone knows that the roads are death-traps over there! It wasn't exactly the Surrey Hills, was it?"

"Panama?" said Laura.

"I mean Uganda..." said Walker. "Uganda and Laos. Panama was Laurence, of course..."

"What do you mean?" said Laura.

"Nothing..." said Walker.

"Laurence? Laurence Pearce?" said Laura. "It was Laurence wasn't it? Has something happened to him, too? In Panama? I thought it was strange that he wasn't here! Jesus Christ, Rob, what is going on? When did this happen? What happened to him?"

Walker raised his cigarette to his mouth, but Laura noticed that it had already burned down to the stub. He spat it out and lit another.

"You were in the States, of course," he said. "Well, Laurence was- he was visiting a very dangerous place," he said. "Utterly reckless of him. Some sort of money launderers' den, apparently. Guns and gangsters everywhere. You know what he was like- obsessed with cutting a dash. Trying to live up to his old man's style. As if Seb Pearce wasn't the biggest shit in London... Not to speak ill of the dead, obvs."

"I know about all that, Rob," said Laura. "But what happened to Lol?"

"Like I say, he was in the wrong place at the wrong time," said Walker. "It seems a notorious money-launderer was staying there too. And then there was this explosion- a business rival trying to take out the competition, they think. Muscle in on his patch. The whole hotel was destroyed. And poor Laurence with it."

"An explosion!" said Laura. "Just like Jules. And Kip Horrocks was killed in a fireball too, in Uganda- only it was the other car..."

"Yes, there was a road accident, you know," said Walker. "You remember how he used to drive. Like hell- like a fucking maniac. Jules always used to say lending Kip your car was like giving a toddler a hand grenade..."

"But it was the car he hit that exploded, Rob, not his own!" said Laura. "Don't you see what means? He would have had to get out of his own car after the crash to get caught in the fire that killed him. Now they think he was actually inside that UN Landcruiser when it went up! None of it makes sense…"

"Yeah, they think Kip went to try and drag the people in the other vehicle out of the wreckage, just as the fuel tank kindled," said Walker. "The soldiers. Quite the hero!"

"Is that what you believe?" said Laura.

"Don't you?"

"I believe that Kip Horrocks was capable of anything," she said. "He could definitely have killed a Government Minister, if he was pointed in the right direction. No questions asked."

"That was in Laos though," said Walker. "Kip was in Uganda. No Ministers there."

"There's a connection though, isn't there?" said Laura.

"What do you mean?"

"Don't be daft, Rob," said Laura. "The fucking Club is the connection! Julian- Kip Horrocks- and now Laurence Pearce. So how about you? Are you a member of this Club too? The Bohemian Sports Club?"

"Me?" said Walker. "Well, I mean, not really. Sort of a country member, you know? Keep up the subs for old time's sake. What with all the other chaps from school being members."

"That's the thing, isn't it?" said Laura. "You're all members. So what is it you do there, Rob?" She took his arm. "I have to know- I have to know what happened to poor Jules. I should have been looking out for him! Is it the Club that arranges these dangerous trips you all keep going on? Do they dare you to go to these places? Double-dare you?"

"Come on, Laura…" said Walker.

"No, you come on!" said Laura. "People are dead here! This is no fucking joke. So tell me what it is. Is it some kind of macho thing? An early mid-life crisis? Why does this keep happening to so many of your friends? For Christ's sake, you must be wondering yourself- if you don't already know. If you'll be next?"

"We're all at that age, I guess..." said Walker. "None of us have really settled down, for whatever reason. Made what we'd hoped out of our lives. So perhaps it is some kind of weird search for fulfilment. For meaning in our lives..."

"Bullshit, Rob!" said Laura, punching his arm. "That's complete bullshit. Because you know what I think? Crazy as it may seem, I think Julian was somehow tangled up in some kind of political assassination out there. And I think Kip was up to exactly the same thing in Uganda. Do you know who he hit with his car? The Head of the UN Peacekeeping Mission in Africa! And you told me just now that Laurence Pearce's death was linked to a notorious money-launderer. Your words. There's motive."

"What motive?" said Walker.

"There are obvious reasons why people- some people- would want each of those men dead," she said. "None of them are civilians. I don't know what links them yet, but I'm sure as hell going to find out. So I'm going to ask you again: what exactly does the Bohemian Sports Club do?"

"Rob! Laura! There you both are!" said Hugo Capstick, loping out through the brick arches of the crematorium, folding a loose lock of dark, curly hair back behind his ear. "Grim business that, wasn't it? Poor old Jules..."

"What does the Club do, Rob?" repeated Laura, ignoring Capstick.

"Now steady on there, Waz!" said Capstick. "The first rule of the Club is: You do not talk to a chap's ex about the Club..."

"Fuck off, Hugo!" said Laura. "That isn't funny. Do you know where we are? At my brother's funeral. I'm surprised you even remember we went out, anyway- you were so wasted the whole time."

"I wrote it all down on my arm," said Capstick. "Kind of like *Memento*. That's what all these tattoos are... Now I'm retracing my steps. In my world, we're actually still dating."

"Christ, you're annoying!" said Laura. "I'm not even going to ask you if you're involved in the Club, Hugo, because I just know you must be knee-deep in anything that's this messed up. And this is very messed up! That

Laotian guy was burned alive, did you know that? Not to mention all those poor soldiers. This has got your finger-prints all over it…"

Capstick held his hands up in mock surrender.

"Just tell me, Rob!" said Laura. "What does the Club do? You were Julian's friend. His oldest friend. Like part of the family. And don't you think his family deserve to know what happened? I, for one, need some closure here. It's Jules' fucking funeral, look around you! If this doesn't put your stupid boys' club into context, then I don't know what could." Capstick glanced at Walker. "Yeah, I know all about the silly vows you've sworn, so there's no need to look sheepish about it now," said Laura. "For the last time, just tell me what happened!"

"Listen, Laura, about the funeral…" said Capstick. "I get that you're upset, of course I do. I know you blame yourself, though you really shouldn't. But I'm afraid that Angela- your Mum- is in a bit of a state about Jules in there. Seriously. I think you better go back in and check that she's doing OK. Because isn't that the important thing right now? It's not about us. Any of us. You have to be strong for her. For all your loved ones."

"You really are a prick, aren't you?" said Laura, stubbing out her cigarette. "To be continued…" She started to make for the crematorium. Then she stopped and turned back to Walker. "I suppose the police in Panama haven't found out any more about what happened to Laurence? Or were they happy with the circumstantial evidence too? That another case closed, is it?"

"Laurence?" said Capstick.

"Yeah, Laurence Pearce, you bastard," said Laura. "You went to school with him, remember? He joined your little club. Now he's dead too. The dots are joining up, Hugo. And they're leading straight to you two. You know a lot more than you're telling me. For now, that is."

"Yeah, right, Laurence…" said Capstick, looking hard at Walker.

"All I know is what I told you already, Laura- what we discussed…" said Walker.

"Strange, don't you think?" said Laura. "With all the information that's been leaked out of Panama recently- you have heard of the Panama Papers, right? You'd think there'd be a lot of digging that could be done into a money-launderer in that particular part of the world, wouldn't you? A lot of open secrets. Loose ends. They're nothing without funds transfers, are they? And it's all available on the internet now. That's where I would start. If I wanted to find out what happened to your friend Laurence, that is. Only I seem to be the only one who's asking any questions about this. So far."

"If she comes back here with a waterboard, I for one am doing a runner," said Capstick. "You're on your own on this one, Waz…"

Laura turned her back on them both and strode back into the brown brick building.

"For fuck's sake, Rob!" said Capstick. "What have you been saying to her? This is no time for flirting with the dead guy's hot sister. We'd better get back to the Club pronto. Bezique is going to have your fucking guts for garters!"

"What's he going to do- kill me?" said Walker.

Capstick stared at him in surprise.

"We're not going to say a word to Bezique about Laura, Hugo- have you got that?" said Walker. "Not to anyone. This has got absolutely nothing to do with her, and it's going to stay that way! Do you fucking understand me?"

"Alright, man," said Capstick. "Cool your boots. I think you've been hanging around with her too long, it's messing with your head. But I guess she doesn't really know anything anyway, does she? She's just a rich chick with a computer. The first rule of the Club is: You do not sweat the small stuff…"

"She's right about one thing, Captagon- you are bloody annoying!" said Walker. "Can't you take anything seriously? Her brother just died. She's going through hell. Blaming herself."

"Oh, I'm taking this seriously alright, matey," said Capstick. "You're the one going out on a limb here, keeping this from Bezique! I just hope you're right about that."

"Enough has happened to their family already," said Walker. "I'm going back to see Angela."

"Really wallowing in this, aren't you?" said Capstick. "She was my girlfriend, not yours. Which is part of the problem here, right? The first rule…"

Walker glared at him.

"OK, OK," said Capstick. "The point is though, it's time to leave the grief behind. That's what this is all about. Turning something shitty into something important. Despair is power!"

"Where are you going then?" said Walker.

"Oh, you can find me in the Club. Bottle full of bub..." said Capstick, ordering an Uber on his cell phone. "Because I'm just about done with fucking funerals for one day, I can tell you! I'm going to get absolutely rat-arsed. Think Prince Harry in Vegas…"

Walker dropped his cigarette and ground it out.

"There are more funerals coming though, aren't there, Captagon?" he said. "There always are."

"That's the life we've chosen now, Waz," said Capstick. "That's chosen us."

"You mean the death," said Walker.

CHAPTER 14

CALIDONIA, PANAMA CITY, REPUBLIC OF PANAMA

The neon skyline of Punta Paitilla sank away into the Bay of Panama, as the cab-driver wrestled his creaking Toyota off Avenida Balboa. They were hurtling into the maze of the Casco Viejo peninsula now. Into darkness. Ben blinked as his eyes adjusted to the gloom of the ill-lit streets. It was like a rollercoaster, free-falling into a different city. Different cities. Outside was chicken-wire, corrugated zinc, naked breeze-blocks- the fringes of the Santa Ana shanty-town. Then a faded ghost-world of crumbling creole mansions, the deeper labyrinth of Spanish Panama. The cobbled roads were claustrophobically narrow now, shut in by the wrought-iron bars rising up from the balconies above, overgrown by straggling cob-webs of black electrical cables. As the taxi bucked and leapt on the uneven surface, Ben watched tantalising shafts of light stealing out into the darkness from between the slats of the shutters.

"What could have brought you down this road, Pearce?" he said. "What rich man's demons were chasing you? Because you found a dead end here."

The rank smoke from the driver's cigarette lingered around the cab, caught up in the cloying smell of decaying mango peel and diesel soot. The unmistakable reek of downtown Central America. Ben remembered it from Belize, Managua, Tegucigalpa, Colón. Especially Colón. Somehow the air cleared when you reached Colombia to the south, or Mexico to the north. On the steaming Isthmus in between, it lingered and suppurated. It never left you, not until you got out. And Makepeace had thought he had got out.

"Here I knew despair…" he murmured.

"*¿Señor?"* said the taxi-driver, turning round.

"*Nada. Siga, siga…*" said Ben, waving him on.

In spite of the cab's humming air conditioning, his hands felt damp with condensation. Nothing could quite keep the humidity out here. It seeped everywhere. Then the cab-driver called out "*Hotel Joya del Istmo, señor,*" and the cab lurched to an abrupt halt.

"Christ!" said Ben, stepping out onto the street. "They really did a job on you, old girl…"

The bombed-out hotel may have been the Jewel of the Isthmus once, but now it looked like a wrecked Spanish galleon, holed below the water-line. The stucco façade of the building had been sheered off by the blast, exposing naked brickwork to the night. Ben stepped back to take some pictures for his claims report, and a passer-by bumped straight into him. He pulled away, protecting his wallet, but the careless stranger had already disappeared into the shadows. It was only when he put his hand in his pocket to check for his mobile phone that he found it. He stepped into a street-light to look at it. A thick, embossed invitation card.

"Tomorrow night…" said Makepeace. "Nothing changes in Panama. You don't have to go looking for trouble here. It comes to you."

CHAPTER 15

OXFORD, UNITED KINGDOM

Harry Schofield gripped the edges of the lectern as if his life depended on it. His head was spinning, but- he had to admit it- there was elation too. Exultation. This was his moment, what he'd worked towards for all these lonely years. It was so close now that he could almost touch it. This was the Divinity School at the Bodleian Library! These vaulted ceilings had housed the world's greatest scholars since the 15th Century- a temple of learning nearly as old as modern science itself. And now Dr Henry Schofield PhD was about to take his own place- his rightful place- in that pantheon. Even if he brought it all tumbling down upon them in the process. The best bit was that he could see the cameras at the back there, the Dictaphones at the ready- the press was here at last. Just as he'd planned it for so long. How do you like me now, haters? Ignorers. No one lifted a damn finger to help me, but look at me now! The stars had finally aligned and at last, at long last, nothing would ever be the same again. Schofield looked up at the cover-slide of his Powerpoint presentation.

"The Oxford Fusion Corporation Welcomes You to Your Clean Energy Future".

His words. His company. Looming large above them all. So this was really happening. We're doing it. You're doing it. Because it's your time, Harry, he thought. This is what you've worked so hard for. Enjoy it.

"Vice-Chancellor, Ladies and Gentlemen," he said. "Let me start with a health warning: what I'm about to tell you is not rocket science. It *is*, however, nuclear physics!" He laughed out loud. "But before I tell you the answer to the future of global energy, let me ask you one question first: What does the term 'inertial confinement fusion' mean to you'?" He looked out with satisfaction at the sea of blank faces before him. "That's just an ice-breaker- and it actually would break ice! Because what we're talking about here are mechanically-induced shockwaves, hitting confined expanses of gas to reach temperatures of millions of degrees! Or to put it another way, the temperature at the core of the sun…" There were some satisfying gasps of awe from the audience at that. "What we've developed in our ground-breaking test facility, right here in Oxford, is the technology to harness nuclear fusion- the most powerful source of energy in the universe! With it, we can solve humanity's looming energy crisis in an instant. One hundred per cent renewable, cheap, abundant energy. Freed from the wasteful diversion of resources to energy production, burning dirty hydrocarbons that destroy our own environment, or building millions of inefficient windmills, mankind can finally reach its true destiny!"

Harry clicked onto his movie stills slide.

"In one great leap we can go from the opening scene of *2001…* " Click. "Straight to the closing one! This, Ladies and Gentlemen, is the most significant energy inflection point since the Big Bang. It will put our country- and our university- firmly back in the fast lane of human development. It isn't so much an Industrial Strategy, as a new Industrial Revolution." Another click, and it was the *Celestia Motherlode* spaceship from *2001*, with the OFC's logo super-imposed on its spherical cockpit. There was a murmur of expectation around the medieval hall.

"This is the Oxford Fusion Corporation!"

CHAPTER 16

CASCO VIEJO, PANAMA CITY, REPUBLIC OF PANAMA

"*Aquí estamos*," said the cab-driver.

"Yeah, that's us," said Makepeace. "For better or worse."

Two suited heavies flanked the front door of a dilapidated mansion. Ben passed a fifty dollar bill to the cabbie, promised him another if he was in the same spot in two hours' time and then stepped out over the deep gutter.

The doormen conferred as he handed over the invitation card, and then escorted him through the hallway.

"*¿Ascensor, señor?*" said one of them, gesturing to an antique cage elevator. Makepeace looked at the buckled concertina door and worm-riddled wooden frame.

"Thanks, but I'll take the stairs..." he said.

At the bottom of the stair-case, another pair of impassive doormen swung open a huge set of doors, to reveal a cavernous hall, already buzzing with anticipation. It must have been an elegant ballroom once, but now what remained of the gap-toothed parquet of the dance-floor was dominated by a circular, sand-floored ring. The ring itself was enfolded by a low concrete wall, topped with a perspex screen. Around it, banks of bleachers led up to plush, armchair-furnished booths at the top. Ringside pundits in sun-glasses and loose-fitting *panabrisa* or *lique lique* shirts chattered to gamblers and bookies, as white-shirted *mozos* scampered all around them, carrying the ubiquitous bottles of white-labelled Seco Herrerano to the Panamanians, raw, smuggled *aguardiente* to the Colombian *illegales* and age-mellowed Cacique rum to the grandees at the back.

A vast banner hung down from the ceiling:

"Welcome to the *Coliseo Gallístico. Morituri te salutant.*"

"Not bloody cock-fighting," said Ben. "Lucky I didn't eat first…"

He sat down in the cheap seats at the front with a glass of *seco*, just as the double doors at the back of the room swung open. The first contenders, wrapped in embroidered blankets like gypsy prize-fighters, were carried down to the edge of the ring. They stared out at the crowd through cross, short-sighted eyes. The bird nearer Ben was a white giant, draped in a synthetic silk shawl embroidered with the words "*El Chiricano*" and a map of Chiriquí Province in western Panama. A *picador*, one of the smaller cocks used to rile up the thoroughbred fighters before the bout, was carried over, craning forward to jab at him with its beak. El Chiricano lunged back at his tormentor with a force that almost catapulted him out of the blanket, sending the *picador* cowering back again. The trainer tried to push it forward for a second assault, but it was already subdued, unwilling to risk another foray. Instead El Chiricano aimed a few vicious pecks at his owner, who cursed and pulled his hand back, then doffed his cowboy hat to the spectators, proud of his fighter's raw aggression.

"*¡Eso! ¡Chiricano!*" yelled the delighted crowd. "*¡Vamos, Chiriquí, vamos! ¡Vamos, super-Chiricano! ¡Mátale, mátale!*"

Ben looked over to the other side of the ring, where the darker, smaller Machete Moreno was held by a nervous youth, clad in a grimy Quaker State boiler-suit. Machete Moreno squirmed away from the *picador* snapping at his neck, moving just enough to twitch his head out of reach. The *picador* lunged at him again, and this time he burrowed back down in his blanket. The crowd laughed and jeered.

"Put your money on *El Machete, señor....*" said a quiet voice from the row behind Makepeace.

Ben restrained himself from turning around immediately. Instead he watched the trainers binding razor-sharp metal blades to the cocks' natural spurs with waxed twine. The horny spurs were formidable weapons without man-made help. With *cola de rata* or *media luna* blades affixed, they were lethal. The kid in the boiler-suit was speaking to Machete in a low, reassuring whisper, stroking his feathers. Beside them an official in an immaculate *pana-brisa* shirt looked on, checking that only regulation-sized gaffs were attached to the cocks' spurs.

"Are you sure?" said Makepeace over his shoulder. "El Chiricano seems to be the crowd favourite. Plus, you know, he's fucking massive!"

The man behind him laughed.

"True! But you saw how aggressive he was to his owner. That makes him an alpha male- a patriarch. A bully… He's not used to being challenged by anything in his own yard, not even the farmer."

"You know, that sounds like a pretty useful characteristic when you're fighting to the death," said Ben. "A bit of swagger?"

"It means he never had to fight, just put on a show. I'm looking for a killer."

"Me too," said Makepeace. "Can you help me with that?"

"That's why you're here. For now, I must place a small wager. Shall I put some money on for you?"

"A thousand dollars on Machete," said Ben, passing a fold of bills behind him. It gave him the opportunity to study the man behind him for the first time. A full, jowly face, with a hint of five o'clock shadow, incongruous with the smart, olive-green suit and silk pocket-square. Money, confidence- probably a professional, Makepeace thought. Lawyer, banker, accountant. Definitely not a cop- or a soldier. But there was something familiar about him anyway.

"You take my advice then?" the Panamanian said.

"You convinced me," said Ben. "Plus, you're the only lead I've got."

"On cock-fighting? Or on *La Joya del Istmo*?"

"Cock-fighting I know about already," said Ben. "They tell me that birds from Bocas del Toro Province win in the first minute- or die in the second…"

"I hope you have better sources in Panama than the Río Abajo bookie who told you that, Señor Makepeace. Meet me in the car lot at the Torre Panabanco at midnight. I have some information for you about the young English milord. I'll bring your winnings then. Pablito the guard will be expecting you. Just give him the word."

"*¿El Chiricano?*"

"*¿Cómo no?* Although he'll be dead too by then. *Ya veremos*."

"I'll look forward to it."

CHAPTER 17

OXFORD, UNITED KINGDOM

The giant prawn dominated the lecture theatre, antennae bristling with hostile intent. There were gasps as it took a menacing step closer to the front row of the audience.

"And now let me introduce you to our scientific inspiration," said Schofield, directing his laser pointer at the screen. "The Pacific pistol shrimp!" The audience looked on in bemusement. "The curse of naval sonar operators in the tropics, the pistol shrimp is best known for the horrendous racket it makes in warm waters, with its freakishly over-developed claw. But to us nuclear physicists, these trigger-happy little guys point the way to something truly amazing."

Elon Musk eat your heart out, thought Harry, as he brought up a labelled diagram of a crustacean claw. Because this is the greatest show on earth. "To the layman, the pistol shrimp's super-sized snapper might look like any old crab or lobster claw. But that's rather like saying that the flux capacitor from *Back to the Future* looks like any old car radio..." He chuckled. "You can see that it's asymmetrical, with two sections, one active and one passive. The passive section- the 'propus', from the Greek for 'forward foot'- has a socket. The other half, called a 'dactyl'- from the Greek *daktylos,* or finger- is the mobile part. It has a hammer, or plunger, that fits perfectly into this socket. The shrimp cocks the dactyl by co-contracting its powerful flexor and extensor muscles. This builds greater and greater tension until another closer muscle contracts, sending the dactyl into the propus at a speed of approximately one hundred kilometres per hour."

Harry clicked onto the next slide, a slow motion video of the pistol shrimp stalking a smaller crustacean along the ocean floor.

"Now in human terms that's pretty damn fast- but it's still not fast enough for the pistol shrimp's purposes. So where this gets really interesting is not in the simple biomechanics, but in the advanced plasma physics. Because when the claw snaps shut, a jet of water is expelled from the propus at about thirty metres per second. The friction between that jet and the still water surrounding it creates a swirling vortex effect. When the vortex reaches the critical spin velocity, which is about thirty thousand rpm, give or take, the centre voids and then collapses. This creates a cavitation effect- a super-low pressure area. The surrounding particles are sucked into the low pressure vacuum with minimal friction or resistance, at a velocity greater than the speed of sound. So we're starting to get really quite rapid now!"

Harry pressed play on the video, and the shrimp claw flashed into action.

"Boom! Now watch this carefully, people, because you won't have seen anything quite like it before…" The water rippled in super slow-mo. "The bursting bubble creates a massive energy release, in which temperatures of up to five thousand degrees superheat the air and water vapour inside the cavity, burning it into a bright plasma core. To relate it back to our own sun, that plasma is now roughly the temperature of its photosphere. Which is why you get the flash of light that you're going to see right about- now!"

There was an intake in breath from the audience, as the screen lit up.

"And this, Ladies and Gentlemen, is sonoluminescence. This is what the Oxford Fusion Corporation is all about. To put it at its simplest- sound has produced light. Energy. And, for those among you with the misfortune to be nuclear physicists, a positive fusion energy gain factor. Which is actually the most important bit of all this."

The footage rolled on in slow motion, the water blurring as a high-pressure pulse careered into the creature in front of the shrimp, stunning it. The pistol shrimp skipped forward to gather it up into its clutches.

Schofield clicked onto the next slide.

"I think we'll pause it there- because what happens next gets quite messy. Definitely not one for the vegans…" He walked down the aisle of the lecture theatre. "Now, I haven't brought you all here today to talk to you about advanced fishing techniques. What we have managed to do at the Oxford Fusion Corporation is to recreate the pistol shrimp's remarkable mechanical shockwave, but hitting a synthetically-induced, helium-hydrogen interface instead of plain old seawater. You can see the process map on this diagram. That's proprietary OFC intellectual property, so no pictures yet please, Lois Lane…" He winked at a female journalist at the back of the auditorium. "In our process, the resultant cavitation forces together deuterium and tritium- that is to say, radioactive hydrogen isotopes- to form helium, in a super-heated gas plasma core. So just like the shrimp, we can now deliver heat and light. But the difference is that we can do it in infinitely greater quantities. So unlike our crustacean friends…"

New slide. The big one. The sun- a beautiful, raging ball of burning gas plasma. The OFC logo flashed up on the image.

"What we are offering is nothing less than the ultimate power source in the galaxy!" said Harry. "A miniature sun. In fact, it doesn't even have to be miniature- it can be at any scale that we choose! We could actually now *replace* the sun, if we wanted to. Which certainly provides some useful future-proofing for this universe. This is a Life Star! And at utility-scale, it's tailor-made for providing clean, baseload power. To put it in layman's terms: this is Energy- solved."

The audience exploded into applause. A standing ovation at the Divinity School!

"Time's up…" said the usher.

Schofield looked at his watch.

CHAPTER 18

CASCO VIEJO, PANAMA CITY, REPUBLIC OF PANAMA

El Chiricano's owner unveiled his fighter in the ring with a flamboyant flourish of the cape. The cock began to strut and swagger like a Spanish *torero*, drawing bays of support from the group of South American businessmen behind Ben.

"*¡Fuerza chiricana! ¡Mátale! ¡Mátale!*"

Machete was in the ring now too. He meandered back to the wall behind him, as though still in the farm-yard, and began foraging around its base. He pried with his beak at some promising cracks in the rough cement. El Chiricano glared at him across the ring, but the phoney war dragged on. Ben watched as Machete, without looking at El Chiricano, began to saunter around his own side of the ring. He was hugging the wall, pecking at the ground in front of him as he moved. El Chiricano started pacing in slow, gradually widening circles around his half of the ring. Then Machete followed suit, mimicking the pattern of El Chiricano's movements. Just for a moment, it seemed like a coincidence. The crowd stopped shouting and looked on in hushed silence as their orbits brought them closer and closer together. They looked like tribal dancers, engaged in some intricate ceremony. Now they were within a yard of each other. Even Machete had given up his studied indifference to the presence of his rival. He cast a barely perceptible glance towards him. There was still deference in the way he held his head away from the bigger bird, but he didn't break his step for a second. Makepeace could hear his neighbours murmuring encouragement under their breath, jogging up and down in their seats. In the ring the circles were now all but intersecting. The South Americans behind began beating a rhythm on the bleachers, until they were hissed quiet by the local spectators around them. El Chiricano stared belligerently at his rival. Machete was still circling slowly towards him, keeping his distance, but everyone knew what the ritual was now. Combat. Then Machete's gaze locked in on El Chiricano. The bigger bird glanced away, distracted by a shout from the crowd, and in an instant Machete rose high up on the front of his feet with a violent, frenetic beating of his wings. Dragging his body off the ground, he rocked back and aimed a whirlwind of raking downward cuts at El Chiricano with his murderous spurs.

"*¡Pechugazo! ¡Pechugazo!*" murmured the South Americans- a cut to the chest. There was a buzz of surprise around the *Coliseo*. El Chiricano, shrugging off the impertinence of the attack, began flailing his wings too, trying to get above Machete and out of the range of the lethal spurs. His own spurs flashed into life, arcing through the air towards Machete, who fell back again, driven onto his heels by El Chiricano's counter-attack. Now there was a murmur of satisfaction around the ring as El Chiricano moved in for the kill.

"*¡Mátale! ¡Mátale! ¡Mátale!*" chanted the crowd. Kill him.

El Chiricano lunged towards Machete again, and the smaller bird gave up more ground. Then Ben saw that for all their relentless power, El Chiricano's heavy blows weren't telling. Despite his size and strength, he had moved too late to get the height advantage on Machete. With every innocuous flurry of white wings, El Chiricano's energy was bleeding away. Machete held his body away for another precious second before rearing up again. Using his muscular haunches to aim more scything blows at El Chiricano, he beat him down again, landing a left and right-foot combination. Then he disengaged and retreated back from El Chiricano, who was lashing out wildly with beak and spurs. The effort was exhausting the larger bird now, and he made one last desperate lunge towards Machete, swiping into the dead air between them, before stopping, drained. The two birds watched each other like punch-drunk boxers between rounds. El Chiricano made a half-hearted feint forward, and Machete stepped back again.

Machete was hurt, his leg gashed by an uppercut from El Chiricano. Then El Chiricano turned to show a chest that was a mass of deep red lacerations, the blood spreading out across his white plumage. The murmur this time was a shocked one, the slow realisation of a partisan crowd that the situation is spinning out of control.

El Chiricano was running on empty, looking for any refuge from the storm of beak and spurs. But Machete had already started the slow, measured walk back to the centre of the ring. He knew that there was a pretender in his yard, and age-old genetic programming drew him straight towards it. He was a natural born fighter, and every instinct told him to finish this now. El Chiricano was sagging to one side. He tried to flap his wings in defiance, but one hung down beside his body, torn and broken. He slunk back to the edge of the ring, staggering round and round the circular wall in a futile search for a corner to hide in. Now death was stalking him. The crowd was on its feet, jeering the defeated white bird and his humiliated owner. Stung by the taunts, the breeder moved over to the edge of the ring to urge his champion into one last stand. As the adrenalin wore off, El Chiricano was in too much pain to ponder the fickleness of the mob. They were whistling at him now, disparaging his lack of *cojones*. The white bird was already slumping to the sand as Machete made his move, jabbing at his head with his pointed beak, then unleashing another devastating combination of lateral slashes with his spurs. A white feather, dislodged by the ferocity of the attack, fluttered through the thickening atmosphere and past the marauding Machete. Now El Chiricano was down. He clambered back onto his feet with an effort, and then fell again. His owner nodded at the judge, before stepping into the ring and flipping the twitching bird over onto its back, checking for signs of life. He turned back and gestured to his assistant behind him to come and pick up the wreckage. A thin trickle of blood ran into the sand below and was swallowed up. The dull sand was as unforgiving, as insatiable, as the crowd itself. Machete stared with cold, expressionless eyes at the flushed faces around him, hardly moving as he was wrapped in his blanket again and carried from the ring.

"Time I was going too…" Ben said. "Back to the twenty-first century."

He swigged down the last bitter mouthful of *seco* and headed for the exit.

"Any luck at the *Coliseo Gallístico*, *señor*?" said the cab-driver.

"Yeah- they left me my shoes," said Makepeace.

The driver laughed.

"So where are we going now, *jefe*?"

"Avenida Pedrarias Dávila- you know the Torre Panabanco?"

"*Claro*," said the driver, smirking. "You can't miss it. You know the ad! Panabanco never fails you…"

CHAPTER 19

OXFORD, UNITED KINGDOM

Harry Schofield wiped the corners of his mouth with his handkerchief. He took a swig of water and looked around him. He was nearly done now, but he wasn't sure he was ready to leave this stage yet. If he ever would be. Because that would mean it was really over.

"Now, I'm sure you all have lots of questions, which I'm more than happy to take at this point?" he said. "Don't be shy!"

A hand straight up in the front row. Yes! It was a young research student, who Harry recognised from the Beecroft Building. Rock and roll.

"Doctor Schofield- thank you so much for your fascinating talk," she said. "You mentioned the fusion energy gain factor in your presentation. Can you please comment a bit more on that in the context of your sonoluminescence process, please? Because we've obviously seen that fusion, and even mini-supernova effects, can be achieved at laboratory scale if cost is no object, at facilities like the Joint European Torus at the Culham Centre, the Wendelstein 7-X stellarator in Greifswald and the National Ignition Facility in California. But in each of those cases, the power required to maintain the gas plasma at steady state far exceeds the actual energy output, with *Q* well below 1. So what makes the Oxford Fusion process different?"

"That's a great question, thank you- is it Brenda?" said Schofield.

The student smiled and nodded.

"Well, for a start the tokamak and stellarator processes that Brenda is referring to are massively energy consumptive," said Harry. "That's because of the truly astonishingly large magnets and electromagnetic fields that they employ, to hold the gas plasma in place for as long as possible. It's rather like spending a billion dollars trying to hold onto a beach ball- with a pair of chopsticks. Superficially impressive, but also largely pointless. What they're trying to achieve is symmetrical cavity implosion, which is quite elegant, because it gives you more efficient fuel compression. In fact it might even be a good idea, if it didn't mean you were using input energy of 24MW for output of 16MW! And when you're looking at laser-driven inertial confinement fusion, like the 'Nefariously Inefficient Fiasco'- I mean the National Ignition Facility- that takes a whopping 422 megajoules of input energy, just to charge up the capacitors that power the laser amplifiers! So ironically, the best hope for the NIF in the short term might just be us- the Oxford Fusion Corporation. Because we're basically the only ones who can make energy cheap enough to power up their laser!"

Brenda was laughing now, and Harry decided to press home his advantage.

"I mean, you would be completely bonkers to use laser-based ICF for energy production," he said. "You would need a dedicated, utility-scale power station running on a rapid-start fuel, just to fire it up. On the other hand, if you wanted to shoot down an Imperial Star Destroyer, then a laser-based process would be a lot more useful than our boring old baseload power generator! What we realised here is that, unlike the mighty International Thermonuclear Experimental Reactor, the plain old pistol shrimp didn't have thirteen billion euros to perfect his sonoluminescence. He's generating the plasma core he needs every time, from simple first principles- and asymmetrical cavity implosion. So maybe we should take a leaf out of his book, and not the ITER's! Does that answer your question, Brenda?"

"Absolutely. Thank you," she said.

"You're very welcome. Now, next question- the lady from the press back there?"

"Thank you, Doctor Schofield. Lois Lane. Not really- Linda Booth, *Daily Mail.* You said in your presentation that your process will change mankind's future. Why is that?"

"Well, some aspects of mankind's future are probably a bit beyond the scope of this lecture," said Harry. "But you will all be familiar with the Malthusian trap…"

He brought up a new slide. It simply bore a quotation:

"*The power of population is indefinitely greater than the power in the earth to produce subsistence for man.* Thomas Robert Malthus, Fellow of the Royal Society."

"Malthus hit the nail on the head, based on prevailing energy economics," Harry said. "In fact, those words are even truer now than when he wrote them in 1798. Energy is one of the main limiting factors on human productivity. We are forced to invest an increasing amount of our resources, just to keep the lights on. But cheap, abundant, emission-free energy would change all that in an instant. Farming and water management processes that are currently far too expensive for most of the world's population would become available to all, overnight. Take the desalination of seawater to produce fresh water. Technically speaking, the only thing keeping the deserts dry is the cost of the power to desalinate the sea and pump it into the sand. Arid countries like Saudi Arabia already produce their water using oil, at enormous financial and ecological cost. That makes the Energy-Water-Food Nexus the biggest conundrum in human history. But you've just seen the answer to that trilemma. Energy- check. Water- check. And with sustainable energy and water, we can feed the world."

There was an impressed murmur.

"One last question?" said Harry. "The gentleman next to Linda?"

"Dave Cooper, *Daily Express.* My question is: Could the shrimps' own energy output be harnessed for human use? A sort of 'Scampi Power'? "

Harry laughed.

"Nice headline, Dave! But you have to keep in mind that these shrimp only grow to about 50 millimetres in size. That makes them a bit sub-scale for any meaningful energy production! You would probably need a creature of at least human size, before it became worth developing the infrastructure to harvest 'Scampi Power in a Basket'…"

"So what we really need is a human pistol shrimp?" said the journalist.

"That would do nicely," said Harry. "The pistol shrimp has cornered the market in biological inertial confinement so far. But get back to me when you find some human-sized pistol shrimps, and I'll generate some fusion power for you! They'll be the most powerful creatures in the world."

Now everyone was laughing. Everyone except for one elderly man in the back row of the lecture theatre. Bartholomew Malthus, Member of the Bohemian Sports Club, looked up at the Malthusian trap on the screen. Then he tapped three digits into his cell phone: '200'.

CHAPTER 20

EL CANGREJO, PANAMA CITY, REPUBLIC OF PANAMA

"The Torre Panabanco, I presume..." said Makepeace as they pulled up in the foot-hills of a mirrored glass and steel monolith, its name emblazoned at the top in neon letters for all the world to see. It towered over the sky-scrapers and apartment blocks flanking it on both sides. A sprawling complex of designer outlets and American fast-food franchises cowered at its feet, covered in mock-terracotta tiles like Walt Disney's vision of a colonial hacienda. The whole development could have been transplanted straight from Miami piece by piece, from the box-fresh TGI Friday's and Häagen-Dazs right down to the manicured palm-trees and peppermint astro-turf. In the darkness it looked like an abandoned theme park, waiting for daylight to reanimate it.

The cab followed the drive-way as it looped round off the street, behind an inert ornamental fountain and then up the ramp into the car-lot. Ben paid the driver and climbed out at the fibre-glass guard's booth by the barriers of the car-lot. The grizzled *mestizo* sentinel inside it was fast asleep. Slumped face-down on his desk, head resting on a bundle of crumpled soft-porn magazines and cheap leather gun-belt slung round the back of his chair, he looked as though he had settled down for the night.

"Pablito?" said Ben. "*¡El Gran Pablito!* Wake up, *huevón*! *¡Despierta, hijo de puta!* The password is *Chiricano. ¡Chiricano!*"

Pablito simply grunted and shifted his head on the makeshift pillow. Ben sniffed at the close air.

"Guess I'm not the only one who's been drinking *seco* tonight, then…" he said.

Ben slipped around the barrier and into the gloom of the car-lot. He stood still for a few seconds as his eyes acclimatised themselves to the darkness, then looked into the void. There was no sign of his source- just endless rows of cars on either side of the central aisle, stretching out into the innermost recesses of the lot. Deep in the bowels of the car-park he saw the illuminated call buttons of elevators, gleaming red like evil eyes against the matt black back-drop of the far wall.

"OK, going up, Pablito," said Ben.

He walked towards the elevators down the central aisle, already beginning to feel the dankness of the lot closing in on him. It reeked of humidity and slicked diesel. Sullen, unlit headlights stared blankly back at him, like the unseeing isinglass eyes of the crack-heads in the Casco Viejo. Suddenly there was an explosion of sound like a gun-shot, ricocheting around the concrete-walled lot. Ben jumped, then swore and kicked the crumpled aluminium soda can away in irritation, sending it skidding across the asphalt. Then he stopped mid-stride, as the lot echoed with the answering sound of a gasp of breath. Barely breathing himself, Ben strained to identify where it had come from. With each sound reverberating like a pin-ball through the blackness, it was impossible to be sure. Turning back, he fought the disorientation and forced himself to scan each row of cars one by one. In the deepening darkness the cars were robbed of colour, contrast and every feature except outline. With an effort, Ben ran his tired eyes down the endless columns of German saloons and hump-backed American SUVs. The deep shadows between them seemed to swallow the light like black holes, obscuring and merging the narrow gaps. He blinked to keep his eyes focussed. He was cursing the source, the lot and everything in it when the pattern was abruptly broken. He could just make out the bulk of an SUV on the right-hand side of the aisle. The contours of its hood were blurred and broken. There was something on top of it. Ben took another step closer, but he still couldn't make it out. He started to turn back into the lot and follow the lights back down the aisle. Then something clicked between his peripheral vision and his brain and he started to run towards the car, feeling in his pocket for the book of matches he had picked up back at the Miraflores Locks. He tore a match out and struck it as he reached the off-roader. It spluttered and then flared into flame. It took a second or two for the dancing light to focus and settle. Then a shape started to form in front of him. The match flickered and burned out. Cursing again, Makepeace lit another match and watched as it picked out the now-unmistakable form of a human body, sprawled out across the wind-shield of the car.

CHAPTER 21

ST JAMES'S, LONDON, UNITED KINGDOM

"There's a reason I ordered lunch *à deux* in the Bullion Room today, old man," said Malthus, looking up at the cast gold kilobars and bas-relief bars mounted on the walls around them.

"There's a reason for everything you do, Malthy," said Bezique. "You may save the geriatric routine for the novices! I am not so easily fooled. Besides, there's no shop talk in the public rooms. And I presume you do want to talk shop?"

"Look at the little trinkets we have in here," said Malthus, running his finger along the glass top of the table. Underneath it sat a king's fortune in sovereign gold coins- Gold Maple Leafs, American Gold Eagles, Britannias, Australian Nuggets and South African Krugerrands. "Our predecessors did not put all their eggs in one basket when it came to accepting gold from government mints. They knew that a sovereign guarantee is only as good as the credit of the country that gives it. What one really needs is diversification."

"You needn't worry about our gold, Malthus," said Bezique. "This is just for show. The Club's real bullion store is all verified by Sharps Pixley- and buried deep in their vaults. But then I don't suppose that's really your point, is it?"

"What I mean is that I don't want to leave anything to chance with this one," said Malthus, ripping a leg off his crab. "You're a man of action, Bezique- and of resolution. But like every man alive, you do have a weakness."

"Well?" said Bezique drily.

"When Plan A fails, you tend to try- Plan A," said Malthus. "When the stakes get this high, you need a Plan B too. That's where I come in."

"So you're going outside the Game?" said Bezique.

"Only for the business side of things. Call it taking out an insurance policy- and with a modest premium at that. Which is all in the Game." Malthus took a swig of white Burgundy and held it up to the light, admiring its deep yellow hue. "Like liquid gold!" he said. "Besides, we can still use a brother to deal with Schofield. This just makes it easier to get to him. In the unlikely event of- failure." He held up a crab claw, manipulating the joint with his bony fingers. "The beauty of it is that he'll come to us. Think of it as two pincers coming together as one, perfectly synchronised." He brought the claw together with a snap. "Boom! To crush our prey between them. All our prey…"

"There is no need for a fail-safe when there is no prospect of failure," said Bezique. "The brothers have not failed the Club within living memory."

"Come now, Bezique!" said Malthus. "What about Simms?"

"That mission was aborted before it even got the green light," said Bezique. "That is why we have such protocols. We were able to find a different resolution to the issue."

"Simms is a loose end," said Malthus. "And what about that dolt, Julian Newman? He certainly won't be getting into any other club I have anything to do with, I can assure you of that!"

"There is only one of your clubs that he could now participate in, in his condition," said Bezique, with an elegant seated bow. "Black ball or no."

"The Hellfire Club?" said Malthus, guffawing. "*Touché*! But my point remains. He left a trail behind him in Laos that a child could follow."

"Fortunately it is a child who is following it," said Bezique. "And besides, even Newman achieved his mission in accordance with my designs. The Minister was eliminated before he could initiate his State-funded testing programme on the Firestarters. In a Communist country, rapidly falling within China's sphere of influence, that could have proved disastrous."

"I remember why we called in the mission," said Malthus. "Just not why you chose Newman to execute it."

"This is spilt milk, my dear Malthus," said Bezique. "I didn't think you the man to weep over it!"

"And yet now you have chosen Walker for this crucial assignment…" said Malthus. "How I despise the youth of today! They are depressed men, not desperate ones. Despair has not yet set them free. And Rob Walker is no warrior."

"He is the right man for this job!" snapped Bezique. "It is horses for courses, Malthus. It has to be. Walker knows Oxford- he even studied at the university for a while. He has been to the kill-zone many times before. He has a clean driving licence, his face fits and he's certainly intelligent enough. I might ask the same question of you- how will you ensure that your own plans do not miscarry?"

"No, my friend," said the old man. "From now on we must ring-fence Plan A and Plan B. But what I can tell you is this: It's lights out for the Oxford Fusion Corporation this time."

"Then here's to Plan B," said Bezique, clinking glasses with Malthus. "The Club is all about evolution, is it not?"

"To evolution!" said Malthus. "And halting it. Now, what news from the Isthmus?"

"Everything seems to be meeting there," said Bezique.

"Oh, it always does…" said Malthus.

"Hernán Cortés said: 'Whoever possesses the passage between the two oceans can consider himself the owner of the world'," said Bezique.

"We will soon see who the owners of this world are," said Malthus.

CHAPTER 22

TORRE PANABANCO, PANAMA CITY, REPUBLIC OF PANAMA

Ben walked round to the front of the car, cupping the match in his hand. Then he recoiled. The body had been mutilated, the throat gaping wide open in a livid gash, tongue lolling out through the cut.

"*La corbata colombiana*," he murmured. "Commissioner Herrera is not going to like this…"

He looked down at the face. It was still hidden in the penumbra, caught in the shadows cast by the dying match. As he leaned in closer, the match burned down, scorching the end of his fingers. He fumbled to light another one. It was his source from the *Coliseo*, staring lifelessly up at him. The sense of familiarity hit him again.

"Snitches get stitches…" said Ben.

The source's eyes were wide open, his expression frozen forever in slack-jawed astonishment. His face, sallow in life, had a shocking pallor to it now. Ben slipped off his jacket and dropped it over him, then started to reach forward to check for a pulse. That was when he noticed for the first time the sickeningly contorted position that the body had been twisted into. He pulled his hand back and dropped to one knee to examine the body. As he did so, he heard another muffled intake of air, this time close by. Cupping the match in his palm again, he rolled over onto the asphalt floor of the car-lot and peered into the gloom. Nothing. He lay still for a second, trying to pick out the angles along the ground. Then, barely a couple of metres away from him, he saw the outline of another discordant shape. Whatever it was lay as motionless as the source's corpse above him. The chemical half-life of the match faded away. Ben groped for another one and inched forward under the car. Striking the match, he waited while the light filled the confined space again. Another body. It had to be. But as he got closer, he saw that it was convulsing. Ben crawled along the asphalt on his elbows, dragging his knee through a greasy oil-slick on the ground as he did so. Now he was within inches of it. There was a low hiss, like gas escaping from a cylinder. The match burned out, singeing the end of his fingers again. He lit the next one, and then found himself looking straight into the wide eyes of a woman in her late twenties. Her face was streaked with tears and oil from the ground, her whole body shaking with suppressed sobs. For a few seconds they stared at each other in silence.

"*¿Quién eres?*" she said.

"You're American?" said Makepeace in surprise.

She shook her head.

"English?"

She nodded.

"Are you alright?"

She nodded again.

"But where's- where's de la Peña?" she asked.

"De la Peña? Is that who he is- was? Shit! Any relation of Gustavo de la Peña?"

"His brother."

"That explains the resemblance…" Ben said. "Were they in the same line of business?"

"Where is he?" she repeated. "Where's de la Peña?"

"I'm sorry- he's dead," said Ben.

She started to get up, her limbs cramping from concealment in the confined space under the car.

"His body's up there," said Ben. "On top of the car. But don't- please don't look at him now, he's..."

Ignoring him, she pulled herself to her feet and ran round to the front of the car. Ben jumped up after her, just too late to stop her from shining the beam of her iPhone torch straight onto de la Peña's mutilated body.

"He's not in great shape," said Ben.

For a while she stood shock-still, too paralysed with horror even to scream. Then she started shaking again, her body convulsed once more with sobbing. She leaned forward to the corpse and Ben grabbed her in his arms, pulling her back from it.

"Let me go!" she hissed. "Get your hands off me! What the hell do you think you're doing?"

"I'll let you go!" said Ben. "I'll let you go. But first promise me you won't touch him."

"What- why not?" she said. "What are you talking about?"

"His body is booby-trapped," said Ben. "Look at the way he's lying. There's something taped to his back. You can see the end of the duct tape under his arm."

"What is it?" she said.

"I can't see- not without disturbing the body. Maybe an anti-personnel mine or fragmentation grenade. Maybe plastique. There seems to be a lot of it going round. But definitely some kind of explosive device."

She stared at him in disbelief.

"You mean a bomb? What the hell is going on here? Who would do something like that- what type of psychopath?"

"Not a psychopath," said Ben. "At least- not an indiscriminate one. This is a deliberate message."

"And what- what is the message?" she said.

"The message is: 'Stop digging'. Listen, are you sure you want to go into this now? Why don't we get out of here, and then talk? We're not safe here."

"First tell me what this is all about," she said. "I didn't come here to run away from the truth."

"The mutilation?" said Ben. "They call it the *corbata colombiana*. The Colombian necktie. It's how the cartels in Colombia punish traitors. Kind of a ritual. If you cross *El Clan del Golfo* or *El Clan del Oriente*, the beef doesn't end with death. They mutilate your corpse, then booby-trap your body, so it has to lie out in the open- out in the street for everyone in the village to see. To disgrace you and your family."

"So this is all a drugs thing?" she said.

"That's certainly what we're supposed to think," said Ben. "I've seen it in Cali, Cúcuta- Little Havana. Never in Panama. But listen- did you see which way the killer went?"

She pointed towards the elevators.

"That way," she said. "I could see the light when the lift opened. He must have gone up to de la Peña's office. I was lying here the whole time. De la Peña told me to hide as soon as he saw him- the killer. I think he knew from the minute he saw him that he was going to… to die. That poor man! He didn't say a word about me- didn't do a thing to give me away. Even when- when this was happening to him…"

"So the killer could still be inside the building?" said Ben.

"Yes, I think so. I think he must be…" she said. "This is the only way out. When I heard you coming- I thought it was him coming back for me."

"We need to leave right now," said Ben. "Do you have a car?"

"Yeah, a rental," she said. "Just over there, by the exit. But wait- I don't even know who you are."

"I'm Ben Makepeace. I was supposed to meet de la Peña here at midnight- to talk to him about the death of an English guy called Laurence Pearce. Obviously that's not going to happen now."

"You knew Laurence too?" she said. "How?"

"Who are you?" said Makepeace.

"My name is Laura Newman," said Laura. "I knew three of the men who've died. And their Club…"

The words died in her throat. The lot was reverberating with the grinding cables and mechanical groan of an arriving elevator.

CHAPTER 23

ST JAMES'S, LONDON, UNITED KINGDOM

Candle-light danced around the wood panelling of the *salle de jeux*, setting free the ambers and coppers of the priceless Millésime Cognac in Bezique's brandy balloon. He hoisted it aloft.

"The Reaper does not sleep- and neither must the Club, when we are charged with his dread business!" he said. "And tonight- this morning- we are honoured to welcome new members. I give you: Brothers Willis; Wright; Tinubu; Pettigrew; Sengupta; Hennessy; De Silva; Baldwin; Sands; Johnson; Shanahan; Stamp; de Mestre; Whitby; Raymond; Graham." Each of the novices raised his glass to the Club with a show of nonchalance as his name was called out. "Brothers Fletcher; Daniel; Jefferson; Hart; Patel; Gregory; Wood; Whitehead; Neale; O'Connor. Their novitiate is now completed. And yet not one of them is truly new to us, for they are bound to us by ancient oaths. By Death itself, which has claimed them for its own- before baseness and dishonour ever could! So let them say of you, too, as our ancient patron wrote of the Thane of Cawdor:

'*Nothing in his life/*

Became him like the leaving it; he died/

As one that had been studied in his death/
To throw away the dearest thing he owned,
As 'twere a careless trifle!"

He drained his glass and then tossed it into the open fireplace. The cracking crystal rang out like a gun-shot.

"And now champagne, Florizel!" he called.

"Beautiful words!" croaked Malthus, clapping him on the back. "I never tire of them..."

"Let me introduce you first to Malthus- our venerable oldest member!" said Bezique. "He has seen the cards pass more times than any man now living- myself included."

"And yet he is still alive? I thought it would come quickly now," said Sands, refilling his glass again. He had the unmistakable air of a soldier about him. Clean-shaven, compact- capable of anything. "The end. I did not pledge myself to the Club to make old bones in Mayfair, like this desiccated fossil..."

"Even Death respects the Devil, Sands!" said Bezique. "So do likewise, and keep a civil tongue in your head."

"Do you think I fear Death- or either of you?" said Sands. "I have sought him everywhere in this world, and I am here to run him to ground in his own lair- not to flee him! If you have a sanction fit to threaten me with, then let me hear it. Otherwise be silent, and show me the way to Death's private door as you have promised."

"Well said, Mr Sands!" said Malthus, clapping his hands together. "That is the way to speak in this company. But Old Frizzle measures his own walk towards us all. It could be one night- or a thousand! Nothing can be certain in the cards. That is the beauty- the art of it. For this is the noblest game of all. The subtlest!" He folded his long fingers together with relish and gazed around the room. "It is the only one that can move me still. Once I loved to hunt- to prey on beasts! To master the proud stag or salmon, the bear or wolverine, in their own elements, and bring them down to our own base level. But now humanity is my only quarry, the brotherhood my only hunting-party. For the faces at the table change- but never the expressions. And never the results."

"There are only so many expressions in this world- and only two results," said Bezique, unwrapping a new pack of playing cards with a flourish. "As a man- and as a species. Kill or be killed. When your time comes, you can't stand still. You must do, or die. When it comes to that final battle, despair is power!"

Malthus looked greedily around the *salle de jeux* for the reactions of the players. Some watched eagerly, the gambler's hungry glint in their eyes. There were men of wrath like Henry Sands, risk-takers who were no tourists out on the edge. They had lived there too long already. Others were pale and drawn, like Simon Pettigrew, who looked as if he would give anything to get out of this hand- if only he hadn't given everything he had left to get into it.

"The rules are simplicity itself, gentlemen," said Bezique. "But our traditions dictate that I repeat our creed each time we are gathered together." He cut the cards. "Whatever your faults have been up to now, whatever your wretchedness- whatever your disgrace. Whoever you have disappointed- failed- betrayed..." A few stern faces paled at that. "Wherever you have been, you have left all that at the door now. You are reborn. You are brothers. And this is our brotherhood. Now drink- and repeat the words of our glorious creed with me!"

The members raised their glasses as one, and chanted together with Bezique:

"I believe in a cruel God;
Who created me in his own image;
I bow to no god or master."

Malthus didn't speak a word. He just moistened his ancient lips with his crocodile tongue and looked around him. Some of the younger brothers glanced up from the creed, then caught Malthus' mocking, gooseberry eye and lost themselves in the mantra again.

"I believe that from despair comes power;

From weakness strength;

And only darkness frees the light."

"Amen!" cried Bezique. He raised his champagne coupe and emptied it once more. "No gods, no masters!"

"No gods, no masters!" shouted the brothers, drinking off their own champagne. Florizel hastened to recharge their glasses and retrieve the broken ones, as they dashed them to the floor.

"Remember now what have we taught you here!" said Bezique. "The lessons have been hard-learned already, and the greatest price of all is yet to be paid. The down-payment may be a million dollars, but the balance is everything that is left to you. The world only has power over a man whilst the trappings of life remain to him. Whilst he has hope. When he truly has nothing, he is free again!"

"Then bring on the Death Card!" cried Sands. "I only wish I held it in my hand already."

Bezique raised his glass to him. "To your hunger, Brother. And to the Game! The Game forever!"

"The Game forever!" toasted the Billionaire Suicide Club.

"The game of life- and death…" murmured Malthus. "You will call out the cards as they turn, won't you, Bezique? The old eyesight is not what it once was. And I should hate to miss a single exquisite twist of the knife!"

Sands looked at the old man in disgust, but Bezique nodded.

"I think we can indulge dear old Malthy in this small matter, don't you, Henry?"

Sands just flipped over the card in front of him by way of reply.

"What do you know, Malthus?" said Bezique. "Mr Sands has drawn the ace of spades."

"You come at an opportune time, Sands," said the oldest member. "In every walk of life, there are gifted amateurs, and there are professionals. It is a professional we need now."

"Despair is power," said Sands.

CHAPTER 24

TORRE PANABANCO, PANAMA CITY, REPUBLIC OF PANAMA

Makepeace blew out the match, just as a bell rang out through the darkness. As the doors of the elevator slid open, spilling light out into the lot, he dropped down onto the asphalt, pulling Laura down with him.

"He's got a gun," said Ben. "Start crawling under the cars. We've got to make it to the lifts behind him."

"Are you crazy!" Laura whispered. "That's the wrong way! We'd have to go right past him. And then we'll be trapped, with him between us and the ramp. We have to go straight for the exit!"

"It's too far to crawl that way- we'll never make it before he does," said Ben. "And if he sees de la Peña's body first- with my jacket on it- then we're fucking dead. Now go! Go!"

Laura paused for a second, evaluating the options, and then slipped under the first car. Ben followed her and suddenly the world was all cars, blocking out everything else, like sprawling trees throwing their canopy over the jungle. Straining every muscle to stay silent, they rolled across the gap between vehicles and scrambled under the second one. All the time the footsteps beat a steady rhythm, three long steps down the aisle in the time it took them to struggle under each car. Ben counted them as they went. The killer was getting close now. Ben looked out across the aisle. He could just make out a pair of legs, striding past them towards the exit. In seconds they would be level with de la Peña's grotesque resting-place. Laura rolled under the next car, gesturing back to Ben to hurry up. They were losing speed against the footsteps now, four and a half steps per car by the time Ben scraped his way under car six. As they forced their pace to match the increased tempo of the footsteps, the effort and tension were sapping their energy away fast. In the humid, unconditioned air of the lot, Ben could feel his forehead dripping with sweat. He forced his aching muscles to push him clear of car seven and towards car eight, only to roll straight into Laura, lying in the gap between the cars. She grimaced back at him and for a moment he didn't understand why she had stopped. Then he saw the feline contours of the Porsche 911 in front of her.

"Bloody Porsche drivers…." said Ben.

The chassis hung low between the alloy wheels, giving it a road-clearance of inches. The end of the road for Makepeace and Laura. If they were going to move now, they would have to break cover to do it. Ben felt the blood thumping through his temples, pulsing in time with the footfalls. Laura swept her dark hair out of her face and then froze, grabbing Makepeace's wrist. The footsteps had stopped dead. They lay completely still, wordless. Ben shuddered as a huge cockroach lumbered towards him and ran its long thin antennae over his face. Laura reached over and flicked it away with her sleeve, sending it scuttling back into the gloom. They looked at each other, suffering through each millisecond of tense silence. Then the pounding of feet on concrete boomed out across the lot.

Ben began to pull himself up, ready to make a break for it, but Laura put her hand on his shoulder. She smiled, almost laughing with relief.

"He's running away!" she whispered. "The footsteps are going in the other direction!

Let's wait a minute, then get out of here."

They listened as the sound of the feet died away towards the exit from the lot, and then lay in impatient silence as the luminous second hand crawled around the dial of Makepeace's watch. 57, 58, 59, 60. Ben sat up on his haunches, peering into the blackness over the hood of a Land Rover Discovery.

"Has he gone?" hissed Laura.

"I can't see- just stay down."

Then there was a high-pitched electrical hum and the whole car-lot was flooded with blinding, neon light. Dropping back down into the gap between the cars, Ben rubbed his smarting eyes and scanned the row of cars they had scrambled under. There was something lying on the ground now. It was a small, crumpled form- too small to be another body. His jacket. Their calling-card had been found.

"Shit!" he whispered. "We really need to move. Now!"

He looked at the Porsche blocking their way. It was parked right up against a pillar on the back wall of the lot.

"There's no space behind it either…" said Laura.

"When I give the signal, we have to get up and run to the lifts," said Ben. "Stay down- stay as low as possible, behind the front row of cars."

"So you think- you think he'll come for us?" she said.

"He's already coming."

Ben could hear the footsteps again now- softer this time, padding along the asphalt. A few steps, then silence. A few more steps, then silence again. He was checking each row of cars, one by one. Methodical, unhurried, and headed straight for them.

"If we wait here, he'll find us for sure," said Ben.

He looked at Laura, her freckled face etched with concentration as she tried to work out their next play. Her elegant trouser-suit was covered in a thick grime of engine oil and dirt from the ground, one of the sleeves of her jacket torn and bleeding at the elbow from scraping along the uneven asphalt. Her long hair was streaked with clay dust from car four, and starting to cling to her forehead from the exertion. I bet she still looks better than I do, Makepeace thought. Laura stiffened beside him as a shadowy figure ghosted into view on the other side of the aisle, dropping down to look under another row of cars. He was getting close. As he stooped down again to look under the next row, Ben could make out the leather grip he was carrying in his right hand. In his left hand he was holding a black automatic.

"M9 Beretta," Ben muttered. "I really screwed us with that jacket…"

Laura grabbed Ben's elbow.

"Forget about that now!" she whispered. "Don't you have a gun?"

"A gun? Who do you think I am?"

"I think you're a spy. Aren't you?"

"I'm an insurance guy."

"A what?" she said.

"Laurence Pearce had a life insurance policy taken out on him just before he died. Fifty million dollars' worth."

"Him too!" said Laura. "Jesus, all this insurance. What were they up to?"

"What about you?" said Ben.

"What do you mean?"

"What are you doing here?"

"I'm an investigative journalist."

"Oh, Christ…" said Ben.

"What were you hoping for? Charlie's Angels?"

"SEAL Team Six would have been good..."

"Sorry to disappoint you. But now what the fuck are we going to do?" she whispered. "Because he's going to find us in about two minutes."

She was right. There were only half a dozen rows to go before he reached them. Then they would be trapped. They watched transfixed as he moved on, never rushing, never pausing. Relentless. Laura shivered as he crouched down beside the next row, training the Beretta into the shadows.

"Do you have anything we could use as a weapon?" she said. "Because I'd rather go out fighting, wouldn't you?"

Ben pulled the book of matches from his pocket again and tore another match out of it.

"On my signal," he said. "Start running. And don't stop until you hit the lifts."

"Then what?" said Laura.

"Then we'll improvise."

Ben struck the match and lit the cardboard cover of the book of matches. The technicolour picture of the Miraflores Locks blackened, twisted and then finally flickered into flame. As the spindly sticks caught light and the flame raced to the volatile chemical tips of the remaining matches, the cheap printing inks sent a spiral of acrid blue smoke twisting up into the air. Using the Land Rover as cover, Ben jumped to his feet and threw his arm up to the corroded metal smoke detector on the low roof of the car-park.

Then he caught a flash of green eyes, as the shadow in the aisle pivoted round towards him. Makepeace stood for an eternity with his arm reaching out into the void, waiting for the rust-eaten alarm to trigger. Waiting for the impact of the first bullet.

"Don't fail me now, Panabanco…" he said. "Don't fucking fail me now."

CHAPTER 25

OXFORD, UNITED KINGDOM

Walker wiped his hands on his trousers again, then replaced them on the steering wheel. Should have worn driving-gloves, Rob, he thought. Any gloves. Idiot! Why couldn't he have planned ahead, for once in his life? He had attention to detail, he could always get lost in it, obsessed with it. Brood over it for days afterwards, with 20:20 hindsight. Like the fiasco of his first year exams… He'd written himself off at nineteen years old. But mastery of detail- that had been a different thing. He'd always wanted to do his best, to fulfil his potential, to right the wrongs of his teens and twenties. To learn from his mistakes and move on. That was what they said, wasn't it? That there was no such thing as a mistake, just another lesson. That experience was cheap at any price. You never lost: you won, or you learned. But Rob had always had a knack for finding more mistakes, mistakes where it didn't seem possible there could be any more to come. That barrel had no bottom, and the price of failure was getting higher all the time. For some people it just never seemed to click, no matter how long you waited. He'd gone to university, he'd always done his best! He wasn't a gambler like Jules, a playboy like Laurence Pearce, a chancer like Hugo Capstick- or a psycho adrenalin junkie like Kip Horrocks. He was the nearly man. Nearly a prefect at school, nearly got a degree, nearly made a go of it in the City- nearly met Laura first, before she had inexplicably fallen for Capstick's reckless charm. He had nearly staked his own claim on life. But even old Horrocks had done his bit when the cookie crumbled, everyone said so in the Club. Toasted him, the big, bold man of action! Cometh the hour, cometh the H-man. Redemption had come to him at the end, and he had lived before he died. So maybe this- maybe this was his potential too. He could be a soldier. Because anyone could lay their life down for the cause. And didn't that have to mean something?

"Cargo 200 is mobile..." came the voice through his earpiece.

Suicide Station. It was what he had been waiting for all morning, but it still took him by surprise when it came. As if there was any way to prepare for this- for the news that your life was over. Nearly over.

"Roger that," said Walker, gunning the engine to pull out of the station carpark, heavy-footed with tension. He over-revved at once, pulled his foot back off the accelerator, and a mini-cab behind him blared its horn. Christ, what if he stalled? Of course an automatic would have been better for this job, it was obvious. And something bigger, with his height he was bent over double in the little Audi. Now his foot felt like a huge, uncoordinated block of wood at the end of his cramping leg, something he had no control of whatsoever. He was going to stall, he could just feel it- and at the critical point in the mission.

"Cargo 200 is approaching the Porter's Lodge."

Walker accelerated down Park End Street and over Hythe Bridge.

"Slow down, Walker! The approach is timed for 20 mph," said Suicide Station. "This is no time for a speeding ticket."

"Sorry..." Walker muttered. "You're overthinking again, Rob," he said to himself. "Focus. Focus. Action."

Only one more set of lights to negotiate, but it could take an eternity in the Oxford traffic. Especially if he stalled at them.

"Come on, come on, change..." he hissed.

"Cargo 200 is in the Lodge," said Bezique. "And the feeder arrow is going green- now."

Now Walker was cornering left and rolling down Worcester Street. This was it. The last obstacle surmounted. He was really going to do this. He felt a flood of adrenalin wash over him.

"Slow down, man!" said Suicide Station. "Cargo 200 is at street level."

There was Worcester College on his left. Walker could remember borrowing a gown to go to formal hall there. Remembered that the food had been so much better than at his own college. Remembered the bar, full of pink rugby shirts and pinker faces. But that was a lifetime ago. A different country. And now he could see Schofield. Subject wears standard academic uniform: tweed jacket and brown suede brogues. Check and check.

"Do you have positive ID?" said Bezique.

"Roger that," said Walker. "But wait- do you? What if it isn't him?"

"You're a go, Brother. It's him."

"Repeat, Suicide Station- do you have positive identification?"

Schofield was crossing Worcester Street now, looking around him, clutching a lap-top bag close to his chest as though ready to defend it against all-comers. Was he expecting Walker? God, what if he was!

"Engage!" shouted Bezique. "Repeat, engage, you fool! Do it! Do it now!"

Walker felt his stomach lurch. Suddenly he realised with a sickening feeling what a hash he was making of this. What had he been thinking? Wasting all this time- and now the window was closing. He could see it slipping away from him. But then he remembered: Despair is power.

"No gods, no masters!" he shouted.

Schofield must have heard him. Heard something. He looked around him in alarm as he crossed the road.

Walker stamped down hard on the accelerator and his foot slid off it, grazing the edge. He stalled, cursed and then restarted the engine. Schofield was running now, sprinting for the Gloucester Green side. Walker spun the steering wheel, sending the car careering straight across the right-hand lane. Schofield dived for the pavement. Walker's hand slipped on the wheel and he lost control. He closed his eyes as the car crumpled into the wall, taking the railings along with it like a bridal train. He had nearly hit Harry Schofield on his way.

CHAPTER 26

LIME STREET, CITY OF LONDON, UNITED KINGDOM

Trevor Braithwaite paced the office, Dictaphone in hand, taking liberal draughts from his Evian bottle as he spoke.

"Message to Benjamin Makepeace, Esquire, from the office of the Chairman. Email thingy. Private and confidential. Starts: 'How the bloody hell are you, old chap? And more to the point, where are you? You'll never guess what the bloodhounds have dug up on the unfortunate Laurence Pearce. Well? You give up? I'll tell you then. It seems that he was a rackets buddy of one Rob Walker. They played at the Queen's Club together- thick as thieves, even paired up for the doubles in the annual Queen's match against the Montreal Racket Club over in Canada last year. But why am I telling you all this, you ask? Neither of us being sufficiently *pukka sahibs* to belong to either club ourselves. Wrong schools, and all that. The reason is this, sunshine: Rob Walker managed to get himself killed in Oxford this very morning. Car crash outside Worcester College. His fault. Which would be strictly local news, had he not in the process very narrowly missed crashing into and killing Harry Schofield, Chief Executive of the Oxford Fusion Corporation, a techy energy start-up with some connection to the University. Where Walker had studied himself, some years ago. According to our friends in the Oxford Constabulary, this Schofield is now telling anyone who'll listen that Walker tried to take him out on purpose, so that evil oil companies can stop him, Schofield, from saving the world from climate change by harnessing the power of- wait for it- pistol shrimps! Nonsense, of course, classic conspiracy theory stuff, and the boys in blue have it firmly in the traffic incidents file- and 'Pistol Shrimp Pete' on the crank callers list." He cleared his throat. "Nonetheless, from our point of view, this is about the size of it: Laurence Pearce and Rob Walker, bosom buddies from London High Society, both contrive to die in circumstances liable to take out prominent members of the business community. Within a week of each other. Oh, and this Walker also happens to have been insured for fifty mill. With us, of course. Thought you ought to know. The researchers- and yours truly- are frankly unable to make any more connection than that at the time of writing. But it sounds very much like the criminal activity exclusion to me. And besides, that's what you do, isn't it, old boy? You see things. So you take care now, you hear me? Yours etcetera, etcetera, Braithwaite. Oh, and P.S. Try not to see things involving oil companies, if you can possibly avoid it. The syndicates don't want any aspersions cast on their biggest clients- even for the sake of that fifty million. Make that a hundred million, now. Discretion is the watchword! P.P.S. No, never mind all that… End of message. Fire away, Amy, my dear! Send it off into the ether. The Isthmus. Or wherever Makepeace may have got to. He hasn't even sent any expenses claims back yet. Most unlike him, because he's normally a canny young fellow!"

Braithwaite dispatched the recording for typing, and then tossed the Dictaphone across the room, the smile disappearing from his face. He cracked his knuckles and stared out across the Lloyd's atrium, lost in thought.

CHAPTER 27

PANAMA CITY, REPUBLIC OF PANAMA

Ben's fingers seared and burned as the flame ate up the remaining scraps of card. El Pishtaco twisted round into cover behind a car and levelled the Beretta at him. Then the whole world seemed to erupt into sound. In the cramped confines of the car-lot, the fire-alarm was gut-wrenchingly, cripplingly loud. Senses supercharged by the tension, Makepeace could hear, taste, feel the dizzying sound-waves vibrating all around him. Even El Pishtaco seemed stunned until, just as instantaneously, the noise cut out dead. The corroded circuit-board had failed them. Before the last echo of the alarm had been swallowed up by the damp concrete of the lot, a volley of 9mm rounds ripped over the top of the Land Rover and thudded into the back wall behind them. For an instant, Ben was sickeningly aware that all he had done was draw the killer straight onto them. Then Laura grabbed his hand and pulled him after her. Running low on their haunches, they sprinted for the elevators. In a quicksilver, liquid movement El Pishtaco was up on his feet too, firing on the run, releasing three more shots that smashed through the Discovery's windscreen. The perspex crumpled, sending fragments skidding across the concrete floor. Laura and Ben dived down behind the Mercedes at the end of the row next to the lifts, just as another shot came screaming into its windshield. Ben braced for the impact, but the bullet deflected off the car with a dull thud, leaving the glass scored but unbroken.

"Bullet-proof glass!" said Ben. "This is our ride…"

They crouched down behind the armoured front panels of the car. Ben looked across at the elevator call-button. It was only a couple of feet away along the wall, in the middle of the central aisle.

"That's what Emerald Eyes is waiting for," said Laura. "For us to make a move."

"Yeah, well we can't stay here for ever," said Ben. "We're in a Mexican stand-off without a gun. Where's your car?"

Laura shook her head in frustration and pointed down the aisle.

"It's the white Toyota over there. Behind him- it might as well be on the moon."

"Give me your car keys," said Makepeace.

"You'll never make it, tough guy- you know you won't," she said. "We'd have a better chance with the lift!"

"Just give me the keys…"

She fished in her bag and passed him a plastic key-fob. Ben took a deep breath and edged to the nose of the Mercedes. He pushed the end of the electronic key out towards the no-man's land of the aisle and pressed 'Unlock'. Nothing for a split-second. He was already pushing the button again when the Toyota's central locking system engaged with a crisp click. It reverberated through the tense stillness of the lot, just enough like a cocking automatic to send El Pishtaco dropping down to the asphalt. As El Pishtaco spun around towards the noise behind him, Ben lunged out and punched the elevator call-button. The heavy steel doors shifted, lurched and then began to inch slowly open. Too slowly- Makepeace was still reaching out to pull Laura into the elevator after him when El Pishtaco wheeled round again and sent one shot crashing into the mirrored interior of the elevator, then another flying inches beyond Ben's out-stretched arm. The bullet ricocheted off the Mercedes' radiator grille and then crashed into the ceiling of the lot. Ben dived back behind the cover of the car, sprawling on the ground next to Laura.

"Did you miss me?"

"Like a hole in the head," said Laura. "Now we're right back to square one..."

The lift stood tantalisingly open, lit up from within. Ben looked across at it again, measuring out the distance in his mind. Laura read his thoughts.

"We might make it if he missed- or hesitated."

"He's not going to hesitate," said Ben.

Pablito the security guard hesitated though, for one fatal instant, as he came jogging down the aisle into the car-lot. Woken by the alarm, the shooting or both, he was still scrabbling with the release clip of his gun-holster as he loped towards El Pishtaco.

"Get down, Pablito!" screamed Makepeace at the top of his voice. "*¡Al suelo! ¡Al suelo!*"

Pablito reeled around. Laura jumped up, grabbed at Ben's sleeve and flung herself headlong into the elevator. Ben leapt in after her, fumbling for the 'Close' button inside it. Pushing his hand aside, Laura leaned forward and pressed '17'.

Through the narrowing gap between closing doors, they watched helplessly as El Pishtaco shot Pablito twice in the middle of his chest. The security guard rocked with the impact, and then crumpled backwards as another bullet exploded into his forehead. His gun clattered to the ground, unused. El Pishtaco whirled back towards Laura and Ben, aiming his own weapon at the shrinking gap between the doors in one fluid arc. They crushed themselves back against the sides of the elevator, but there was nowhere to hide as El Pishtaco squeezed the trigger. There was a hollow click and then silence. Empty clip. El Pishtaco stared at them as the elevator doors slid together with a ponderous thud, fixing their faces in his memory. For an instant the green eyes seemed to pierce right through the brushed steel of the doors, and then they were lifted clear of the slaughterhouse below.

"Sorry Pablito," said Ben. "*Descansa en paz, compañero.* Rest in peace."

"Ben- what would have happened if I'd touched de la Peña's body back there?" said Laura.

"Maybe nothing," said Makepeace. "Bombs fail. People fail. That's one thing you do learn in the insurance business."

"But if it hadn't failed?"

"Then we'd both be dead."

"So you did save my life then. Thank you."

Makepeace smiled, as the lift hurtled up into the Panama sky.

CHAPTER 28

OXFORD, UNITED KINGDOM

"More wine?" said Malthus, pouring out a brimming glass of Cheval Blanc without waiting for an answer. "1998 was a superb year for 'the Horse'. And the best thing is that it was such an average year for the other Bordeaux *châteaux*! To savour abundance, there must also be scarcity- want. Whether it is merlot in the Médoc, or energy. But then of course you know that, my dear fellow! You're lucky to have this place so close- they keep a pretty decent cellar, I find."

"I don't come to the Randolph for lunch very often," Schofield admitted.

"You really should make the effort," said Malthus. "I always stay here when I'm up. It's rather plusher than it was in my day, of course. It was a draughty old barracks in those days, styled on the bleaker type of Yorkshire boys' boarding school. The food was terrible, and the sex was worse…"

Schofield spluttered into his wine glass.

"Here's to you, young Harry!" said Malthus, toasting him. "It's wonderful to hear how much progress you've made with your sonofusion research. Through sheer bloody hard work! And all in perfect secrecy, whilst these other fools have fiddled about with their white elephant stellarators and National Ignition Facilities, and broadcast it to the four winds!"

Schofield struggled to contain his self-satisfaction.

"Oh yes, secrecy was of the essence of the operation!" he said. "Secrecy and security. Right from the outset, I knew that there would be dark forces opposing my work. So I spoke to my college friend who used to work at GCHQ, and he gave me a few inside tips. Tradecraft... And then I bided my time. I waited until I was ready before unveiling my discoveries- but even now I'm surrounded by spies. Do you know I was nearly killed this morning? An attempted hit and run on Worcester Street. In broad daylight! You wouldn't normally expect that kind of thing in Oxford. If I hadn't kept my wits about me, I'd be a dead man now."

"My dear fellow, I did hear about that," said Malthus. "Most upsetting for you. And for all of us in the BCS Ventures family, of course. But what makes you think it was deliberate? Didn't the wretched driver just lose control of his car, as the police said?"

"It must have been intentional," said Harry. "I studied the angle of impact myself. The car was nearly perpendicular when it hit the railings. And from the damage to the vehicle and barriers, he must still have been accelerating into the impact. They had to cut the driver's body out. Besides, I saw him looking right at me as I crossed the road! The vultures are circling..."

"Good Lord!" said Malthus.

"Of course the oil companies are out to get me," said Harry. "They'll stop me any way they can. They must be terrified of what our technology can do! What use will anyone have for their oil or natural gas, when they can use our sonofusion to generate limitless, emission-free electricity? Fossil fuels will be a thing of the past. Unless they can take me out first, of course..."

"You must be protected at all costs!" said Malthus. "And I was meaning to talk to you about precisely that. It goes without saying that we will need Key Man Insurance for you, to come on risk as soon as our investment goes in. You- personally- are a very valuable man, Mr Schofield. And getting more valuable all the time. A key man, if ever there was one. To us- and to all humanity!"

Schofield beamed.

"Of course. And about your investment, Bartholomew- do you have any more due diligence you need to complete?" he asked. "The other investors had endless questions- endless bloody lawyers! They wanted us to get patents for the compression technology, the confinement chambers, the wave generation software, you name it- all before they would give us a penny. There were always more forms to fill in, boxes to tick, warranties to review- until I started losing the will to live. It was like having two jobs!"

"We're a very different kind of investor, Harry," said Malthus, clapping him on the back. "We're all about the will to live. We're what you might call 'high conviction'. The highest of all. We take a view on a brilliant young scientist- someone like yourself- and we back them to the end. Oh, to the very end. Our investments are not done by bean-counters- they're done by true believers. And now, about your own salary..."

"I haven't been taking a salary, of course- just while we got things up and running," said Schofield. "It seemed more appropriate to waive it. And of course the college have been jolly generous in letting me keep my fellow's rooms all these years, whilst I've been working on Oxford Fusion..."

"Just what we like to see from our CEO!" said Malthus. "But the days of sack-cloth and ashes are over for you now, old chap! *Finito.*" He beckoned the waiter over. "In fact, we'd like to start by paying you arrears on the salary that you should have been drawing over the past five years. If you'd been filling your boots, working for some faceless City bank, like so many of your peers."

"Sell-outs..." said Schofield.

"So what if we said- two hundred thousand pounds a year, for the sake of an argument?"

Schofield choked on his wine again.

"You mean you're- you're going to pay me a million pounds?"

"Call it a 'golden hello'..." said Malthus. "For our golden boy! You are very important to us, Harry. So if you could just sign this insurance policy for me- as a formality, I'm not even going to speak to our lawyers about it- then I think we can manage to keep the contract-monkeys out of the rest of it..."

Schofield reached for the fountain pen.

"That's a good chap!" said Malthus. "I rather think a sticky is called for…" he said to the waiter. "The Château d'Yquem 1976- the year of young Harry's birth."

"You have made an excellent choice, sir," said the waiter.

"That's what I do," said Malthus, draining the last of the Cheval Blanc.

CHAPTER 29

TORRE PANABANCO, PANAMA CITY, REPUBLIC OF PANAMA

"Aren't we going the wrong way?" said Ben. "Up, I mean?"

"Man the fuck up, Makepeace- we just set a fire alarm off in Panama's tallest building!" said Laura. "Every cop in town is on their way here."

"I still don't like this," he said. "Pros don't run out of bullets. And you get fifteen rounds in an M9."

"He didn't know Pablito was going to show up like that," said Laura. "But you're sure he was a professional?"

"Would you cut a man's throat and rip his tongue out through the hole?"

"I can tell you what I'm not going to do, and that's leave empty-handed," she said. "Not after everything we've been through! Two men were killed down there, to keep a secret. That means we must be getting close to the truth. And it's this way. Up."

"So where are we going now?"

"De la Peña's office is on the fifteenth floor," said Laura.

"Why are we going to the seventeenth then?"

"Do you really want that psycho to follow us up? What if the elevator display shows what floor we've gone to? The seventeenth is the bank's reception.

We can take the stairs down to the fifteenth. That way Emerald Eyes has got thirty floors to search before he finds us. By which time, I suggest we're long gone."

"Isn't there any security in this building?" said Ben.

Laura held up a plastic key-card.

"There was Pablito," she said. "I borrowed this from him on my way in. I thought it might come in handy."

"You must be a very good journalist," said Ben.

"I need to know what happened," she said. "What's happened to everyone! My brother and two of his best friends have all died in the last two weeks. We don't know how many more people could die before this is over."

"Well, us, for a start…" said Ben, as the lift doors slid open. He peered outside. "Ladies first?"

Laura scowled at him, and then stepped out into the ornate seventeenth floor atrium, luxuriant in mock porphyry and lurid Romero prints. She waved the key-card at the electronic sensor beside the door, and the LED flashed green.

"Open Sesame," she said, opening the door that led to the stairwell. "Quick, let's go."

"They should really build a lift in here…" said Ben, as they hurried down the stairs to the fifteenth floor.

"Shut up, idiot!" said Laura.

She tapped the key-card on the reader on the door into the fifteenth floor.

"And we're in…" she said.

"What exactly are we looking for?" said Ben.

"De la Peña's office will do for a start."

It was easy enough to find, the corner office, decked out in the hardwood opulence of Panamanian privilege.

"You didn't manage to get his password too?" said Ben.

"This was supposed to be our first meeting," said Laura, rifling through the papers on de la Peña's desk. "He arrived in a taxi. I introduced myself, but before we could come up to his office, Emerald Eyes arrived, and de la Peña told me to hide. You know what happened next."

"Did you notice anything about the killer?" said Ben. "Except the eyes?"

"I could only make out one word he said, and I don't even know if I heard that clearly- what it means…"

"But what do you think it was?" said Ben.

"It sounded like- *pistacho*."

"*Pistacho*? As in a pistachio nut? What do you think he meant by that?"

"Like I said, I don't know if I heard it properly," said Laura. "That's what I thought it was. But in Latin America they call the nut *pistache* anyway. I think maybe in Spain they say *pistacho*."

"Do you think this guy could have been Spanish?"

"You saw his face, Ben. Do you think he looked Spanish?"

"No. Whatever he is, it isn't Spanish."

"He was tall though- much taller than any *indígena* I've ever seen."

"So it could have been a code-name?"

"I don't know," she said. "But look at this…"

She passed Makepeace a framed photo from the desk.

"The brothers de la Peña," said Ben. "I recognise Gustavo from the Pearce file. They were very alike."

"And now they're both dead," said Laura. "That's what this is about- why Severo agreed to meet me. He wanted to speak to me. To both of us, clearly. He wanted justice for his brother- just like me. The police aren't even investigating the *Joya del Istmo* case."

"That's odd," said Ben, picking up another photograph. "Because this one's Severo with the Commissioner of Police- Omar Herrera. These guys were seriously connected. But no one's asking any questions."

"You don't ask questions when you already know what happened," said Laura. "Just like my brother's death. And I bet just like Kip Horrocks' too."

"What happened to them?" said Makepeace, scrolling through his messages.

"Julian was killed at the Rocket Festival in Laos," said Laura. "A freak accident- which just happened to kill a Government minister at the same time. Kip died in a car crash in Entebbe."

"Was anyone else involved in that?" said Ben.

"General Mohammed Al-Jaber- the Commander in Chief of the African Union's mission to Somalia. He was in a Landcruiser full of Moroccan Navy commandos on an empty road, when Kip somehow managed to crash into them, killing them all."

"Laura, this may seem like an odd question," said Ben. "But do you happen to know someone called Rob Walker back in the UK?"

"Rob- yes, of course!" she said. "I saw him at Jules' funeral. What's happened? Is he alright?"

"I'm sorry to have to tell you this," said Ben. "But he's been killed too. My boss just messaged me. There was a road accident in Oxford this morning, UK time."

"What on earth was he doing in Oxford?" said Laura. "He hated the place! He vowed he would never set foot there again, after he made such a mess of his Mods."

"Well, he broke that vow," said Ben. "And nearly killed a pioneering nuclear physicist into the bargain."

"God..." said Laura, sinking down into de la Peña's chair. "His poor family. Are the police investigating?"

"Case closed," said Ben. "A traffic accident."

"Can't you see there's something horribly wrong here?" said Laura, flicking through de la Peña's Rolodex. "All these deaths! What's going on?" Then she stopped and stared at a card in amazement. "I don't believe it..."

"What is it?" said Makepeace.

Laura tore the card off the Rolodex and passed it over to him.

"It's the connection, Ben. It's the thing that draws every one of these deaths together."

"Bezique. Bohemian Sports Club," read Makepeace. "50 St James's Street, St. James's, London SW1."

CHAPTER 30

QUEEN VICTORIA STREET, CITY OF LONDON, UNITED KINGDOM

"Black Velvet, old boy?" said Trevor Braithwaite, standing up and emptying his silver tankard as Ben and Laura walked in to the restaurant. "The drink of heroes! And you, Miss Newman?"

"Champagne and Guinness?" said Laura. "Ugh. What a complete waste of good champagne..."

"Have it your own way!" said Braithwaite, holding two fingers up to the waitress. "I thought you'd been in tow with young Benjamin here."

"Yeah, but we've been working," said Makepeace.

"Yes, about that..." said Braithwaite. "Lobster bisque all round!" he mouthed to the waitress. "You do realise that you're actually supposed to close these TPT files, not just bring us back more?" He buttered a piece of brown bread with a silver knife. "If you carry on generating three new cases for each one I assign you, the TPT will be on its knees by the end of the month! I'm on two bottles of Evian a day as it is... I'm getting here earlier every lunch-time."

"Come on, Trevor," said Ben. "We can't just ignore this. They all had life insurance with Lloyd's syndicates, set up through multi-layer trust structures. There's a huge conspiracy going on here. Someone insured Laura's brother for fifty million dollars, and then sent him to his death in Laos. The blood money is mounting up."

"Keep your voice down, man!" said Braithwaite. "This place is full of Lloyd's people." He took a gulp of Black Velvet. "I'm not ignoring anything-certainly not when it comes to claims on our underwriting syndicates! I was the one who tipped you off on the Rob Walker case, remember? Sent you an email myself. But I've looked at the Julian Newman file already. The Metropolitan Police say it's a matter for the Laos authorities, and the Laos authorities don't acknowledge that anything untoward happened. They're calling it a freak accident with fireworks."

"They denied that the Saddle Dam D burst!" said Laura. "And that killed nearly a hundred people. They were hardly likely to advertise the fact that a West End club could fly in and assassinate a member of the Politburo under their noses, were they?"

"Forget the cops," said Makepeace. "What we should be investigating is the insurance angle. Follow the money. We need to run the Laurence Pearce case to ground, anyway. Whatever you do about Horrocks, Newman and Walker, that's an open Technical Performance Team file."

"I'm well aware of that, Benjamin," said Braithwaite, draining his tankard. "You're not the one with half the syndicate chief executives in London breathing down your neck!" He nodded to a pin-striped diner further down the wooden counter. "That's the head honcho at Syndicate 601… Being Chairman of Lloyd's isn't all beer and skittles, you know. Your old man could tell you that!" he said to Laura.

"It's funny you mention that," said Laura. "Because I've been wondering what I should be telling my father about all this. You know he's still one of the biggest Names on the market?"

"That sounds rather like a threat, doesn't it?" said Braithwaite. "Yes, yes, Chablis of course- the Grand Cru…" he said to the waitress.

"Listen, Mr Braithwaite," said Laura, gesturing around the restaurant. "I don't really give a shit what you and the Old Boys' Club get up to here. Knock yourselves out with your boarding school puddings and Bubble and Squeak, for all I care. But my brother is dead, and so are three of his friends, and I seem to be the only one who's asking why. So if I have tread on a few toes to get to the bottom of it, then so be it."

"I stand duly chastened!" said Braithwaite, tasting the wine. "Jolly good…" He turned back to Laura. "So why don't you tell me your bright idea for closing some of these damned files?"

"It's perfectly simple," said Ben. "I'm going to join the Billionaire Suicide Club."

"You're going to join what?" said Braithwaite, choking on his Chablis.

"The Bohemian Sports Club," said Laura. "That's what's on the name plate. But the insiders- the members- call it the Billionaire Suicide Club. I've been doing some digging. They have tentacles everywhere: the public schools, the universities, the investment banks- the Army. Recruiting new members who've reached the end of their tethers. Preying on desperate men, like my poor brother."

"And so you're going to join a suicide club, Benjamin?" said Braithwaite. "Can you hear yourself? Are you out of your mind? It would vitiate every insurance policy you have. And even if this far-fetched club of yours exists- which I can scarcely credit- how on earth would you go about becoming a member? You're not a billionaire, the last time I checked."

"You pay one million dollars, for one thing," said Laura. "That ought to go a pretty long way to getting in."

"And just how do you know that, Miss Newman?" said Braithwaite.

"I have power of attorney for my brother's estate," said Laura. "I've been through the transaction records. He transferred a million dollars in gold to the Bohemian Sports Club six months ago. Those bastards robbed him of his money, before they took his life away too."

"A million dollars a head, eh?" said Braithwaite. "Not too desperate then, these clubmen?"

"Desperate rich men," said Laura. "Surely you can get your head around that? How do you like your life?"

"Steady on!" said Braithwaite, holding his hands up. "So what does this million bucks buy you, then?"

"We don't know exactly how it works yet," said Laura. "We never will, unless we can get Ben on the inside. For obvious reasons, it's a clandestine organisation. They swear the members to secrecy, insure their lives and then brain-wash them into going on these insane assignments. They're protected at the highest level- all over the world. They've covered up all these deaths. Laurence. Kip. Rob. My brother. And dozens more like them, no doubt. The only way to get to the bottom of it is to get in there and see for ourselves."

"Be that as it may, I can't justify risking Lloyd's money just to assuage your sisterly guilt, my dear!" said Braithwaite. "Who knows whether we'll ever see it again? The whole thing sounds like a huge fraud! Reeks to high heaven of it. I mean, you can just imagine the auditors' meeting can't you?" He poured out another three glasses of Chablis and waved the empty bottle at the waitress. "Another of these, I think... I can hear the bean-counters picking holes in it already. They'd have a bloody field day!"

"Fine," said Laura. "No one asked you to pay. I'll put the money up myself."

"You?" said Braithwaite. "You have money like that sloshing around? A million dollars?"

"I'm the Newman heiress, aren't I?" she said. "I'm richer than ever, for what that's worth. And that shady club just killed my brother. The only person in the world I had to look after." She took Makepeace's hand. "So if Ben is brave enough..."

"Mad enough..." said Braithwaite.

"If he's brave enough to go in there, then I for one am right behind him- with everything I've got," she said. "Because right now that's the only chance I have of finding out what happened to my brother. What you don't know is that when Julian died, he wrote me a letter. He told me that he was leaving me what's left of his trust fund, as an apology for all the trouble he'd caused me over the years. But of course, as soon as he had gone the first thing I realised was that he hadn't been any trouble at all. The only trouble was not having him in the world with us anymore."

"Our condolences, of course..." said Braithwaite. "Terrible business. But let's imagine for a second that we do accept this generous offer to fund Makepeace's membership, and the TPT decides to invest his time in this- project. How would we even go about it? Making contact with this club? Presumably they're not advertising membership in the Yellow Pages?"

Laura held up Bezique's business card.

"That's easy," she said. "We just send this guy an email. From Julian's account. That should get his attention, don't you think?"

"Right-oh, then!" said Braithwaite. "And how do I get hold of you if any new leads come in, Benjamin?"

"You can find me in the Club..." said Makepeace.

CHAPTER 31

ST JAMES'S, LONDON, UNITED KINGDOM

It was a filthy morning in the West End. The rain was already soaking through the delicate leather soles of Newman's black Church's brogues, lifting spatters of dirt off the St James's pavements. Julian's Brioni suit also seemed better equipped for a fragrant Roman spring than a London rainstorm. Ben was still glad that Laura had forced him to borrow her brother's clothes though, Hermès jacquard tie, Longmire cuff-links and all, when he reached the yellow brick and Portland Stone façade of the Bohemian Sports Club. Florizel opened the imposing, gull's egg blue-coloured door and appraised him. This was no place to be ill-dressed.

"Time to start thinking like a billionaire…" Ben muttered to himself.

"Mr Makepeace?" said Florizel.

"You were expecting me?" said Ben.

"Of course, sir. We know all of our members here. This isn't a restaurant- or the RAC Club."

"No. They tell me it's the most exclusive club in London," said Ben.

"Oh, it's more than a club, sir," said Florizel.

"But I'm not a member yet."

"No, sir. And indeed Mr Bezique asked me to pass you a message- before you do cross this threshold."

"Go on."

Florizel cleared his throat.

"He said: 'There is still time to make good your escape into thraldom. Reflect well before you take another step: and if your heart says no- here are the cross-roads.'"

"Thanks for the message," said Makepeace. "Now take me to him. I am not the man to go back from a thing once said. I'm here to join the Club, not to haggle over the terms."

Florizel inclined his head.

"That's what Mr Bezique told me you would say, sir," he said. "He has been conducting his own due diligence on you- as you would expect, given the discretion that our membership demands."

"Of course," said Ben. "This is no place for tourists."

"Indeed, sir," said Florizel. "And if you'll permit me: I have met many men at this door in forty years, and yet I have never seen anyone enter it so calmly as you do."

"*Vogue la galère*!" said Ben. "I follow the game…"

"Then follow me, sir," said Florizel, leading Makepeace down an oak-panelled corridor, lined with brown leather chesterfield sofas. "The Game is this way."

The walls of the club were lined with oil portraits from all over the world, Japanese Samurai, red-coated East India Company officers, dead Kennedys, leather-clad rock-stars and pin-striped businessmen.

"There is but one brotherhood, sir," said Florizel. "Drawn from the whole world around us. The cards fall where they fall."

Ben studied the portrait of a hard-bitten Victorian gent sporting a frock coat, lamb-chop whiskers and a monstrous cheroot. The plaque simply read: 'To The Most Corrupt Rogue In Christendom'.

"It was meant as a compliment, sir," said Florizel, following Ben's glance. "And graciously accepted as such. He was the president of the Club in Robert Louis Stevenson's time. Mr Stevenson was rather an indiscreet gentleman- an author, you see. But Mr Raffles there was the president who refined the Game to the pitch of perfection that we know today."

"And Stevenson himself survived their meeting?"

"He had just been diagnosed with tuberculosis, sir. In his despair, he was introduced to the Club by a friend of Mr Dickens, and even entered the *salle de jeux* to play the Game. But he didn't draw Old Frizzle in that hand, and he never again returned to the club afterwards."

"That's allowed by the club rules?" said Ben.

"He took himself off to Western Samoa to convalesce," said Florizel. "In those days, the South Seas were considered far enough to go- if a gentleman wished to resign his membership, and was prepared to leave London forever."

"And now?"

"Hardly, sir. The world is a smaller place, these days. And the Club's hand far longer. We find that the member who is tired of London now is tired also of life."

"So Stevenson was the last member to leave the Club alive?" said Ben.

"There was a certain Mr Simms who sadly chose to leave us," said Florizel. "He languishes in some benighted Emirate or other now, unable to return."

"Not even for the Season?" said Ben.

"Perhaps the shooting season, sir."

"Christ, is that Lord Lucan?" said Makepeace, peering with astonishment at another portrait outside the cloakroom.

"A very elegant gentleman, sir," said Florizel, taking Newman's overcoat and hanging it up with practised ease. "Always beautifully turned out. He favoured Ede & Ravenscroft himself, though."

"I'm sorry?" said Ben.

"The tailors, sir," said Florizel. "I see that you favour Messrs. Brioni, yourself. Many of our younger gentlemen do. I feel myself that there is something not quite right about the hang of their trousers though. Perhaps it is due to this modern use of a belt, rather than braces. And look at your jacket- you must have spent a lot of time in the gymnasium since you were measured for that. But I may have become parochial in my old age. Now, if I might trouble you, I suppose that Mr Newman would have mentioned the practical side of matters to you? Before he- passed to the other side…"

"You mean the money?" said Ben. "The joining fee?"

Florizel inclined his head.

"One million United States dollars. How would sir prefer to pay?"

"In one ounce, mixed-year Krugerrand coins," said Ben. "No paper-trail, you see…"

"That will be quite satisfactory. And where does sir hold his gold?"

"In my vault with Messrs. Sharps Pixley, 54 St. James's Street."

"Naturally, sir. Next door. Most convenient. The club keeps all its gold with S and P. Except that you will see displayed in our Bullion Room, of course."

"Then it's settled," said Ben. "My assistant Laura is waiting for you in their private reception, if you would be so good as to join her there. She has my power of attorney, and the code to make the transfer into the Club's account."

"It would be my pleasure, sir. I will step round to Sharps' as soon as I have announced you."

He opened a panelled door.

"Mr Makepeace!" he called.

"But of course it is…" said Bezique. "Do step in, my dear fellow."

"That's an unusual fish tank," said Ben. "What are those things?"

CHAPTER 32

EDINBURGH, UNITED KINGDOM

Andrew Fairley allowed himself to day-dream for a minute about the trip as he strolled down over South Bridge from the Medical School, the icy wind whipping up his overcoat. Peru! The very name had always fired his imagination. When he was a child his older siblings had watched endless re-runs of a 1980s Japanese animated series, *The Mysterious Cities of Gold.* Somewhere through the preposterous soundtrack and painful dubbing, the show had tapped a latent fascination with Latin America in Andrew- the blurred lines between history, science and myth, the secrets lost high up in the Andes. Truly a New World. Especially when you came from Edinburgh, Andrew thought. Growing up, the old place had seemed like one great reprimand of age-weathered sandstone and Presbyterian rigour, designed to suppress exoticism in all its disreputable forms. Now he would have the opportunity to explore Cusco, Nazca and Huaraz for himself, with a respectable stipend from the University behind him. Following in the footsteps of Mendoza, Esteban and Zia, Andrew thought, laughing at the recollection. It was ridiculous. But in a way he was doing exactly that- looking for the secret of a longer, better life. Would he be the one to discover a heart of gold in those mountains? Professor Carmichael had always said that he thought differently- that he was a right-brained thinker, an innovator. Sometimes just a dreamer, and now the seagulls riding the gusting wind off the Firth of Forth seemed to double for the Latin seabirds gliding above the good ship *Solaris*.

"*Some day we will find/ The Cities of Gold...*" Andrew sang under his breath.

He was so engrossed in reveries of El Dorado that he didn't see Brother Hennessy stride over to him, shove him towards the wall of North Bridge and then tip his legs up over his head.

"Compliments to the Reaper," said Hennessy, lifting his feet over the side. "No gods, no masters!"

Suddenly Andrew found himself tilting head-first over the wall, looking down at the clear glass roof of Waverley Station twenty-one metres below, too shocked even to scream. The sheer sense of powerlessness as his centre of gravity shifted towards oblivion was numbing. And then Hennessy crumpled to the ground, Andrew's ankles were yanked sharply back down towards the pavement, and he was catapulted back onto solid ground.

"Come with me..." said the girl, helping him up to his feet. Andrew winced as she hit Hennessy again, his inert form shuddering under the impact.

"Who are you?" he said. "And who is he? Is he going to be alright?"

Laura turned around and tossed the rubber black-jack over the wall.

"We'll talk in the taxi," she said. "And don't worry about him. Believe me, it's the way he would have wanted it. It would have been kinder to kill him."

CHAPTER 33

ST JAMES'S, LONDON, UNITED KINGDOM

Florizel ushered Ben into the office and then backed out, closing the door behind him. A slim man with greying hair stood with his back to Ben, looking out of the sash window into the rain lashing down St James's Street.

"Please forgive me the little test of your resolve, Makepeace," he said. "But a man should enter this place with his eyes open, or not at all. Don't you agree?"

"Even if he leaves with them closed?" said Ben, holding out his hand. "Bezique, I presume?"

"Your servant," said Bezique, turning around and shaking Makepeace's hand.

"I paid my subs at the door," said Ben.

Bezique laughed.

"Of course you did- or Florizel would not have shown you in here. He is a stickler for such things. I don't know where he gets it from..."

"He was christened Florizel?"

"Oh, no," said Bezique. "So few people are, in these benighted times- even in Bohemia. But it is a club tradition. There is always a Florizel, to act as our steward and our bursar. Some would say our keeper… I am too old to worry about money myself. I think of these little contributions more as a- deposit. To focus the minds of our new members on the commitment they are making. For what greater commitment could one man make to another?" He lifted a crystal decanter off the Chippendale commode by the door. "Whisky?"

"I see my reputation precedes me," said Ben.

Bezique laughed and poured out two generous tumblers.

"I prefer a drop of Speyside, in the morning. And you?"

"I'm an Islay man, myself," said Ben. He nosed the whisky. "But I'm always willing to make an exception for a thirty year old Macallan."

"I do find that single malt helps separate the sheep from the goats," said Bezique. "In former times the Club used to run a black-ball system, like the Chauffeurs' Club and our neighbours here in St James's. But now I prefer to rely on my own experience of whether a man will go through with it, when his time comes. A man who drinks Scotch whisky can never be completely unaware of his own mortality."

"The million dollar down-payment must help too," said Ben.

"Indeed," said Bezique, sipping his Macallan. "Though that is not a great consideration for many of our members these days. We must look a little deeper than their pocket-books to divine their hearts. That's why your message beyond the grave from Julian Newman caught my attention! That was quite the calling card. We normally prefer living introducers, but a man so at ease in the company of the fallen…" He drained the tumbler of whisky. "It makes me think you might be the kind of man we can use."

"I trust to be with him soon," said Ben. "He only has a head start on me. And I believe that you can help me on my way."

Bezique studied his face.

"Whatever do you mean, Mr Makepeace?"

"I think we understand each other perfectly, Bezique," said Ben. "Julian told me everything."

"You were in his confidence, then," mused Bezique. "So he failed us again. And yet- you are very different kinds of men, you two. That much is already clear."

"There is but one brotherhood," said Ben.

"Indeed! You are a cool hand, my friend..." said Bezique, looking at him. "That is a good thing in the Game."

"What exactly is the Game?" said Ben.

"What do you think?" said Bezique. "You who have spoken with Julian."

"I think it does what it says on the tin," said Ben.

"It is both as simple as that- and deeper than you can yet comprehend," said Bezique. "The Club does not give up its secrets all at once. Even to those who seem- born to it. You're a soldier?"

"A Royal Marine."

"What's the difference?"

"In IX we were trained to operate beyond the front line- behind enemy lines."

"So much the better," said Bezique. "The lines are not always easy to make out here.

But I must warn you that it is not unknown for novices to experience a certain- remorse- when they first look into the void. Can you be sure that your resolve will not falter, when your own card is dealt?"

"For my part, I never took back my hand from anything, nor so much as hedged a bet," said Makepeace. "You must know why I am here, and that I will not be toyed with. I have lost my money, my marriage and my reputation- all through drink." He held up his whisky tumbler. "And yet even now, it isn't done with me. So if this is another test, dispense with it and lead me to the table. I am a desperate man, and I assure you that I did not come here to be trifled with."

"I like you, Brother!" said Bezique. "That is the way our brothers of old once spoke. They were men who did not pledge their word lightly, or rise from the table until the Game was done. And so you too shall take your place there. But first come with me- there is something I should like to show you. It may hold a certain professional interest."

"Lead on then, Bezique," said Ben. "I have nothing to linger here for."

CHAPTER 34

VICTORIA ISLAND, LAGOS, NIGERIA / ST JAMES'S, LONDON, UNITED KINGDOM

"Brother One in place," said Whitehead, turning his head camera on. "We have positive identification on the West African social cell. Repeat, positive identification."

"How many 200s?" said Bezique through his earpiece.

"At least ninety inside the main building. Some late arrivals just admitted. Must be the traffic…"

"Not late enough to save them," said Sengupta. "Brother Two in place. Locked and loaded. On your call, Brother One."

"Correction, Brother Two- it is my call," said Bezique, switching on the bank of screens covering the entire wall of the St James's operations centre. "Now have visuals through your head cameras. Looks like there's rain coming, chaps."

"There's always bloody rain coming here…" said Sengupta. "We've had two weeks of it."

"Lagos?" said Ben.

Bezique nodded. He flicked off the audio transmitter switch and then pointed to one of the monitors feeding live video, satellite and thermal imaging data back to the Club.

"That's the weather in-country. Sometimes I feel like I'm there myself, when we're up on the wire," he said.

"I'd stick to St James's, if I were you," said Ben. "This is quite a set-up you have here. It seems there's a fine line between being president of a London private gentlemen's club- and a warlord..."

"Indeed," said Bezique. "And sometimes, there's no line at all."

Ben studied the monitor displays.

"Where do you even buy this kind of kit?" he said. "The Queen Anne furniture I was expecting. But this is a full-scale tactical operations centre. You could invade a small country from here."

"It may yet come to that," said Bezique. "We call it Suicide Station. A nod to our illustrious past. It takes its name from the old Metropolitan Police suicide watch on Waterloo Bridge, which many of our earliest members had reason to thank- or to curse..."

"Only you're not here to fish them out," said Ben.

"Nothing so frivolous as that," said Bezique. "We are here for a much higher purpose- to make sure they go through with it. Here we curate a brave man's last hours. Death is light- the lightest thing of all! But life, that can really be a burden. It is a fearful responsibility to make sure those precious drops of life are not wasted."

"Isn't waste what the Club is all about?" said Ben.

Bezique looked at him.

"No, my friend- it is about alchemy. About taking something base, something broken and turning it into something glorious. And it all starts here..." He adjusted a monitor. "All our field operations are directed from here. Destinies are shaped- the balance between the species maintained. And yet not many living people have ever seen it."

"I'm honoured," said Ben.

"You should be," said Bezique. "But next time, you'll be on the other side of the cameras. Think of this as basic training."

"I've already done basic training," said Ben.

"Of course," said Bezique. "That's the only reason you're not in our training seminary right now, lifting truck tires with the novices. But our operations do have a certain- refinement- of their own."

"So what happens next?" said Ben.

"Brother One is already inside the compound," said Bezique. "On the wall, behind that big fig tree in the corner. He has neutralised the external security. Now he's going to set a charge to open the gates for Brother Two. Then he'll place an oxy-acetylene torch- as a slow-burn fuse on the diesel storage tank for the back-up power gensets."

"To vaporise the diesel and then ignite it…" said Ben. "That's going to be messy. But why bother opening the gates, if he's inside already?"

"Brother Two will bring the main payload in by car. He's waiting outside at street level."

Makepeace whistled.

"Sounds like a pretty tricky assignment for two operators…"

Bezique laughed.

"What did you expect?" he said.

"Success," said Makepeace. "What else matters? This approach puts a lot of execution risk on Brother One. Why didn't you just put him in solo with some high explosives? He could light that place up easily enough with a few keys of Semtex, if he's already infiltrated the main wall. Assuming that he isn't too bothered about coming out again?"

"This is not a military black op, Makepeace," said Bezique. "It's far blacker than that. We continually update our operational methodology, to stop the intelligence analysts finding patterns. And if the CIA or MI6 get any swabs from ground zero, I want them to find diesel soot and ammonia like Boko Haram might leave behind- not trace RDX, like the SAS or Spetsnaz. I don't care who you are, military-grade plastique in a Western sphere of influence means questions from the wrong people. That's one lesson we learned from Panama..."

"Panama?" said Ben.

"Never mind," said Bezique. "We're going to live audio again."

"Charge is in place," said Whitehead over the monitor. "Igniting the oxy-acetylene burner now. If they have thermal sensors on the bogey side, this is going to light up like a fucking Christmas tree..."

A red light flashed on in the control centre, and the infra-red monitors around them snow-stormed as the torch's heat signature intensified.

"Switching to visual," said Bezique. "And you're a go, Brother One. Engage."

Whitehead slid down to ground level and approached the sprawling two-story building at the centre of the compound on foot. There was a guard walking around the corner of the building, cradling his AK-47 on its shoulder-strap. Whitehead stepped behind the screen of masquerade trees in the garden. As the guard walked past, Ben saw the thin wire of the garotte flick out and creep around his neck. Whitehead dragged the body back behind the masquerades and hid it from sight.

"Last external guard is a 200..." he whispered.

"200?" said Ben, flicking the audio off.

"*Gruz dvésti*," said Bezique. "Cargo 200. The Russian air force slang for a body bag- and the dead bodies they had to ship back from Kandahar air base. The Club borrowed it as a code-word for our own targets. We had a lot of Russian brothers after their campaign in Afghanistan."

"And now?" said Ben.

"Now we have a lot of British brothers- after your campaign in Afghanistan," said Bezique. "The PTSD generation. The Hindu Kush has always been a fertile recruiting ground for the Club. Now watch- on Brother One's head camera …"

Whitehead advanced towards the window of the main building and then peered in to the meeting-hall inside. It was full of people, laughing and chattering, vibrant with the colour and flamboyance of traditional dress from all over West Africa. Men, women and children, Ben saw. He was starting to feel uneasy.

"That projector screen… The screen at the front there," said Bezique, squinting at the monitor. "Close in on that. What does it say? Go in closer, Brother One… Closer. I need to see that."

Whitehead took another step forward, then stumbled and put his hand out to stop himself from falling. As his hand touched the window-frame, an intruder alarm shattered the quiet.

"Shit! Alarm is live! Pressure sensor…" said Whitehead. He dropped down below the level of the window. Ben could hear voices over the audio feed, shouting in English, Hausa, Yoruba and Ibo, the volume surging as the people inside crowded towards the glass. "We've got to initiate!" said Whitehead.

"No!" said Bezique. "Keep looking. I must see that screen first."

Now small-arms rounds could be heard, cracking and hissing through the microphone. Whitehead cried out and rocked back.

"I'm hit…" he said.

"Brother One is hit," said Sengupta. "Brother One is hit."

"The screen!" said Bezique. "I need to see it."

Whitehead struggled up to his feet, clutching onto the window-frame, directing the head camera into the hall inside.

"What can you see?" said Bezique. "Tell me what you see!"

"Hell!" gasped Whitehead. "It's hell on earth in there… They're on fire! People are burning alive!"

"Jesus Christ!" said Makepeace, staring in horror at the monitor. "He's right. They're in flames! But the explosives haven't even detonated yet." He turned to Bezique. "Did you know about this? Is that what this is all about? Your big secret?"

"Never mind that now," said Bezique. "Look at that screen, Brother One. Read it for me. You are the Club's eyes now. Read it!"

Whitehead was slumped forward against the window, hit by multiple pistol rounds, and there was a great smear of blood down the glass. Even so, Ben could just about make out the projector screen against the back wall of the room inside. Three huge words dominated the others:

"Project Light International."

"What does that mean?" said Ben. "Project Light?"

"Project Light! *Proyecto Luz...*" said Bezique. "It means they're coming together everywhere. Finding each other. And much, much faster than we thought. Burn it down, Brother One!"

With a painful effort, Whitehead lifted the detonator up into view of the head camera.

Now there was a rattle of semi-automatic weapons.

"AK-47s..." said Makepeace. "That's going to put him down."

A heavy rifle round slammed Whitehead against the wall.

"Brother One! Come in!" said Bezique. "Do you copy, Brother One? Do it! Complete your mission!"

The camera jolted and flickered as another round ripped through Whitehead and into the wall.

"He's gone," said Ben. "No one can take that kind of punishment."

"Do it, Brother One!" said Bezique.

"No... No gods, no masters!" spluttered Whitehead, blood flecking the camera, and then hit the tilt switch.

"Now, Brother Two!" said Bezique, switching over to Sengupta's camera monitor. "Now, now, now, now, now!"

The gates of the compound exploded off their hinges as Whitehead's charge ignited, one flipping up over the windscreen of Sengupta's Land Rover and the other blown back into the concrete driveway running up to the building.

"No gods, no masters!" shouted Sengupta, stamping down hard on the accelerator, ramming the Land Rover straight up the ramp and crashing into the entrance hall of the house. "Together we greet the Reaper!"

Then the welding torch ignited the diesel vapour in the storage tanks and power generators, ripping one side of the building off like a chicken leg. The night was suddenly full of horror- screaming, burning, flame and death, until the fuel oil and ammonium nitrate fertilisers packed into the Land Rover went up in a vast, mushrooming fireball and obliterated everything.

"Bang!" said Bezique. "Despair is power."

Makepeace watched the carnage unfolding on the monitors. The buildings had been blasted into rubble. A raging, diesel-fuelled fire was gutting the ruins of the compound, black clouds swirling around the charred walls. No one could have survived that explosion. That meant that nearly a hundred people had already died in the day he had been a member of the Club. He was in way over his head here. It was starting to feel like Central America all over again.

"Fucking hell…" he said.

"Something like that!" said Bezique. "But very much on this earth."

"I've got some questions for you," said Ben.

"Oh, I ask the questions here," said Bezique.

"Yeah, but in this case I'm starting to see why you would need someone like me," said Makepeace. "And I really need to understand what the fuck I'm doing here."

"Tomorrow we play the Game," said Bezique. "Be here. Your questions will be answered then."

CHAPTER 35

EDINBURGH, UNITED KINGDOM

"That guy back there- on North Bridge. Is he dead?" said Andrew.

"He's just resting…" said Laura, looking out of the taxi window as the traffic stuttered out of the City Centre. "He's going to have one hell of a headache when he wakes up. And some very difficult questions to answer, if the police find him first. But he's still an extremely dangerous man. Largely because he's willing to die to achieve his mission. In fact, he actually wants to die. And I think he's going to get his wish pretty soon now."

"What?" said Andrew. "Why?"

"He was sent to kill you- and make it look like suicide," said Laura. "I guess he would have jumped after you, if he'd got you over the edge. Either way, they won't stop now until you're dead."

"But why? Who are they?" said Andrew.

"They call themselves the Billionaire Suicide Club," said Laura. "I trailed Hennessy from their HQ in London. As soon as he left Central London, I knew he was going to find the next target. Black cab out to Heathrow, one way ticket to Edinburgh. Tram to Waverley and then stake-outs of the University, the Bridges- and your flat in Leith. It was easy enough to trail him."

"So you've been following me too?" said Andrew.

"Yeah," said Laura. "It sounds a bit creepy when you put it like that, but obviously I was trying to keep you alive. It actually took me a while to figure out who they were trailing. And I still don't know who you are, or why they were after you."

"Me?"

"Now we know it was you they wanted, right?" said Laura. "But as to why, I think you better tell me who you are. What you're doing. What it is that you know, and they don't want the world to find out. There must be something special about you. They kill for a reason."

"But this is insane!' said Andrew. "I mean, I'm just a cardiovascular researcher. At Edinburgh University School of Medicine. Though I guess you know that bit already…"

"What species do you research?" said Laura.

"Humans!" said Andrew, laughing in spite of himself. "What do you think? I'm not a vet."

"So you've never had cause to look at any other animals- say pistol shrimps?"

"Well, no," said Andrew. "Pistol shrimps? They're the ones that stun their prey with shock-waves from their claws, rights? Like mini-explosions, underwater."

"So I hear," said Laura.

"Prawns, shrimps and other crustaceans have an open circulatory system- completely different from humans," said Andrew. "There's no real analogue there to what we do."

"Alright," said Laura. "So what else have you been up to recently- that might make you stand out?"

"I'm not sure," said Andrew. "Nothing! I'm just not that special. I mean, I'm off to Peru with work next week. That's a big adventure for me- you know, the biggest of my life- but I don't see what difference it would make to anyone else. I've never been there before. Or anywhere really. I've only been to London twice."

"Who's funding the trip?" said Laura.

"The School of Medicine," said Andrew. "And there's a grant from the Institute for Energy Systems too, which I suppose is a bit unusual. Professor Carmichael there is- was- very interested in the project. It must be the kinetic energy angle, I guess."

"So why Peru then?" said Laura.

"Because of what they've discovered there!" said Andrew, his pale blue eyes lighting up. "A Peruvian heart surgeon operated on a woman there after she was seriously injured in a traffic accident- up in Huaraz, in the Central Andes. She found something truly extraordinary. The patient had a super-developed mitral valve in her heart. Then Dr Veragua tested the patient's daughter, and found the same abnormality in her heart."

"So what does that mean?" said Laura, as the cab moved down the Glasgow Road and past Edinburgh Zoo, headed out to the airport.

"What it means is that there are people living out there- people being born- with far more powerful hearts than the rest of the human population," said Andrew. "And with clear genetic links to connect them. This could change everything! Over six hundred thousand people die of heart disease in the United States alone every year- that's one in every four deaths. Heart disease is the leading cause of death for both men and women. This could mean that the species is evolving to combat heart disease! If we can find out how, it could revolutionise heart surgery- preventive medicine- even prosthetic hearts. It could save millions of lives all over the world."

"But that's good, right? Why would anyone want to kill you to cover that up?" said Laura. "Religious fanatics? Creationists? Pharma companies?"

"There's something else too," said Andrew. "The material of these heart valves is different from anything we've ever seen before. It's tougher- more pressure-resistant. It has to be, to support the contraction speed. The strength of the contractor valves."

"What is it made of?" said Laura.

"It seems to be a hardened form of keratin," said Andrew. "That's a fibrous structural protein. It's the key material making up human hair- and animal claws and hooves."

"Like pistol shrimp claws?" said Laura.

"Pistol shrimps again?"

"Just answer the question!"

"I don't know. I suppose so…" said Andrew. "Keratin monomers bundle together to form intermediate filaments- a bit like chitin, which is what bi-mineralised arthropod exoskeletons are made from. The chitin bonds with calcium carbonate to strengthen the structure of crustacean claws. But that's more a question of marine biology. There is data to suggest that subjects showing the heart valve abnormality can experience an audible clicking sound from the mitral valve when agitated, though. Which is a bit like the noise the pistol shrimps' claws make underwater, I guess… But why do you ask? That's a pretty specific question."

"One of the people the Club targeted was developing a form of nuclear fusion- derived from that natural sonoluminescence," said Laura. "And I just had a message from Ben, my friend inside the Club. He says that the president has a tank of pistol shrimps inside his office. The questions are all starting to join up."

"What about the answers?" said Andrew.

"Let's start with the questions," said Laura. "What happened to Professor Carmichael? Why did you say he 'was' interested in your project?"

CHAPTER 36

ST JAMES'S, LONDON, UNITED KINGDOM

"You are already closer to our inner sanctum than I intended," said Bezique, leading Makepeace up an elegant Regency flight of stairs to the *salle de jeux*. "Than many of our members ever will be. That's a gamble with a new man. But then we're all gamblers here- we have to be! Our work is reaching its critical juncture. And you may yet have a role in the biggest mission of all."

"Bigger than splashing a hundred people in Lagos yesterday?" said Ben. "What do you have in mind- regime change? Genocide?"

"Genocide has become a dirty word," said Bezique. "And yet it is but the battle between two races. It does not apply to a battle between species. Different rules apply to that, for each species develops a value system to fit its own capacities."

"What about the duty of the strong to protect the weak?" said Ben.

Bezique laughed.

"That's just what I mean. There is no common ground between the species. For only the weak value mercy- and only the strong ruthlessness. How could it be otherwise?"

"Are you saying that all those people in Nigeria weren't the same species as us?" said Ben. "Because I didn't just pay a million dollars to join the London chapter of the fucking KKK."

"You misunderstand me, my friend," said Bezique. "It is not their colour that separates us- but something much deeper than that." He pointed up to a portrait on the wall, hung high above the two great double-doors at the top of the stairs. "Learn at the feet of a master…"

"Charles Dickens?" said Ben. "I'm not a big reader."

"That is not his lesson to us," said Bezique. "Or his legacy. Only in a few places does his mission appear through his work. You must know where to look."

"What do you mean?" said Ben. "Philanthropy?"

"Of a particular kind…" said Bezique. "He was a great patron of the Club in his time-

a custodian of its secrets, and an inspiration for its mission. As a boy, I was fascinated by his *Bleak House*- obsessed."

"You must have been a better student than me," said Ben. "That's how I ended up in the bloody Marines in the first place."

"That scene changed my life," said Bezique. "Even at first reading, I knew that it was true. That it had to be confronted, in all its horror." He took Makepeace's arm in his own. "Take a walk with me through London, on that fateful night. The greatest city in the world- that the world has ever seen. And yet monsters already walk arm-in-arm with the shadows… They creep along its gas-lit streets. They rub shoulders with the greed, the anger- the violence. And this night, there is a black soot falling like snowflakes, a demonic Jack Frost stalking a stifling City night. A smell, an oily film of tainted meat that lingers in the air. Fearful smuts of grease that besmirch a man's skin, and won't be washed away. Yellow fat that drips down the wall like candle tallow… There is a reek, a breath, a taste, an overwhelming atmosphere of decay. When you carry it in your own heart, you can't escape it anywhere. And so those wretched conspirators, Mr Weevle and Mr Guppy, try to bar the feeble doors of their own souls to the truth. To lock out what has happened to the hideous

'Lord Chancellor' Krook, in his dingy shop on Cursitor Street. To out-run reality, as it pursues them down that dreary close. But they can't escape the horror either, and their fears crowd in on themselves, crushing them against the bars of their own imaginations. Their fears, their revulsion- their disgust. They see the shin bone, the feet, the hands- the cat, lapping at the congealing puddle of its master's body fat. The waxy residue of a human flame that has burned itself out on its wick. For that is the truth- the only explanation- the one thing that is left, once the excuses, the hopes, the illusions, have all melted away! Krook has burned alive, he has burned from within, Makepeace, he has spontaneously combusted. They tell themselves he was consumed by his own, by Chancery's, putrid moral corruption. But he wasn't, and they know it- and now you know it!"

"Then what was it?" said Ben. "What killed him?"

"Krook was one of them!" said Bezique. "He was a different type of creature altogether. A Firestarter. That is the truth we guard here. That we have always guarded. Now you share our burden, Makepeace. We must destroy them all, strong or weak- man, woman or child- before they destroy us."

CHAPTER 37

WORCESTER COLLEGE, OXFORD, UNITED KINGDOM

"Where are Doctor Schofield's rooms?" shouted Laura, as she and Andrew sprinted through the Porter's Lodge. "We have to speak to him. He could be in danger!"

"Main Quad, Staircase 10," said the porter. "But, Miss! Sir! You can't leave your car out there like that! It's blocking the whole road!"

"Come on!" said Laura, grabbing Andrew's hand and running out past the library into the Main Quad. They tailgated a student on her way into Staircase 10 and then scrambled up the narrow stairs, scanning the names painted on the doors as they ran.

"Here it is," said Andrew. "Doctor Harry Schofield." He rapped hard on the wooden door. "Doctor Schofield!" he shouted, banging on the door again. "Harry! Doctor Schofield, please let us in! Your life is in danger! From the same people who tried to run you over. Open the door!"

"Stand back!" said Laura. She lifted her leg back and then kicked the door in. The flimsy wood splintered under the impact.

"Oh God..." said Andrew.

Inside the study were two bodies, collapsed on the floor.

"Are they alive?" said Laura.

Andrew felt each pulse in turn, then switched off the gas fire, stepped over to the window and flung it wide open.

"What are you doing?" said Laura. "Don't alter the crime scene!"

"They're both dead," said Andrew. "And I don't really want to join them. Did you see the way that gas fire was burning? And the door- it was locked from the inside. There's no sign of any weapon- or a struggle. I think this is carbon monoxide poisoning. Or at least it's supposed to look like it..."

"Jesus..." said Laura. "The Club."

"But do you know who they are?" said Andrew.

"That's Doctor Schofield," said Laura, pointing to Harry's body, a sheaf of papers scattered around him. She took a burst of photos of the scene with her iPhone. "And I've seen the other one before too. He came out of the Bohemian Sports Club with Hennessy. They must have been assigned their missions at the same time."

"Hennessy- the guy who tried to kill me?" said Andrew.

Laura nodded.

"Schofield is on the same track as Professor Carmichael was... As you are! It's these new people- their hearts. The power they might have, if they could channel it! The energy they could generate. It all fits together. Because whatever the police and the college authorities are prepared to conclude- this was not an accident."

Andrew leafed through Harry's papers, the last testament to his genius.

"Let me read through these..." he said. "Maybe I can find something."

"Look at this!" said Laura, picking three silver laughing-gas canisters out of Harry's waste-paper basket. "There are more down there... Could that be how they got the carbon monoxide in here?"

"Could be," said Andrew. "Then let the faulty fire take the blame. Or maybe it was just to make sure. And take a look at this..." He held up one of Harry's slides. "Your pistol shrimps, madam?"

"Let's take them to go," said Laura. "We need to get back to London. You believe me now, right, Andrew? As crazy as it all seems?"

"Yeah, I believe you," he said. "I guess being dangled off the North Bridge by your ankles can focus the mind that way."

"Thank God!" said Laura. "You're the only one who doesn't think I'm losing my mind- except for Ben and his alcoholic boss."

"Where is Ben now?' said Andrew.

"He's at the Club," said Laura. "Playing for his life."

CHAPTER 38

ST JAMES'S, LONDON, UNITED KINGDOM

The members processed into the *salle de jeux*, each stooping to touch Richard Harding's shin-bone for luck as they passed the champagne stand by Bezique's chair.

"Club port and madeira are served," said Florizel, carrying a crystal decanter in each hand. "The port to travel left around the table, and the madeira right, if you please. The President would be obliged if members did not rest the decanters on the card table until they are empty."

"To the Game!" said Bezique, raising his port glass. "Now take your seats please, gentlemen. We have pressing business on our hands this evening. I have a private jet on the tarmac at Biggin Hill airport, waiting for the man who draws the Death Card."

There was a murmur of excitement around the green baize table as Bezique unwrapped, shuffled and cut a new pack of playing cards with practiced ease.

"The first card, we burn, in tribute to the Most Corrupt Rogue in Christendom!" said Bezique, flipping up the top card in the deck.

"The king of hearts- the Suicide King!" he said.

"Why is it called that?" said Ben.

Bezique held up the card. The King of Hearts gazed out impassively, almost disinterestedly, caught in the act of thrusting his sword deep into his own head.

"I've never noticed that before," said Ben.

Bezique smiled.

"He is something of a mascot here. A fitting Master of Ceremonies for the Game tonight. Burn…" he said, discarding the Suicide King.

Not many of the members smiled back. They were in too deep now. And so was Ben, he realised with a jolt. He took a gulp of port and watched the cards fly across the table with the rest of them. Now one card lay face-down in front of each of the members.

"Gentlemen, the Club calls you!" said Bezique. "Mr Pettigrew, if you would do the honours for us?"

Simon Pettigrew turned over his card, face grey but rapidly colouring to match the card in front of him.

"Three of hearts…" said Bezique. "Turn."

"Mr Stamp- four of diamonds. Turn."

"Mr de Mestre- queen of spades, Calamity Jane. Turn."

"Mr Whitby- seven of clubs. Turn."

"Mr Raymond- ten of diamonds, Big Cassino. Turn."

"Mr Graham- king of diamonds, the Man with the Axe. Turn."

Graham mimed a chopping motion with his hand in his relief. Bezique smiled. Clearly a certain licence was allowed in the heat of the moment. But now the play was getting closer and closer to Ben's own chair. He could feel the unholy, feverish excitement of the Game. This was a sport to madden- to drive a man to his death, still begging for the chance to risk it all one more time.

"You deal an elegant hand, Bezique," said Ben. "Almost too good for an amateur. You move the cards like a Monte Carlo *croupier*."

"You have a good eye, my friend," said Bezique, giving Ben a dangerous look. "An eye for weakness! In this game, I am always *banco*... But that was not the case when I worked the casinos. I was caught stealing from them. I was beaten up, thrown out, disgraced." Ben stared at him. "You're surprised? That I would reveal my shame?" Bezique laughed. "I revel in it! I cling to it. It is my strength. For I have been to the brink, and come back. I sat on the edge of the Yacht Club de Monaco Marina with a bottle of cognac. The sands of my time were running out with the brandy. When I finished it, I was going into the water. But then one man found me. He was a gambler too- a gambler in humanity. Somehow he saw through my misery, to my true potential. He brought me back from the brink- lifted me up to my feet. He gave me my new name, bought me a train ticket to the French Foreign Legion headquarters in Aubagne and set me free from my past. I survived the Legion, just as I had survived the Marina. And I learned that despair is power."

"Malthus?" said Ben. "Then that means that..."

"What?" said Bezique.

"I should like to meet him," said Ben.

"You will- when the time is right," said Bezique. "He plays the deepest game of all. I have walked with monsters- but he is fit to walk with the gods."

"The Suicide King?" said Ben.

"That's right," said Bezique.

"So when did you read *Bleak House*?" said Ben. "I thought that changed your life?"

"We all invent ourselves, Makepeace," said Bezique. "You need to decide what you can be. What the Game can make you. It is only three cards away from you now."

"*Vogue la galère*!" said Ben.

Bezique inclined his head.

"Mr Shah- Four of clubs, the Devil's Bedpost. Turn."

"Mr O'Shaughnessy- Nine of diamonds, the Scourge of Scotland."

O'Shaughnessy sprang to his feet and performed an impromptu Scottish reeling step.

"Bravo, Mr O'Shaughnessy- good form!" said Bezique. "Turn, Mr Makepeace."

Ben's stomach lurched. He took a swig of port to calm himself. The rich, old wine sent his head spinning. He looked at the swirling geometric pattern on the back of the card in front of him, as though if he stared hard enough he could look straight through it. It couldn't be the ace of spades already. On his very first hand. The chances against that were overwhelming, fifty-two to one. Unless…

"Mr Makepeace?" said Bezique. "A gentleman does not wait to be asked twice."

"Apologies, Mr President," said Ben. "But I think this port is slightly corked. Easily done at that age. Florizel, would you be so good?"

He held out his glass, flipping his card over as he did so.

Unless…

"The ace of spades- the Death Card," said Bezique.

Unless it was fixed.

"Hold the port, Florizel," said Ben. "Champagne for the Club! Tonight we drink like soldiers of fortune- as though tomorrow will never come! *Vive la mort!*"

"Bravo, Makepeace!" said Bezique. "The old Foreign Legion toast. *Vive la mort, et vive la guerre!* And now, your chariot awaits you."

CHAPTER 39

BAYSWATER, LONDON, UNITED KINGDOM

"I'm just saying the timing feels a wee bit suspicious, doesn't it?" said Andrew, sipping his tea. "I mean, first you save my life. Then you narrowly fail to save Schofield's. Ben leaves at the drop of a hat, and now this ex-boyfriend gets in touch in the middle of the night, saying he's had a 'come to God' moment and wants to bare his soul to you."

"That's not quite what he said," said Laura. "That really would be suspicious. And horrific- like the picture of Dorian Grey or something…"

"So you trust him then?" said Andrew.

"Oh yes- about as far as I could throw him…" said Laura. "I've known Hugo Capstick for a long time, and he makes a loose cannon look like a fun deck game. The boys all called him 'Captagon', because he took so many drugs at school."

"Like the amphetamine? Nice," said Andrew.

"I used to think him such an enigma- such a charming rogue. Someone worth saving from himself. Now I don't see the charm. But the one thing he isn't is a killer."

"Was your brother, though?" said Andrew. "A killer, I mean?"

Laura looked at him.

"I'm sorry…" said Andrew. "But would you have thought him capable of what he did in Laos? Of killing all those people? Whether or not he meant any harm to them- innocent bystanders died there. It sounds to me as though the Club is brainwashing these guys. Do you know what that man who tried to kill me- Hennessy, you called him- said? 'No gods, no masters'."

"No gods, no masters!" said Laura. "That's exactly what my brother said over the phone, just before he died. What do you think it means?"

"I don't know…" said Andrew. "I suppose the people with these new heart-valves could seem like gods- or devils. Like they were struggling for mastery of their environment. But how would they know about them? The Club? No one does. I mean, I've been spending the last two years researching nothing else, and there are no medical papers about them- nothing in the journals. No one wants to know. Professor Carmichael couldn't believe it, when he found out about our research. That's what makes it so exciting! Why I just had to get out there to Peru."

"But what if they do know, Andrew?" said Laura. "And they just don't want anyone else to find out? I found an extraordinary story in the *Hounslow Chronicle*- about an arson in Isleworth Crown Court, the same week Laurence Pearce died! The defendant claimed that his friend had spontaneously combusted in the diamond vaults they both worked in. But before he could finish giving his evidence, he was burned alive himself- in open court."

"Who did it?" said Andrew.

"A former submariner called David Mason," said Laura. "And get this- Mason had been described by the Royal Navy as one of the best officers of his generation. They trusted this guy with Trident nuclear missiles!"

"Jesus!" said Andrew. "So why was it not all over the press?"

"There was a D-Notice- citing national security," said Laura.

"The Club again…" said Andrew.

The intercom buzzer sounded.

"That'll be Hugo…" said Laura, peering at the video display. "On time for once- that's ominous. But it looks like it is just him, at least. Like he promised."

"So what are you going to do?" said Andrew.

"Let him in, of course- I have to!" said Laura. "I have to know what happened to Julian. Complete shit or not, Hugo is still one of the last people who saw Jules alive."

"Do you want me to stick around?" said Andrew.

"Would you mind?" said Laura. "I know it's a lot to ask- on top of everything else. I've put you in danger so many times already."

"It's actually going to be quite difficult to get out now without seeing him, isn't it?" said Andrew. "I'd feel a little silly hiding in your kitchen. I mean, you could say I was the cleaner, but I forgot my marigolds…"

"Thank you!" said Laura.

"It's the least I can do after you saved my life," said Andrew. "It looked an awful long way down to the station…"

The buzzer sounded again.

"He always was an impatient little prick…" said Laura, pressing the entry button.

"Charmed, I'm sure," came Capstick's voice over the intercom. "I've missed you too, darling! I'll be up in a jiffy."

"He doesn't sound too repentant to me…" said Andrew.

He waited next to Laura while she opened the door.

"Thanks for agreeing to see me, Lazza…" said Capstick, stepping in. "We really do need to talk. I didn't bring flowers, but it's the thought that counts, right?" He hesitated as he saw Andrew. "And who might this be?"

"This is a friend," said Laura.

Andrew nodded at Capstick.

"Enchanted to meet you, Friend," said Capstick. "Though I had rather hoped that we could speak alone, Laura. It's such a private matter- and then there's poor Jules to think of …"

"You can speak in front of him," said Laura. "I'd feel more comfortable if you did, actually. I don't know who you are right now, Hugo. And I certainly don't trust that club of yours."

"Fair enough," said Capstick. "But does Friend here know we used to go out together? I'd hate to cause any awkwardness. And I'm just the type to make people jealous. Always have. I think it's the hair…"

"He doesn't care about that!" said Laura.

Andrew blushed.

"Oh really?" said Capstick, laughing. "Does he know that? He actually looks rather like- you. Are you getting narcissistic in your old age?"

"Did you come here just to wind me up, Hugo?" said Laura. "Because if so, you could have saved yourself a Tube ride. Your message did that already."

"Touchy!" said Capstick. "Why don't you put the kettle on, and we'll all have a nice cup of tea?"

He followed Laura and Andrew into her kitchen.

"You haven't done much with this old place, have you?" said Capstick. "It hasn't changed since you moved in here! I dread to think what your mother would say. She'd probably have an interior design SWAT team in here, before she took her Fendi coat off."

"I've been travelling," said Laura.

"So we heard," said Capstick. "That's one of the things we wanted to talk to you about."

"We?" said Laura.

"Your famous curiosity has been getting the better of you, hasn't it, Laura?" said Capstick, tying his hair back with a band. "And you know what curiosity does, don't you?" He pulled the Glock 18 automatic out from under his jacket. "The first rule of the Club is: Curiosity kills the kitty-cat…"

CHAPTER 40

CARTAGENA DE INDIAS, COLOMBIA

Ben drank in the spiced evening air and watched the local kids playing football. They loped with languid grace across the scorched pitches that stretched from the colonial city walls down to the shore of the Caribbean. He was in no great hurry to reach his own destination either. The playing fields looked more like the Serengeti than the Santiago de Bernabeu, the grass worn away around the centre spot and penalty areas. Once Cartagena's ramparts had guarded the Spanish galleons shipping Nueva Granada gold and Potosí silver to Europe. Now they looked out over the next generation of Colombian *galácticos*, a lucky few perhaps destined to break into the big leagues in the Old World. But even these prodigies were struggling to make out the ball now, as the delicate pinks and oranges of the evening sky were blotted out by the inky black of the Caribbean night. Finally the last players started to melt away, hailing down rickety *chiva* buses on the coastal highway. Time was up- for them and for Makepeace. It was as good a place as any for a last night.

"Time to face the music," he said, setting off down Calle Belén on foot. He stopped to watch an elegant, ironwork street-lamp flicker into life above him. A wizened lizard stirred and ambled up inside the glass of the lamp. Insects fluttered around it, making feints and dashes towards the mesmeric bulb, bouncing off the glass before succumbing to the snare and flying up inside it. The lizard crouched motionless for a minute, then launched itself through the air to the opposite side of the lamp in a curious, sideways leap. For a split-second the long, lanky toes on its back feet seemed to slip, and then the balled feet splayed on the glass again and stuck to the pane. Now Ben could see the fat moth in its mouth, snatched mid-flight. The moth leapt and thrashed its wings, trying to dislodge itself from the lizard's jaws. For a second it seemed that the heavy insect might drag the lizard off its perch and tumbling down to the cobbled street below, but the reptile just tossed it from side to side in its mouth like a dog worrying a rat. It held its prize aloft, then rocked its head back to swallow it whole.

"*¡Olé!*" said Ben. But the show was already over- night insects were jostling around the lure now, and the lizard just swivelled its head to pick off the plumper moths and flies that blundered by. It basked in the light behind its protective glass walls, the jagged scales on its back harvesting the precious warmth. The Spanish *conquistadores* had had a similar idea when they founded Cartagena de Indias. Red-faced English and Dutch pirates and privateers dashed themselves on its massive sea walls, whilst the plundered interior of Spanish America filtered along endless mule-trains into its markets and counting-houses. The agents of the great Seville trading houses had taken the profits of their Creole kleptocracy and built themselves a new town, fit to shame the drab port of Cartagena back in the old country that had given it its name. It looked like Cadiz, Havana- or Old Panama, Ben thought. And now the Billionaire Suicide Club was here too, pursuing some nameless quarry through the swamps of the interior. Ben looked up and down the street, and then turned into an elegant doorway. There were three letters engraved into the stonework: 'B.S.C'.

"Welcome to *La Heroica*, Señor Makepeace," said an impeccably-dressed Colombian man in a white *lique lique* shirt, opening the gate into a stone-flagged courtyard with an ornate well in the middle. "And welcome to the Cartagena chapter of the Club. *Más que un club*. I am Geraldino, at your service."

"*Gracias*, Geraldino," said Ben. "Is that your own name, or the Club's?"

The steward smiled beneath his moustache.

"The Club gave me my name- together with everything I have. You could call me the Colombian Florizel."

"And is there a Colombian Bezique?"

"There is only one Bezique, *señor*," said Geraldino. "He sits in St. James's, like the spider in the centre of the web."

"But there are lots of flies?" said Ben. "Of Makepeaces?"

"We shall soon see, shall we not, *señor*?" said Geraldino. "Perhaps you really are a special one, as they say in St James's. Desperate times bring desperate men."

"I'm desperate for a drink," said Ben.

"Señor Bezique said you would be," said Geraldino.

He led Makepeace to a table, covered with a gleaming white cloth.

"Ties are not required here, *señor*," said Geraldino.

"Just as well," said Ben. "I didn't bring any. I didn't think a tie would matter too much where I'm going."

"Oh, ties always matter," said Geraldino. "But they are not required before dinner in the tropics."

Ben laughed.

"You really are the Colombian Florizel! Have you two ever met in person?"

"But of course," said Geraldino. "You know he's a fellow South American?"

"No!" said Ben. "Where is he from?"

"Cochabamba," said Geraldino. "*La Llajta*… In Bolivia."

"He's very fair though, isn't he?" said Ben. "You'd take him for a European."

"*Sí, muy mono*…" said Geraldino. "He trained me in St. James's. There is nothing like the Bohemian Sports Club in Colombia- in all of the world! I was taught about wine, language, service, history- literature. The Club is a legend, and legends require curation."

Makepeace sat down and Geraldino poured out a cut-glass tumbler of aguardiente with 'salad'- green mango, sliced coconut, grapes and lime.

"Heavy fuel..." said Ben, raising his glass to Geraldino. It was only then that he noticed the thick steel plates welded on to the street door, and the tungsten alloy brackets reinforcing its hinges. The picturesque painted wooden shutters of the town-house were backed by metal blast-shields.

"What is this place?" said Ben.

"It is *La Heroica*," said Geraldino. "The home of the Club in Latin America. This is not like St James's- it is the front line of the Brotherhood. The enemy is very close here. Once you have entered *La Heroica*, you're a soldier. Like all of us here."

"Thank you for your paramilitary service," said Ben.

"Are you ready, *señor*?" said Geraldino. "As ready as you can be?"

"Well, this ain't my first time at the rodeo," said Makepeace.

"So I have heard, *señor*," said Geraldino. "Also that Bezique himself granted you an exemption from your novitiate. That he invited you into Suicide Station to sit by his side. And that you only drew the *as de espadas*- the Death Card- a few days ago. And yet here you are already! That is why I say- maybe you are a special one."

"Is that a compliment?" said Ben. "Maybe Bezique just wants me dead in a hurry."

"Maybe- but if so, I don't think he would have assigned you this particular mission, *señor*," said Geraldino. "Project Torquemada is the Club's number one priority- anywhere in the world. Failure is not an option. And you are the Grand Inquisitor now."

"What more can you tell me about it?" said Ben. "Torquemada."

"You read the mission dossier I prepared?" said Geraldino.

"Yeah, it was a long plane journey," said Ben. "But now I'm here. On the ground. It feels more real. So tell me about Cargo 200. They call him 'Jairo Paisa'. Which I guess is a bit like 'John Doe' in Antioquia?"

"It is a *nomme de guerre*..." said Geraldino. "A mysterious name for a mysterious man."

"He's a medical doctor?" said Makepeace.

Geraldino smiled.

"Yes, *señor*, he's a doctor- like Mr Kurtz was an ivory trader. He is a doctor- a warrior priest- a warlord. A visionary and a believer, who has killed more men than he will ever heal. A very dangerous man."

"You find belief so frightening, brother?" said Ben.

Geraldino shook his head.

"It depends what the belief is, *señor*. Jairo Paisa believes in *La Nueva Raza* above all else- and he is ready to kill to protect it. That makes him dangerous to us all."

"We're dangerous too, Geraldino," said Ben, draining his aguardiente. "We have one foot in the next world now."

"You're a quick learner, *señor*," said Geraldino. "For one who completed no novitiate."

"I'm not sure about all this 'Despair is Power' stuff," said Makepeace. "But they're right about one thing. You can cause a lot of trouble when you don't give a shit."

CHAPTER 41

BAYSWATER, LONDON, UNITED KINGDOM

"Who do you have to sleep with to get a cuppa around here?" said Capstick. "No need to answer that, Friend... But I'd still like that tea, love, if it's not too much trouble?"

"Why don't you make it yourself then, you fucking prick?" said Laura.

"Suit yourself, Germaine Greer," said Capstick.

He put Laura's kettle on to boil, turning on all of the gas taps on the hob as he did so. The gas hissed out into the kitchen. Capstick closed the door, wedging Laura's tea-towels underneath it, training the Glock on them as he worked.

"So now you're interested in house-work?" said Laura.

"Oh, I'm very well-trained now," said Capstick.

"What is it with you guys and gas?" said Andrew.

"When you come to think of it, there are only so many ways you can accidentally die in a West London flat, aren't there?" said Capstick. "It says it all about the bourgeois condition. Believe me, the Club has been working on it for years. We thought about the old toaster in the bath, but then how do you both get into it? Awkward. And pills. Why would two people just decide to take pills together? The suicide pact is always possible when there's romance in the air, I suppose. You know, more than just friends..."

"Is that a threat?" said Laura.

"Just making conversation," said Capstick.

"I'd say some fresh ideas are long overdue," said Andrew. "I mean, the carbon monoxide poisoning in Oxford? That's like an old episode of *Casualty*."

"What is it with you and the 80s TV references?" said Laura.

"I was a medical student for a very long time..." said Andrew.

"Ah- so it's you, is it, Friend?" said Capstick. "The mysterious cardiovascular researcher. Two birds with one stone! Hennessy made a bit of a hash of your mission, I'm afraid."

"What happened to him?" said Laura.

"It seems he decided to greet the Reaper after all," said Capstick. "He jumped off the North Bridge in Edinburgh. The good folk at ScotRail were none too pleased to find a passenger on Platform Thirteen without a ticket. Even less so than usual, as he had entered straight through their new glass roof."

"Jumped?" said Laura. "That's strange- because he was unconscious when we left him."

"You really are a pair of eager beavers, aren't you?" said Capstick. "Made for each other. Jumped, fell, was thrown- what's the difference, between friends? And you've clearly seen the good Doctor Schofield too. The late Schofield. Finding out what you know was part one of my assignment."

"What's part two?" said Laura.

"I'm sure you can put two and two together, can't you, Laura?" said Capstick, looking at her along the barrel of the gun. "A clever girl like you. I'm just a killer for your love..."

"Why don't you just get on with it then, if that's what you came here to do?" said Laura. "I'd prefer that to listening to you crow."

"Feisty, eh?" said Capstick. "I like that... You would have been a great asset to the Club- much better than poor old Jules!" He turned round a kitchen chair and sat down, leaning over the back of the chair. "The silly sod came as near as dammit to screwing it all up, of course. Only I'm afraid the first rule of the Club is: No girls allowed…"

"Why not?" said Andrew.

"Because no woman would be so bloody stupid as to join!" said Laura. "It's the ultimate boys' club! But how on earth did you get involved in all this, Hugo? You're not as thick as you pretend. You certainly never seemed like the kind of person who could be influenced so easily- brainwashed…"

"Unlike your brother, you mean?" said Capstick. "You really don't know then, do you? What the Club is really for. The work we do. Otherwise it wouldn't seem so hard for you to understand. The purpose it gives you… And let's face it, I never had any purpose to speak of before, did I? Too damn rich. So why bother working? There were always too many other options- clubs, drugs, clothes, cars. Women. So many that I could never settle down with any of them. Or with myself."

"Poor little rich boy…" said Laura.

"I thought you of all people might understand!" said Capstick. "Your own life hasn't exactly been- normal."

"Oh, I do understand!" said Laura. "I'm stupidly rich too, remember? And as spoilt as you, let's be honest. I've just been lucky enough to do work that most other people couldn't afford to take on, even if they wanted to, when they need to earn their living."

"Work!" said Capstick. "Your crusading investigative journalism. Suitably noble fare for a martyr! Well, the news-flash is that I've found a purpose too, Laura. Found myself, in something bigger. And not just pious words, either- in action! Saving our whole species from an invasive one. A parasite that has been infiltrating us for years. Choking us, preparing to take over from us."

"What do you mean?" said Andrew.

"Oh, you know all this, Friend- it's why you had to die!" said Capstick. "A new type of human, with hyper-developed hearts. Firestarters. They can do incredible things! Live for generations. Generate power. Even burn everything around them! Speaking of burning…" He sniffed. The smell of gas was filling the room now. "They're gathering their forces. But we can stop them, if we strike now. We're the only ones who can. We have the funds, the manpower- the will- to root them out, before they get too strong. That's our mission. Our destiny!"

"What makes you think they want to harm anyone?" said Andrew. "They're just people with different heart valves, for Christ's sake! It's evolution at work. Humanity rebooting itself, to fix a glitch. We're learning incredible things from them! And who knows what glitches they may have, as the genes evolve? They might be the ones who need help from us."

Capstick winked at him.

"You know your stuff," he said. "So that's why you're Laura's new friend… She always did know how to get what she wanted from a man!" He coughed, the gas catching his throat, and Andrew lunged for him, knocking him off his chair and down onto the floor.

"Andrew! No!" shouted Laura.

The two men wrestled on the ground for a moment, struggling for the gun, tumbling over and over. Capstick coughed again, the gas crowding out the oxygen in the room. And then the shot rang out. Andrew rolled over, blood racing across his chest faster than Laura would have believed possible.

"No!" she screamed.

She smashed a chair over Capstick's head, looking around for another weapon as he struggled back to his feet. She picked up a can of furniture polish and blasted the aerosol in his face, filling his eyes and nose with the pungent chemicals.

"Fuck! You've blinded me, you bitch!" shouted Capstick, clawing at his face and tripping over the fragments of chair.

Laura took one look back at Andrew's lifeless body and then ran, out through the flat, down the stairs and out onto Westbourne Terrace.

"Shit!" said Capstick, sprawling on the floor, eyes burning. "We have a runner, Suicide Station. Repeat, Cargo 200 has left the scene on foot…"

"Torch the place!" said Bezique. "Where is she going? Where would she look for a hiding-place?"

"She won't be fucking hiding!" said Capstick. "I know her too well for that. She'll be looking for payback."

CHAPTER 42

LA HEROICA, CARTAGENA DE INDIAS, COLOMBIA

Early morning in Cartagena, the cool breeze ruffling the drooping fronds of palm-trees, caressing the lightest of ripples from the flattest of seas.

"Paradise found..." said Ben, sitting down in a wicker chair on the roof-terrace on top of the Club. He looked out over the undulating terracotta tiles of the city, as they hoarded the orange glow of the rising sun. Dirty grey pelicans were waking up, trawling the water near the shore. With their long necks and bills and stunted little bodies, they looked ungainly on land, time-forgotten pterodactyls hunched together in shambling colonies. Once airborne though, they sliced open the sky, plummeting down onto the water like dive-bombers. They shared their fishing-grounds with lobster-boats and swimming children, at ease with the less natural fishermen milling all around them.

Geraldino stepped out onto the terrace with a covered tray.

"*Desayuno, señor.*"

He poured coffee out of a silver Asprey pot engraved with the Club's initials, and then lifted monogrammed white napkins off a plate of fresh fruit and a basket of steaming *empanada* pastries.

"Say what you like about the Club," said Ben. "The catering is first-rate. Though they did try to palm me off with some corked port in St James's..."

"Detail is important, *señor*," said Geraldino. "That's one thing that Florizel taught me. If you can't take the trouble to crumb down a table, how will you clean a murder scene?"

"Words to live by..." said Ben.

Geraldino laughed. He followed Ben's glance out over the waking city.

"You like this place, don't you, *señor*? I can tell."

"Yeah, I could live here," said Makepeace.

"Only living isn't why you're here, is it?" said Geraldino.

Ben laughed.

"Die here, then. Taste life for the last time."

Geraldino stared out to sea in silence.

"Is there something else you want to say to me, Geraldino?" said Ben. "I won't tell anyone."

This time it was the steward who laughed.

"No, *señor...*" he said. "But even after everything you have lived through, you may see things out there that shock you- things that seem impossible," he said. "That is when you must find the strength within yourself, to do what seems impossible for you. To keep your reason when it seems easier to go insane. To complete your mission."

He poured Makepeace another cup of coffee.

"Cream, *señor*?"

"*Solito*," said Ben. "Don't you ever resent the control they've taken over your life, Geraldino? What you've given up for the Club. Your name. Your freedom. Your humanity?"

"You don't know what I was before, *señor*," said Geraldino. "The wreck of a man I was, before the Club picked me up and made me whole again. Behind every brother is a story of moral collapse- and redemption. That is what makes the Club what it is. Despair truly is power, you see. Whatever you believe, believe that!"

Ben nodded.

"And now you should enjoy your last few minutes of peace up here, *Señor* Makepeace," said Geraldino. "I have received the word from Suicide Station. Project Torquemada is a go."

"A go to where?" said Ben.

Geraldino smiled.

"To a jungle settlement called Riosucio. The interior, *señor*. Into the heart of darkness. It is always calling us. Your Kurtz is waiting for you there. Jairo Paisa…"

"But what if this Kurtz is the god?" said Ben.

"Then we're all doomed, *señor*," said Geraldino. "You must judge that for yourself, when you meet him. And then you must kill him."

CHAPTER 43

THE CORNICHE, ABU DHABI, UNITED ARAB EMIRATES

"So why come here?" said Laura, squinting into the sunshine.

"Somewhere they can't reach me," said Ian Simms. "Isn't that why you came?"

"I came for information," she said. "A long way, Ian. Then I'm going wherever it leads me. I'm past caring about where the Club can reach me."

"You sound just like they do!" said Simms.

"I'll take that as a compliment in this case," said Laura. "But are you really safe anywhere now?"

"The brothers may be expendable- but the Club still doesn't pick fights with the big dogs," said Simms. "Super-rich sovereign governments. Not if it can help it, anyway."

"So you're protected from the outside," said Laura. "But who protects you from the inside?"

"I have some collateral that makes me valuable to certain people here..." said Simms. "Let's just say that my Cargo 200 had royal connections. I realised as soon as I saw the mission dossier that it was a way out. To get out- and stay out. Staying alive is an expensive business."

"Even here?"

"Especially here. Look around you..."

He traced a pale finger along the line of luxury hotel names dominating the sky-line behind them, smart glass winking in the Arabian sun.

"OK, so there's a Four Seasons," said Laura. "But how can I trust you, Ian? Hugo Capstick contacted me too. Then he tried to kill me. He succeeded in killing my friend. It's given me some real trust issues with members of the Bohemian Sports Club."

"I'm a former member," said Simms.

"And how many former members are there?" said Laura.

He laughed.

"Just me. Look, I get it," he said. "I'd be worried if you weren't suspicious. But I'm sticking my neck out here too. My enemy's enemy is my friend, right? That's why I reached out to you. Besides, your brother was in the Club too, wasn't he?"

"Yeah, I remember that," said Laura. "Everyone keeps reminding me. I'm treating him as a special case, so far as my personal safety is concerned."

"Fair enough," said Simms, lighting a Davidoff cigarette, his hand trembling. "But Capstick was still an active member when he tried to whack you. He hadn't cut his ties. That makes all the difference in the world. From the point of view of your personal safety, I mean."

"Where is Hugo now?" said Laura.

"He's gone," said Simms, watching her face. "I'm sorry. His ace was up. They say it's a long-haul '200'. Mission, I mean. He won't see Chelsea again-not in this life, anyway."

"RIP," said Laura.

"At least he gets to die with his boots on," said Simms. "Hennessy got dumped off a bridge."

"So I heard," said Laura. "But aren't you rather well-informed for a former member?"

"Like I said, I have some protection from the Club here," said Simms.

"That doesn't mean I can afford to forget about it. Let's just say I sleep with my eyes open. And the novices do talk- particularly if they need a bit of help paying their joining fees. Not everyone is as rich as Julian- or you."

"And what do they say?" said Laura.

"Walk with me," said Simms, taking her arm as they strolled along the water-front. "This is the tolerable time of year. You know, with the breeze. In the summer- it's like a fucking oven. It reminds me of the Club, actually. The *salle de jeux*. Stifling- intense. Unbearable."

"Why did you join in the first place?" said Laura. "That's what no one can ever tell me. It makes no sense!"

Simms stopped walking.

"Because- because it's a club…" he said at last.

"More than a club," said Laura.

"More than a club," repeated Simms, his pasty face flushing. "Because everything we live, everything we struggle through- everything I failed at for the first twenty-five years of my life- it's all about belonging. When it comes down to it, it's just belonging. Finding some form of fellow feeling. Some way to make sense of the whole confusing mess of existence. Finding people who you can share something with, just for a few moments!" He crushed his cigarette out and lit another one. "People who you can huddle together with, to shelter from the solitude. The void. Even if it means that you have to set yourself outside the pale of normal life. I mean, especially if you do! If you have to become men apart- brothers in death. You can use that wall to keep the darkness out. And when you reach out and touch it- you know that you're finally something more than yourself. You've chosen your own path, however twisted it is. However insane! When you finally meet the Reaper, you will greet him together. Isn't that something? Well, for the first time in my life, I felt that bond! I had escaped the loneliness. Death made sense of everything."

"And you were willing to kill for that feeling?" said Laura. "To die alone- at the age of thirty?"

"You never think it will be your turn…" said Simms. "There are fifty-two cards in a standard deck. Besides, death was our sacrament. Our touchstone. Despair is power. I still find myself saying those words every day! A hundred times a day. Because it's true. When you've lost everything, you are free again. My life could finally mean something."

"You still believe that?" said Laura.

He nodded.

"Help me, Laura," he said. "I'm so lost. I'm just so lost now..."

She took his hand.

"If you really believe that, you need to help me," she said. "Before more people die. You can still make a difference, Ian."

"What do you want to know?" he said.

"I'll be in touch," she said.

"Will you stay for lunch?"

"Lunch is for wimps, Simms," said Laura.

He laughed.

"Take this to go, then," he said, holding out a manila envelope. "Pay dirt."

"What is that?" said Laura.

"Consider it a goodwill gesture," he said. "You should know what your friend is facing out there in Colombia. The members are all talking about it. This isn't just another public schoolboy caper, Laura- like Horrocks playing toy soldiers in Entebbe. The Club has upped the ante. This guy has killed more people than cholera. He's like the fucking angel of death. Makepeace needs to get out of there while he can."

"What if he's found him already?" said Laura.

Simms put his sun-glasses on.

"Then you need to put a firewall between Makepeace and yourself as fast as you can," he said. "Because he's gone, and they'll come for you next."

"Let them come!" said Laura. "I'm tired of watching them hurt the people I care for. We'll see who blinks first."

CHAPTER 44

RAFAEL NÚÑEZ INTERNATIONAL AIRPORT, CARTAGENA DE INDIAS, COLOMBIA

"You know what the funny thing is, Señor Makepeace?" shouted Geraldino over the high-pitched engine whine, cradling his AR-15 in the crook of his arm. Ben shook his head, grimacing as they battled through the blast of whipped up grit and dust in the rotor wash. "We're about to fly there in a chopper- when it's the FARC's shoulder-held surface-to-air-missiles that cut this area off in the first place! They call Riosucio 'The House that SAMs Built'. Now we really are in the front-line!"

"Thanks for sharing!" Ben yelled back, as they ducked their heads and clambered into the back seats of the Bell helicopter. "Did I tell you I'm a nervous flyer?"

Makepeace could feel the deafening sound of the blade slap vibrating through his entire body as the chopper lifted up off the ground with a sickening lurch, nose tipping forward, and then accelerated forward. For once it wasn't the familiar sensation of parting company with his stomach that made him want to throw up. He re-read the encrypted file that had just hit his email inbox. Laura had scrawled one line on the front of Simms' dossier before she scanned it to him:

"De la Peña didn't say *pistacho*. He said *Pishtaco*. *El Pishtaco*. Don't go anywhere near Riosucio, Ben. He's waiting for you."

"Have you ever heard of *El Pishtaco*?" shouted Ben.

Geraldino stared back at him.

"Who told you that name, Señor Makepeace?"

"I'll take that as a 'yes' then."

Geraldino nodded.

"Have I heard of the Devil!" he said. "Yes, I've heard it. It is not a lucky one in Colombia. But he does not come here anymore. During *La Guerra Sucia*- the Dirty War- the Peruvian came here many times. He crept through these jungles like a sickness, killing men from all sides. The *indígenas* say that he is damned by God. That he steals the souls of the living…" He crossed himself. "But since peace has come, he has left this country alone."

"Peace has gone then, Geraldino," said Makepeace. "Because he's back."

CHAPTER 45

DUBAI, UNITED ARAB EMIRATES

"And where are you, my dear?" said Braithwaite through Laura's Bluetooth. "Somewhere nice and warm, I trust?"

"The Abu Dhabi-Dubai highway," said Laura, overtaking a matt-black Lamborghini. "Sucking diesel." She accelerated hard to get past a glinting metal tanker truck, then cut back out into the fast lane. Julian would have hated this. For a gambler, he had made for a very nervous traveller. Not the ideal passenger for Laura. "Mangroves to the left of me, desert to the right."

"I think you mentioned you had a message for Benjamin?"

"Yeah, I did."

"Well?"

"For Ben, I said. Now he has it."

"Charmed, I'm sure!" said Braithwaite.

"Do you know where he is now?" said Laura.

"Of course, of course," said Braithwaite. "Somewhere out in the jungle. Riosucio. Northern Antioquia- up near the border with Panama."

"But you're still in touch with him?" said Laura.

"He's actually a tad incommunicado, just at the mo, to be honest..."

"Christ!" said Laura. "Do you have any idea what he's up against in there? That's bandit country. It's one of the FARC guerrillas' last strongholds in

Colombia. There's no law there, except the gun and the machete."

"My dear lady, you were the one who insisted on sending him there- who funded this whole madcap plan of yours!" said Braithwaite. "If you recall our meeting at Sweetings, all this was very much against my better judgment. Besides, Makepeace is still alive."

"So you have heard from him?" said Laura.

"No, but I- I haven't heard anything to the contrary either!" said Braithwaite. "Let me speak to some of our contacts in the old cloak and dagger business... The spooks. I'll get right back to you. Can I call you on this number?"

"Sure. My UK mobile," said Laura, flooring the car as she streaked by the Baker Hughes campus. "Now if you'll excuse me, I have a very long flight to catch."

"Where to?" said Braithwaite "Are you coming back to Blighty?"

"Pick a fucking lane, you moron!" shouted Laura.

"I beg your pardon?" said Braithwaite.

"Sorry- some Emirati boy racer trying to cut up the little lady driver... Who drives an Escalade anyway?"

"Ah! But where are you headed for?" said Braithwaite.

"Colombia, of course," said Laura. "We put Ben in there, and now we need to get him out, Mr Braithwaite. I'm not losing anyone else."

She turned off the Bluetooth and stopped at the traffic lights. Then she noticed that the black Chevrolet Escalade had rolled up right next to her again.

"Shit..." she said, revving up to accelerate away when the lights changed. Suddenly the tinted passenger window of the SUV rolled down and there was a flash of light. Laura closed her eyes as the flicked cigarette butt span through the air and hit her window, sending a shower of sparks over the roof of her car. The four Emirati men in the Escalade howled with laughter at her discomfiture. Then the lights changed and Laura pulled away. She slammed her foot on the accelerator and undertook the gleaming SUV on the right hand side. As the driver blared his horn at her, Laura lowered the driver window and tossed out her half-drunk can of Diet Coke. It caught in her car's slip-stream and thudded straight into the Escalade's windscreen, the soda exploding all over its glass and paintwork. The black SUV pulled off onto the hard shoulder to lick its wounds, and Laura switched on the car radio. Black Sabbath.

"*People think I'm insane/ Because I am frowning all the time...*"

"It's not paranoid if they really are out to get you," she said.

CHAPTER 46

ANTIOQUIA DEPARTMENT, COLOMBIA

Makepeace gazed down at the swamp system festering below. The interior. It was like the surface of a different planet. Suddenly he felt a very long way from home. Geraldino handed him a map in a water-proof case. There was a compass taped to the plastic.

"In-flight reading, *señor*!" he shouted over the rotor chuff. "If Jairo Paisa doesn't show up, this is all you'll have to orient yourself for twelve hours in the bush."

"It's kind of hard to know what to hope for…" said Ben.

"Just stay calm and take your bearings as often as you can," said Geraldino. "It's very easy to get disoriented in the jungle."

"I know," said Ben. "But do you think he'll break the date?"

"St James's says this is a go," said Geraldino. "That's the best intelligence anyone is likely to get in this region. Suicide Station has access to restricted US spy satellites. Eyes in the sky that even the Colombian government doesn't get to see."

"They can see through trees?" said Ben, looking down at the virgin green baize of the jungle, rolled out as far as the eye could see. Like the table in the *salle de jeux*, he thought. This was no place to hedge your bets. It was overwhelming- all-enveloping. "It's beautiful," he said.

Geraldino pointed down at a black hole in the jungle canopy below.

"Watch out for the clearings, *señor*!" he shouted. "That's where the SAMs come from. A puff of smoke, like the caterpillar's smoke rings in *Alice in Wonderland.* Then… Boom!"

"Can I turn your radio off, Geraldino?" said Ben. "I feel like it would improve my travelling experience. Is there a switch for that?"

"*¡Sí, cállate, huevón!*" said the pilot over the radio. "We're not all fanatics here! For me this is just in and out- no questions asked. I don't want to hear about fucking SAMs when we're flying out over the boonies like this." He turned around in his seat, and held up all ten fingers. "*¡Diez minutos, gente!* Ten minutes. Time to make your peace with God, *gringo*."

"I believe in a cruel God…" said Ben.

Geraldino held out an ugly black hand-gun in a side-holster, like a club *sommelier* presenting a bottle of wine for inspection.

"Smith & Wesson M&P semi-automatic, *señor*," he shouted. "Compact and reliable. You might fail it, but it won't fail you. You know how to handle it?"

Makepeace nodded.

"*Gracias*," he said. "I'm still fucked if I need to use it though, aren't I?"

Geraldino grinned.

"*¡Ay, sí- jodido, señor! Muerto*. You could scare away some dogs though, right?"

"Maybe I'll use it to shoot a chicken, if I get hungry in the bush," said Ben.

"Take this too," said Geraldino, passing him a machete. "In this country, the machete is man's best friend."

"What are his other friends?"

"NODs, luck- and water," said Geraldino.

"Right- I don't have any night optical device," said Ben.

"Then we must hope that you're really lucky, *señor*," said Geraldino. "Or that the job is done before nightfall. Take this, anyway." He handed Makepeace a two-litre bottle of Dasani mineral water. "And these..." he said, passing him a flip-top carton of Marlboro cigarettes. "For bribes- there aren't many convenience stores out here."

"Thanks," said Makepeace. He put them in the sports bag Geraldino had given him back in Cartagena. It was filled with bricks of white powder, wrapped in clear plastic and sealed with duct tape.

The helicopter banked left, tilted its nose and then began to drop down into a sink-hole in the tree cover. The rotors beat up the loose grit and foliage of the jungle-floor, branches and leaves whirling up all around the clearing. Geraldino leaned over to Ben and pushed the stop-watch button on his watch. He shook his shoulder.

"*¡Doce horas, señor!* Twelve hours. Time enough to root out the heretics, Torquemada! Then we meet you back here- or you'll have met Jairo Paisa first, and you'll be dead already. Either way... *¡Buena suerte, señor! ¡Viva el Club!*"

"Don't forget to ignite the green rescue flare when you're ready for extraction!" shouted the pilot. "Because I don't plan on landing here if I don't have to."

"You can light a candle to my memory," said Ben.

"OK, but I'll do that in the Iglesia de San Pedro Claver!" yelled the pilot. "No need to risk my own neck in this hell-hole..."

Makepeace laughed.

"Good luck, *carajo*!" he shouted.

"*¡Vete, soldado!*" said Geraldino. "Despair is power. So make us all proud, special one. No gods, no masters!"

Ben pulled open the door and dropped out onto the ground. As the helicopter lifted off again, he made for the edge of the clearing, head low, buffeted by rotor wash. He turned around and Geraldino gave him the thumbs-up. Then the helicopter rose vertically up towards the overcast sky above, leaving Makepeace behind. It had nearly cleared the tops of the trees when something flashed out of the forest. The rocket-propelled grenade hit the tail of the helicopter, ripping it off and sending the chopper into a flat spin. Then gravity took over, and it plummeted straight down, rotors colliding with the trees on the edge of the clearing and sending it pin-balling to the other side.

"Fuck!" Ben said. "RPG…"

"Time to move, Makepeace," said Bezique's voice through Ben's earpiece. "Now, now, now!"

"Rest in peace, Geraldino," said Ben, as he scrambled into the cover of the trees. "Together we greet the Reaper."

The helicopter's rotor blades were still thrashing around as it slammed down onto the forest floor, scoring deep grooves into the earth. Then the explosion scoured it all away.

CHAPTER 47

REDWOOD CITY, NORTHERN CALIFORNIA

Victor Onyechi watched another perfect California day creep up over the horizon, robed in tangerine and indigo. He never tired of it. He had always been an early riser back in Nigeria, and now that he had finally made it to Silicon Valley, he didn't want to waste a single minute of it. Why would you? The perfect business environment, the perfect climate- the perfect life. The sun was rising, and it was all coming up Victor. At last. He turned on his enormous Californian TV. And right on time, there was the smiling face- his own smiling face.

"Well, you know what they say, Jim!" said TV Victor. "It takes a lot to haul your ass into the Valley. And then it takes a lot to buy a pint of milk here!"

Jim Cromwell was loving it and so, quite frankly, was Victor.

"So, Victor, we've been hearing a lot about these awesome gadgets of yours! Can you tell our 'Breakfast in the Bay Area' viewers a little bit more about how those are going to work for them?"

"Sure thing, Jim," said TV Victor. "First up, we call it 'Alchemy 2050'."

"Like the ancient quest for the philosopher's stone?" said Jim. "To turn base metals into gold?"

"That's absolutely right, Jim," said TV Victor. "Only this is far more valuable than that! What we're doing is capturing ambient, environmental radiation to produce energy. There are power sources all around us, all the time. We're giving people a simple, cheap tool to capture that and use it to power their life. To power their dreams! Just like the Bay Area has powered mine."

"Wow! Just, wow," said Jim. "Tell me more, Victor."

TV Victor held up the Alchemy prototype.

"I guess most of your viewers will be getting pretty familiar with wireless charging for their iPhones and Androids by now," he said. "What we call inductive charging. Well this, Jim, is wireless charging for your whole life!"

Cromwell leaned forward to study the fist-sized device.

"Wireless charging is based on one of the bed-rocks of modern physics," said TV Victor. "To get technical on you for a minute, Faraday's principle of electromagnetic induction. If you build a magnetic induction loop, like the one in this prototype, into a cell-phone charging pad, that will establish an alternating electromagnetic field. When it's within distance of the base, the receiver induction coil housed inside the cell-phone can convert that electromagnetic force back into electricity."

"And that's going to recharge that thirsty battery of mine?" said Jim.

"Right!" said TV Victor. "Staying in touch with all those celebrity buddies of yours takes a bit of juice, am I right, Jim?"

"You tell me, Victor! So this sounds great," said Jim. "But how does that even happen?"

"What Faraday demonstrated was that if you install a magnet in a wire coil, it will generate an electric current by moving electrons through a conducting wire. Where we've topped off his work a little is by using high frequency superconducting diodes, to grab even more of that ambient electromagnetic radiation."

Cromwell beamed to camera.

"So you've topped Michael Faraday, and all right here in the Bay Area!

That's quite a feat right there, Ladies and Gentlemen…"

TV Victor laughed and took a modest sip of water to let that sink in.

"He was a pretty smart guy, but I guess he didn't have superconductors in his tool-box back in 1831!" he said. "That's real important to Alchemy 2050, because it gives us super-efficient conversion from alternating current to direct current, which is the key to harvesting environmental radiation. So now we are sucking this stuff straight out of the cosmos! That means that if you live anywhere near high voltage cables, shopping malls, tall buildings, subway lines- or even an area with frequent lightning strikes or electric storms- you're never paying another electricity bill in your life! Period. This really is that life-changing. And just think of the environmental benefits!"

"Sounds good to us, right, folks?" said Jim.

"In your case, Jim- using our device, you could even use your famous personal magnetism to create power!"

"Thank you, Victor!" said Jim. "Gee, look at me blushing! That's all we've got time for now, folks, but I hope that Victor will come back again soon to tell us about his hot new plans for ambient heat pumps?"

"You bet, Jim!" said TV Victor. "We're going to do for heating and cooling what we've done for power. So now everyone in the Bay Area can stay cool, just like you! And all without burning any fossil fuels, so we can save the environment- and put an end to those nasty forest fires we've been having here! Thank you for having me on the show this morning."

"Thank you, Victor Onyechi and Alchemy 2050!" said Jim. "We'll be back right after this message from our sponsors, Pacific Energy…"

Victor clicked the TV off, and punched the air.

"Thank you, Jim!" he shouted.

Then there was a slow handclap behind him, and he turned around in astonishment. "Very clever, Victor!" said Hugo Capstick. "Very clever indeed. Almost- because this can be a thing, you know- too clever for your own good."

CHAPTER 48

RIOSUCIO, COLOMBIA

Ben counted as one by one his senses were overloaded by the jungle. He felt like he was wading through quicksand, picking his way through labyrinthine mazes of vegetation, hopscotches of roots, nightmare tangles of clinging vines and Elephant Man tree-trunks.

"Stop walking like a *gringo*," he told himself, as the perspiration drenched through his shirt. It was murder moving in the jungle, physical and mental torture. Barbed creepers clutched at his face and limbs, a thousand, thousand evolutions of thorn and bur all vying for mastery of his skin at once. The heavy, damp air all around him reverberated with the maddening cacophony of the jungle. A troop of howler monkeys set up a disorienting, demented wail, screaming wide-mouthed from the canopy roof. Their dark forms flitted into view through the sun-dappled upper leaves, obscured by thick fronds and tangled lianas. They stopped to add their yell to the disjointed chorus, and then hurtled headlong on to the next vine. The din of the jungle intensified to answer their call, the cicadas beating out a manic, accelerating rhythm. It seemed to come from every corner of the forest, ringing in Ben's ears as if coming from inside his head as well as all around. Some nameless creature screeched out a long plaintive cry, the horrifying lament of a tormented soul in bedlam. Hideously over-sized mosquitoes surfed the waves of heat and moisture loading the air. They swarmed in black and white speckled clouds around Ben's sweating face and hands, heedless of the chemical reek of diethyl toluamide in which his shirt had been soaked overnight. The insect repellent caught in his throat in the stifling atmosphere.

"The only one this shit is killing is- me…" muttered Makepeace.

The high-pitched scream of marauding mosquitoes was ringing constantly in his ears now, making him turn and fidget, twisting and slapping at his back as he made his way along the rough-hewn track to the rendezvous point. He was losing time. As the sweat pooled on his body, the ravenous insects sought out the patches forming on his clothing, biting him through the wet fabric. Distracted, he lost his footing and skidded down into the mud on the jungle-floor, his knee thudding into a fallen tree.

"Bugger!" said Ben, gritting his teeth against the pain and hauling himself back to his feet. The track was almost unpassable now, so he slashed at the vegetation with the machete, progress slowing to a crawl as he cut his way through.

"Christ, this is hard work," he said, mopping away the sweat running down his face and splashing onto the precious map. The plastic cover had already steamed up from the ambient humidity. Ben hacked at a thick screen of greenery looming large above him, and then stepped out into a clearing. For a moment he saw three men and a woman in combat fatigues, floppy hats and 'MAC' armbands, assault rifles slung around their shoulders. Guerrillas in the mist.

"MAC," Ben murmured. "*Muerte a Capitalistas…*"

Even through his fatigue, Makepeace felt a nauseating shock of realisation. There had to be a sentry watching the path. Then a rifle butt swung into the side of his head, and his legs crumpled down underneath him.

CHAPTER 49

REDWOOD CITY, CALIFORNIA

"Bravo, Victor! Quite a show you put on for us all..." said Capstick, putting his feet up on Victor's De La Espada coffee table. "I, for one, thoroughly enjoyed it. And as for Jim, I actually thought he was going to cream himself! Should bring you quite a bit of extra publicity, don't you think? Drive the share price up? Although all that's a bit irrelevant now, to be honest. Which is why I thought I'd drop in. A stitch in time, eh?"

"How the hell did you get in here?" said Victor.

"I climbed over the fence, to be perfectly honest," said Capstick. "It seemed easier than a lot of tiresome explanations."

"What- what do you want?" said Victor. "You don't exactly seem like a house-breaker."

"With the plummy accent, you mean?" said Capstick. "You'd be surprised. But actually, what I'd like is to buy Alchemy 2050. We'll pay you ten million dollars on the nose. Cash down. Today."

Victor laughed.

"You broke into my house to make a low-ball offer for Alchemy?" he said. "Man, venture capital sure has gotten brutal in this town! You guys are animals! Although you really would be robbing me if you paid me ten million dollars for this baby. Don't you know that Amazon have offered me a hundred mill for a minority interest, just to let them trial it in their global data centres?"

"Yeah, we know all about that," said Capstick. "But there is one important difference between us and Amazon that you should be aware of."

"Oh, really?" said Victor. "What's that? You break and enter? They won't be doing any jail time? They're remotely credible?"

"Some of that may also be true," said Capstick. "But my point is that they won't burn your house down, with you inside it, if you don't sign today. And by today, what I mean is- right now."

"OK, funny guy," said Victor, pushing Capstick. "Play time's over! Get the fuck out of here, will you, man? Right now! Who do you work for anyway? Because I am going to make sure you never work in this damn town again, do you hear me?"

"I hear you," said Capstick. "And that's probably also true. But I'm representing the Billionaire Suicide Club in this matter. So long-term job security isn't a big problem for me."

"Billionaire?" said Victor. "You're seriously delusional, buddy! The only person in this room who's going to make a bill is me! You hear me?"

"And that can still happen, Victor," said Capstick, holding up the detonator. "That's fine by us. Just not with Alchemy. For that, you get ten million. But the billionaire door is still open to you, if you make the right decision in the next thirty seconds."

"What's that in your hand?" said Victor.

"The California forest fires have made you a rich man, haven't they, Victor?" said Capstick. "They've turned cleantech into big business here! Moved it into the mainstream. But the first rule of the Club is: If you play with matches, you get your fingers burned..."

"What are you talking about?"

"Look out of the window, Victor."

Capstick pointed out of the picture window at the front of the house.

"The woods? What of it, man?" said Victor.

"Those trees and bushes are bone dry," said Capstick. "Except for the fifty-five gallon drum of gasoline I just poured out there. I actually left the barrel outside, if you look. The whole thing would go up like a tinder-box if I pressed this little red button. Only I'm not going to, am I? Because you're going to sign this contract."

He passed a document over to Victor.

"Ten million dollars!" he said. "And we're not asking for a single warranty. We just don't want this to fall into the wrong hands. Imagine what a mutant Firestarter with a nuclear reactor in their heart could do with a gadget like yours! They would have limitless power- and money. So sign the piece of paper and move on, Victor. Do something completely different. Live long and prosper!"

"What are you trying to tell me, crazy man?" said Victor. "There is no fucking way in the world I'm signing a damn thing on your say-so! So, if you'll excuse me, I'm going to call the cops now..."

"With this phone?" said Capstick, holding up Victor's cell phone. He dropped it on the floor and ground it under his heel.

"That's enough clowning, Capstick," said Bezique's voice through the ear-piece. "You're on a gated estate. Finish this!"

"Last chance, Victor," said Capstick. "As an old friend of mine used to say: Is it better to burn out, or to fade away?"

"Fuck you!" shouted Victor.

Capstick smiled and pushed the button.

"Guess Kip was right: it's burn out every time..."

The two of them watched the wave of fire sweep down from the wood and wash straight over the house. Victor ran to the front hall.

"Not that way, Victor..." said Capstick. "Not that way! I thought you were supposed to be smart. Geniuses are really not all they're cracked up to be..."

The fireball blasted straight into Victor as he opened the front door, the gasoline-fuelled flames enveloping him. He screamed and ran back through the house, clutching at his burning hair and clothes, straight out onto the balcony, and then toppled over it. Capstick watched as he tumbled three storeys down into the swimming pool below.

"Finally, some peace," said Capstick. "I thought that guy would never stop talking."

"Status, Hugo?" said Bezique.

"Oh, Victor is sleeping with the fishes," said Capstick. "Cargo 200. Does anyone have a light?"

He lit a cigarette, sat down on Victor's sofa and waited for the inferno to reclaim his restless soul.

CHAPTER 50

RIOSUCIO, COLOMBIA

"You took a wrong turn, *gringo*," said a Colombian voice. It came from about a foot above Makepeace, as he lay prostrate on the jungle floor. "Somewhere around Miami. What do you think you're doing here? Ecotourism? This way is closed."

"*Soy el primo de la costa,*" said Ben, rubbing his head. It felt like it was about to split in two. "I'm the cousin from the coast…"

"*¡Bienvenido, primo!*" said the Colombian. "You're very welcome, cousin. You're just not what I was expecting. We jungle people don't like surprise visitors."

"Next time I'll write ahead," said Ben.

"You're alone?"

"You know what they say," said Ben. "*Mejor solo que mal acompañado.* Better alone than in bad company…"

"That's just it," said the Colombian. "I think you have been keeping bad company.

Where's de la Peña? It was his radio frequency we picked up. His signal promised me antibiotics. It didn't say anything about a *gringo*."

"You're *el primo de la selva*?" said Ben.

"Yes- the cousin from the jungle," the Colombian said.

"Jairo Paisa?"

"People call me that."

"Your mother?"

"That's none of your business, *gringo*. What do they call you?"

"Today they're calling me Torquemada," said Ben. "But normally just Makepeace."

"You're here to make an inquisition?" said Jairo Paisa.

"That's right," said Ben. "And purge some heretics. If they don't purge me first."

"If! 'If' can be the longest word…" said the Colombian.

As the throbbing in Ben's head died down and his vision cleared, Jairo Paisa's face began to take shape. Mid-forties, intense dark eyes set deep in a weathered face. Steel-coloured hair and beard beneath a bush-hat. Wearing a camouflaged combat smock, like the other guerrillas. And holding Makepeace's earpiece in his hand.

"Is that thing still working?" Ben asked.

Paisa shook his head.

"You're all alone now, *primo*," he said. "In the deep, dark, woods."

"Well, that's a relief," said Ben. "We can speak frankly. And you found the drugs in my bag?"

"Yes," said Jairo Paisa. "Penicillin and amoxicillin. Worth their weight in gold! Here you can find the purest cocaine anywhere in the world- but no generic antibiotics."

"You haven't give them to anyone?"

"Not yet," said the Colombian.

"That's good," said Ben.

"In fact, I was about to propose a little test before we consider them- how shall I say it- FDA-approved?" said Jairo Paisa.

"Let me guess," said Ben. "You want me to taste it first?"

"You'll think me untrusting," said Paisa. "But I've learned to fear *gringos* bearing gifts."

"That's what they want you to do," said Ben. "But I'm afraid I can't oblige."

"And why is that, *primo*?" said Jairo Paisa.

"Because the packages have all been tainted with powdered thallium," said Ben. "Enough to kill us all out here, a hundred miles from the nearest hospital."

Jairo Paisa leaned towards him.

"Why thallium?"

"Because it's highly toxic, but the symptoms of heavy metal poisoning are delayed for twelve to twenty-four hours," said Ben. "Long enough for you to observe the drugs' effect on me- and to conclude that they're safe. By the time I got sick, I would either have gone- or I'd be dead already. Either way, it would be far too late for you to do anything about it."

"You have Prussian blue with you then, *gringo*?" said Jairo Paisa. "To treat the thallium poisoning?"

"No," said Ben. "You'd have found that too. They couldn't risk that. And they were guessing that you don't have any either."

Paisa looked at him.

"You're an unusual assassin, *mono*..." he said. "Very few facilities in Colombia have access to medical-grade Prussian blue. You can't just cook up pharmaceutical potassium ferric hexacyanoferrate in a jungle coca lab. Which is the best scientific equipment we have access to, out here."

"You know your stuff," said Ben.

"We can drop the pretence, *no*?" said Jairo Paisa. "You must know that I'm a doctor. Your whole plan depends on it. What I want to know is who you are- and who sent you to your death. You're quite a rarity, you see."

"Why is that?" said Ben.

Jairo Paisa shook his head.

"All of us here have enemies. But you're the only one in this jungle who everyone on every side seems to want dead."

"What do you mean?" said Ben.

"Someone smoked your helicopter, didn't they?" said Jairo Paisa. "You didn't take that as a hint?"

"Yeah, I did," said Ben. "Only I thought it was you."

"Why would we do that, *mono*? We wanted the product, and we didn't know it was spiked. If it was good, we'd want more. That helicopter could have brought it. It's not going to now, is it?"

"So who was it then?"

"A very brave man!" said Jairo Paisa. "To come in here and fire off an RPG right under our noses like that. He was also a very stupid man. We'll have him hung up by his *cojones* before nightfall. One way or another, we'll find out where he came from. Just as we'll find out why you came here, ready to take a poison- without bringing the antidote."

"That part is easy enough," said Ben. "It's because of where I came from."

"And where was that?" said Jairo Paisa.

"From the Billionaire Suicide Club," said Ben.

Jairo Paisa grabbed him by the throat. The wry humour was all gone from his voice.

"You dare to call it a club?" he hissed. "Those murderers!"

"More than a club," said Makepeace.

"You have achieved your ambition then, *gringo*," said Jairo Paisa. "You were dead the minute you landed here."

Then the jungle erupted with gun-fire. The howler monkeys above yelped and scattered, screaming out alarm calls as they went.

"What the fuck is going on?" shouted Jairo Paisa. "No one jumps us here!"

CHAPTER 51

ST JAMES'S, LONDON, UNITED KINGDOM

"Florizel! Bring me flesh…" shouted Bezique.

The steward carried a silver salver through the panelled door into Bezique's office. Bezique sprinkled shreds of decaying meat from the platter into the huge tank that formed one whole wall of the room. The pistol shrimp all scrambled to devour it, snapping at each other and sending localised explosions reverberating around the room through the hydrophones in the tank.

"The net is closing," said Bezique, fishing a shrimp out of the aquarium. He laughed as it clicked its claw at him. "Oh no, no- your party piece only works under the water, my pretty. Outside it, you are as weak as the rest of us! As vulnerable as any human…"

"Well?" said Malthus. "What was so important that you had to drag me across London?"

"The Peruvian has made contact," said Bezique, dropping the shrimp back into the water. "Torquemada is in."

"Alive and kicking?" said Malthus.

"Are you getting sentimental in your old age, my friend?" said Bezique. "Or do you just take a particular interest in your latest protégé?"

Malthus laughed.

"I will take that as a joke," he said, cracking his knuckles. "I left sentiment behind a very long time ago. You of all people should know that…"

"They shot down the helicopter," said Bezique. "Geraldino is gone."

"The Colombian Florizel?"

"Rather a waste..." said Bezique, replacing the lid of the aquarium and handing the net to Florizel.

"You will find another Geraldino," said Malthus. "Any fool can bow and scrape, and slavishly uphold tradition. Those are the sheep. The wolves are what we need. The ruthless, hungry men who can forge new legends for the Club. It is nothing to us if they savage a few sheep along the way. A few million!"

"That will be all, Florizel," said Bezique. Florizel hesitated for a moment, then nodded and backed out of the room. "Yes, then- Makepeace is still alive. For now. Though why you set such store by that is still a mystery to me, I confess."

"He is as expendable as anyone else, when it comes down to it," said Malthus. "But the price must be right. I'm not interested in wasting an asset like Torquemada to wipe out one small jungle settlement."

"You would rather waste another helicopter?" said Bezique.

"A helicopter!" said Malthus. "A thousand more helicopters. Helicopters you can insure! But Torquemada is something precious. Unique. This is the best chance we've ever had to infiltrate *La Nueva Raza* in South America- in their heartland. This is a golden opportunity to find their headquarters and root it out for good. After the Panama fiasco, it may be the only chance we get."

CHAPTER 52

RIOSUCIO, COLOMBIA

They were moving too fast to pinpoint in the gloom, but Makepeace knew they were out there. He could sense their presence, glimpse the stealthy movement in his peripheral vision. Nightmare predators moving through the trees. Even if you don't blink, you miss it.

"Bloody bats..." he muttered.

It was all part of the total sensory assault of the jungle. The path was treacherous, with only the occasional glimmer of moonlight to illuminate the obstacles, and Ben scraped his shins time and time again on hidden snags. No time to stop though- not even when he felt the fabric of the combat fatigues ripping on a sharp root, the blood dripping down his leg into his boot. He winced with pain and willed himself to catch up with Jairo Paisa again. The doctor was his only chance of staying in touch with humanity now, and he was maintaining a relentless pace. Every part of Ben's body was screaming out for rest- from his blistered feet, up through swollen ankles and shredded shins. His frazzled mind. Still Jairo Paisa's wiry frame weaved on through the bush, not missing a step. Ben himself was stumbling every few paces now, the gap between him and Paisa growing all the time, the mental monkey on his back getting heavier. Then he saw the red dot laser sight. It probed its way through the dense undergrowth before disappearing again, flickering and darting like a hellish firefly in the growing gloom of the night. There it was again, flitting through the mass of vegetation. The bright red spot rested for a moment on the tree above Makepeace's head, before roving on again. He was being hunted. Panic drove him forward, crashing through the foliage as he tried to escape the evil eye searching him out through the forest. The extra rush of adrenalin brought him up to within a couple of metres of Jairo Paisa.

Then Ben heard a new sound, a machine-like, Terminator rhythm, pursuing him through the jungle. Someone was hacking through the undergrowth with a machete, forging a different path to cut them off as they ran. Accelerating towards them. It was metronomic, methodical, an alien beat ringing out above the pounding of the blood through his ears. It seemed to be coming from all around the forest now, in front as well as behind, soundwaves playing tricks on him. Getting into his head. And getting louder and louder.

Jairo Paisa was still running with a measured, energy-conserving stride, balancing speed and concealment. It was too late for Makepeace though- in his exhausted state, stealth was far beyond him and he could only keep up by throwing caution to the wind, lumbering on with heavy legs. As he struggled to keep sight of Paisa, he caught his foot on a jutting root and tumbled down onto the rough track. He looked up from the ground and saw Jairo Paisa's bearded face staring back at him through the gloom. The Colombian paused for a second and then shrugged, turned and was swallowed up by the jungle.

Ben struggled back to his feet. Even as he looked up, he knew he wasn't alone. The shadowy figure in front of him was so well camouflaged in the dark jungle that he could only just make him out at point-blank range. Just the outline of night-vision goggles, and the webbed barrel of the long sniper's rifle. It was aimed straight at Ben's head. El Pishtaco held his finger up to his lips. Suddenly there was a flurry of activity in the bush behind him, and a machete blade came crashing through the undergrowth. Two men in MAC armbands burst out through the gap, machetes in hand. The first one saw Ben late, dropping his machete and unslinging his assault rifle. He still hadn't seen

El Pishtaco when the shot from the sniper's rifle ripped through his chest, the high-powered round sending him flying back into the bush. The second guerrilla swung his machete at El Pishtaco, hitting the rifle and knocking it from his hands, but even as he was swinging his own assault rifle up in its sling for the shot, El Pishtaco was pulling a hand-gun from his side-holster and putting two rounds through his head. The guerrilla crumpled to the ground. El Pishtaco wheeled back round to Makepeace, and Ben set off his signal flare. As the powdered copper fuel kindled, the pyrotechnic burned phosphorescent green, dazzling El Pishtaco behind his night-vision goggles. He tore them off his head, but Makepeace was already careering down the pathway back into the jungle, panic coursing through his veins like nitrous oxide. Never run in a jungle at night. But behind him Ben could hear the loud, staccato rattle of automatic weapons fire and the answering thud of suppressed single shots. He ran. From the screams, he could guess whose rounds were taking the greater toll. More of Jairo Paisa's guerrillas were pouring through the undergrowth all around, flooding the jungle with gunfire. Makepeace ran on, calling on every reserve of fear and adrenalin. Five minutes further down the path, even panic was failing him. The visibility was horrendous, low branches catching at his face in the darkness, raking his skin. A trailing thorn-bush caught his trouser-leg as he shaped to leap over a dry creek, and he tripped and lost his feet. Putting out his hands to save himself, Ben caught his left arm in the clinging thorns and tumbled hard to his right, striking his head on a rock. He started to push himself off the stony creek-bed, before sinking back down onto his knees. He heard the harsh whine of the first mosquito, circling in towards him through the shadows, and then the darkness swallowed everything.

CHAPTER 53

THE OLD SMOKING ROOM, BOHEMIAN SPORTS CLUB, ST JAMES'S

Malthus brushed his way through the screen of tobacco plants, brooding in the humidity.

"I'm not sure about this new contraption of yours, Bezique," he said, closing the door of the walk-in cigar humidor behind him. "Not all change is for the better. My Cohiba tasted like a wet sock last night."

"I'll have Florizel look at the humidity settings," said Bezique, trimming the end of his *Romeo y Julieta* cigar with a razor-sharp cutter. "My own misgivings are more focussed on Project Torquemada. Why would Jairo Paisa trust Makepeace enough to lead him to *Proyecto Luz*?"

"Why does anyone do anything?" said Malthus, smoothing the lapels of his smoking-jacket, as he lit his own Havana. "You have seen a lot of life, Bezique- of hope, of irrational faith. Of desperation! I believe Paisa will see something in Makepeace, just as El Pishtaco did in you. Something of himself. You survived, and so will Makepeace. I'm counting on it."

"But they must have found the earpiece already," said Bezique. "We have had radio silence from Torquemada for hours. And even if they don't know about the GPS sensors in Makepeace's smartphone, *La Nueva Raza* would still be taking a huge risk in revealing any of their secrets to him. Or ever letting him leave the jungle…"

"A risk! Oh, a ludicrous risk! Of course they would," said Malthus, puffing on his cigar. "They would be risking everything. But then we're all risk-takers here, aren't we? That was the true genius of your illustrious forebear, when he introduced the Game. You don't need to a deck of cards to get one man to kill another. But you do need it to build an army of gamblers." He cracked his knuckles. "I don't need to remind you what stakes we're playing for, Bezique. These are the things that men risk everything for. What else is there? Besides the very survival of your people- your species?"

"And you are gambling that Makepeace will win his trust?" said Bezique. "This shaman- this jungle doctor?"

"The best operators work with what they have," said Malthus. "With everything they have. They turn their weaknesses into strengths, and they never stop improvising. Makepeace must have told them about the thallium already, or he wouldn't be alive even now." He paused to re-light his cigar. "Almost certainly he has also told them about the Club- all that he has been allowed to learn about it so far. That would be the natural way to distance himself from Project Torquemada. All of this is valuable information to *La Nueva Raza*. They can't just ignore it. The question is how long it buys Make-peace. Only time will tell us that. Things are different in the jungle…"

The upholstered door opened and Florizel glided noiselessly up to Bez-ique, bearing a piece of paper on a silver tray.

"An encrypted message from Suicide Station in Cartagena de Indias, sir," he said. "Torquemada is mobile."

"On foot?" said Bezique.

"The GPS sensor system shows movement back towards the exfiltration site," he said. "Should we green-light the helicopter?"

Bezique looked over at Malthus, who inclined his head in assent.

"Very well then," said Bezique. "Let's hope this one proves more- durable…"

Florizel bowed and backed out of the room again, pulling the heavy door closed behind him.

Malthus rested his cigar in the ash-tray and topped up his tumbler with Scotch whisky from a monogrammed crystal decanter. He rubbed his hands together.

"The Game is afoot!" he said. "Makepeace is good- that's the part you keep under-estimating. He's a Royal Marine Commando. He'll find a way in, and once he's in, he won't stop until he gets to the truth. He's adaptable- used to operational autonomy."

"Autonomy..." said Bezique. "That's what worries me. Where will his loyalties lie when he's with the Firestarters? If you're right, then he is no true brother. And the Club depends on absolute loyalty!"

"There's one problem with the blindly loyal, my friend," said Malthus. "They're blind!" He ground his cigar out in the ash-tray. "I don't care which side is Benjamin is on, and I wouldn't believe him if he told me. I only want him to reach *Proyecto Luz-* his journey terminates there. He will never see London again. The only question is who kills him first: the Peruvian; *La Nueva Raza-* or us." He shuffled the deck of cards on the Chippendale occasional table next to him. "Time to play the Game again, don't you think? We must not get preoccupied with any one sphere of influence. Not when we have a whole world to curate!"

"Of course," said Bezique. "South East Asia is in train as we speak. Sands is mobile. And, unlike your protégé, his loyalty is beyond question."

"Henry Sands' loyalty is to Death..." said Malthus. "But then it comes to the same thing, in the end."

CHAPTER 54

RIOSUCIO, COLOMBIA

Morning, and the deafening sound, the smell, the taste, of AK-47 rounds. Nearby- but not in the hut. Cover. Respite, just not much. Ben rolled over to the wall of the shack. He groaned and forced his eyes open, only to see the yellow eyes of a huge rat on the rafter above his head. It scampered along the wooden beam, tail slithering, and disappeared into the matted palm-fronds of the roof of the hut.

"Guess I'm still alive then," said Makepeace, touching the mass of clotted blood above his right eyebrow. The movement sent another spasm of pain rushing through his temple. It bored in behind his eyebrow, and he sank back down onto the mud of the floor. His ankles were swollen and itching with the ravages of the dawn mosquitoes. He reached down to scratch them, but every movement threatened to tear his head apart, battering him into submission. He huddled in a foetal position, fighting the rising nausea, shielding his eyes from the shafts of sunlight streaming through the palm roof of the hut. The roof rustled and bulged with scuttling rats.

"And this place fucking stinks…" he said.

"*¡Bienvenido!* You are very welcome, *primo*!" said a voice from the doorway of the hut. "After all the trouble it cost us to find you out there. You have a certain knack for staying alive."

Ben pulled himself up into a seated position, grimacing with pain. His head was throbbing, splitting. He jammed his thumbs into the upper hollows of his eye sockets, trying to relieve some of the pressure on his aching brain.

"*Tranquilo, gringo- tranquilo,*" said Jairo Paisa. "I'd offer you a pain-killer, but as you know we're a little short on medical supplies at the moment."

"I've had such a curious dream…" Ben said.

"Here the nightmares tend to come true," said Jairo Paisa.

For the first time Ben could see the contents of the room. Two dead bodies lay on the ground next to him. What had once been a man and a woman. They were burned and blackened, fragments of clothing and melted weaponry scorched and branded onto twisted flesh.

"Jesus! What the fuck happened to them?" said Ben, recoiling. "They look like they've been incinerated…"

"They are of *La Nueva Raza,*" said Jairo Paisa. "You must know about the Achilles Effect- to have come so far. To have taken such a risk…"

"I saw it when the Club attacked the Lagos cell," said Ben. "But I didn't understand it. People were burning alive."

"Then West Africa is gone?' said Jairo Paisa.

"I'm sorry," said Ben. "They showed me the operation in London. There was nothing I could do."

"You!" said Jairo Paisa. "What could you do?"

"They were scared though," said Ben, rubbing his head. "The Club was. Of Project Light International."

"*¡Proyecto Luz!*" said Jairo Paisa. "So it is happening! Our brothers in Africa will be avenged."

"The Club is making its move too," said Ben. "Everywhere. You need to move your cells. Or get ready for a war."

"Ready for war!" said Jairo Paisa, crouching down next to him. "We are at war. You think anyone would choose to live like this? Evolution is a war! Look at these people here…" He pointed to the bodies in the hut. "It's like an abattoir in here. I could do nothing to save them. They were warriors! But the tension- the stress of being hunted- it was too much for their physiology."

"So that's the Achilles Effect," said Ben. "The fatal flaw- like Achilles' heel! All that energy is difficult to control. And the Club knows it… That's what they fear so much. That one day you learn to harness it- and turn it into power. That you use it against them, in this war they're waging on you!"

Jairo Paisa nodded.

"Already there is a new strain of *La Nueva Raza*, who can control it better," he said. "Just like in the time of the Cro-Magnons and the Neanderthals, there are different breeds of human walking the earth now. But there is a difference this time…"

"What's that?" said Ben.

"We are all one!" said Jairo Paisa. "We have learned to find each other, to trace the genes that unite us- and to co-operate, for the greater good. *¡Por La Nueva Raza- todo!*"

"That doesn't sound much like the humans I know," said Ben, spitting out a mouthful of blood.

"No!" said Jairo Paisa. "That is the difference between us. We are pledged to protect all forms of *La Nueva Raza* from the people who hate us and fear us. From people like you…"

"If you believe that, why are you telling me this?" said Ben.

"*Gringo*, you must know now that you're already dead," said Paisa. "Nine of my people are corpses, lost out there in the jungle. These two didn't make it through the night. So before I kill you, you will tell me why. Perhaps in that way you, too, can make a contribution to the cause."

Makepeace glanced around the room.

"I have your gun, if that's what you're looking for," said Paisa. "You're not protected by Smith & Wesson anymore, cowboy."

"I wasn't planning on shooting my way out…" said Ben. "But how many people do you have left now, Jairo? Do you know who's out there? Who's hunting us?"

"Hunting us?" said Jairo Paisa. "We will soon see who is hunting who…

But are you trying to tell me that this man, this hunter- he's not another *gringo*? That he didn't come here with you?"

"He's not an American- or a Colombian," said Ben. "I don't even know what his real name is. Except for one thing- people call him *El Pishtaco*. That seemed to mean something to Geraldino, the Club's man on that chopper. Now he's dead too."

Jairo Paisa sat down on a camp-bed.

"The Peruvian?" he said. "The *pesetero*… Mercenary. That's not possible! He has not been seen in Colombia for years."

"So you do know him?"

"What is he doing here?" said Paisa.

"I don't know," said Ben. "I saw him in Panama. He killed de la Peña's brother- to stop him talking to me."

"But he let you go?"

"He put a slug over my head, then ran out of bullets."

"You were lucky, *gringo*," said Jairo Paisa. "But now you've run out of luck. He may have followed you here, but he's never going to get his bounty on you."

"There must be more to it than that," said Ben. "There was no need to come into the jungle to kill me. He could have killed me in the Torre Panabanco, in Cartagena- anywhere. It must have something to do with you. With my mission. Project Torquemada."

"Don Jairo…" said a guerrilla, stepping into the hut. He whispered something to Jairo Paisa.

"This *pishtaco* of yours has killed another three of my people, *gringo*," said Paisa. "If he wants you so much, maybe we should just give you to him."

"If I die now, these questions will never be answered," said Ben. "In the end, they will succeed in burying you out here in the jungle. And I'm the only one who can get you out of here."

"Get me out of here?" said the Colombian. "Why would I want to leave? Or to go anywhere with you?"

Ben shrugged.

"If it was me, I'd want to be a part of it," he said. "To make a stand. Can't you see what's happening here? It's genocide in motion- they're just picking you off, region by region, before you can join forces. Africa, Asia- South America. As long as you're apart, you're playing into their hands. They're not afraid of a few guerrillas in a hut in Colombia. They're afraid of Project Light International! You must be some of the best troops *La Nueva Raza* has. So are you ready to fight back? To light up the Billionaire Suicide Club?"

"*Coño, gringo…*" said Jairo Paisa. "I don't know who's more crazy. Them- or you! What do you really want?"

"I want to stop the Club," said Makepeace. "Too many people have died already, and they're just getting started. I won't just sit back and watch it happen, this time."

CHAPTER 55

OLD PEAK ROAD, HONG KONG SAR, PEOPLE'S REPUBLIC OF CHINA

The security guard was lighting the first Salem cigarette of his watch when the slim wire of the garotte snaked down over the wall of the compound. He saw it in his peripheral vision, a millisecond before it jerked tight around his neck. By the time he reached up with his hands to clutch at the razor-sharp metal, it was already far too late.

"I'm inside," said Sands, dropping down into the compound. "Mobile."

"Head for the front door of the main building," said Suicide Station. "Go, go, go, go."

Two armed guards flanked it. They started to unsling their assault rifles as Sands approached, so he rolled a phosphorus grenade down the path between them. They dived for cover and Sands gave each of them a short burst with the silenced MAC-10 where they lay.

"Two 200s..." said Sands. "Still mobile. Loading."

He changed clip, scooped up the unexploded grenade, ignition pin still in place, and stepped into the ornate hall-way of the villa.

"Clear," said Sands. "And mobile."

He moved fast down the corridor, ignoring the priceless Chinese artefacts lining the walls. He was in his element now. There was no better reason to live than the fact that other people were trying to kill him. There was no space or time for questions, no way for the PTSD to catch up with him now. Not unless he stopped moving.

"There's a set of double doors at the end of the corridor," said Suicide Station. "Two more guards. Then you're in the red zone."

"I see them," said Sands.

He removed the pin from the grenade and sent it skidding the last ten metres over the shiny marble surface of the floor towards the guards. They watched it skim off the surface of the stone and then slide between them. Sands sent another grenade after it, then pressed himself back in the shelter of a doorway to the left of the corridor to avoid the blast. He felt the shock-wave as the grenades splintered the heavy wooden doors and everything else in their way.

"Two more 200s, and I'm going in…" said Sands.

He stepped through the mangled wreckage of guards and doorway, and down onto the mezzanine landing at the top of a double flight of stairs. The marble staircases on each side of him led down into a cavernous room below.

"Bloody hell…" said Sands.

"Status?" said Suicide Station.

Sands gazed out into the sea of faces below, all staring up at him.

"There are hundreds of them!" he said. "Hundreds…"

"You're sure?" said Bezique.

"That could be a whole battalion down there!" said Sands.

And then all hell broke loose, as the guards below unleashed a hurricane of small-arms fire up at him. The marble splintered and sent rounds ricocheting all around the landing. Already gunmen were racing up the staircases on each side of them, shooting at Sands as he dumped a precious MAC-10 clip on them and then reloaded.

"Are they all Firestarters?" said Sands.

"Yes," said Suicide Station. "It is worse than we feared. But you know what to do."

Sands cleared the staircases with arcing sprays of 9mm rounds, and then climbed up on the balustrade at the edge of the landing. He spread his arms wide in a Jesus Christ pose, body rocking as the pistol rounds slapped into him. Somehow he managed to keep upright, until the spell was broken and he crumpled like a broken puppet, tumbling forward off the balustrade.

"No gods, no masters!" he shouted. "Together we greet the Reaper."

The men below continued to shoot at him as he fell, until they saw the packages of plastique underneath his shirt. Ten 1.25 pound blocks. They scattered as his body crumpled onto the floor below. Then Sands' finger slipped off the pressure switch on the detonator, the product gases from the high explosive expanded at thousands of metres per second and the walls of the villa were levelled. As the gas was sucked back into the low-pressure blast area, the rest of the building collapsed in on itself.

"Your struggle is finally over, Sands," said Bezique. "But where will we find the soldiers like you, to stem this tide?"

CHAPTER 56

RIOSUCIO, COLOMBIA

"Disorientation is the killer," Makepeace muttered to himself, as they hurried down the tunnel of vegetation ahead. It felt like they were falling, tumbling into a green whirlpool. "Disorientation is the killer. Don't lose sight of the light…" His mind lurched back to Central America. There had been no light left there by the end.

The guerrilla in front of him was jumpy, on the edge, staring out into the forest. He was more dangerous than El Pishtaco right now, Ben thought-safety off, swinging his rifle towards every rustle. One trip, and he would take them all out. The walls of jungle were closing in on them. Then there was a sharp crack, from somewhere out of the green. Makepeace watched as the trigger-happy guerrilla collapsed to the ground in slow motion. He didn't even have time to clutch at the wound, the head shot killing him instantly.

"Man down!" said Ben, diving behind a tree. The guerrillas were shooting wildly, cyclically, back into the brooding undergrowth. A burst of heavy Kalashnikov rounds splintered a *higuerón* trunk near Ben, sending the canopy crashing down towards him. Ben braced for the impact, but the garland of vines around the fig tree snagged on the surrounding trees and arrested its fall. He got up and hurtled down the path. Then there was another rifle shot, and a loud, prolonged screaming from up ahead. The guerrillas started firing again, just dumping rounds now, emptying their magazines into the trees. Two of them stopped and bent down, trying to pick up the man ahead of Makepeace.

"Keep moving!" shouted Ben. "He's gone! *Está muerto*…"

Two shots rang out in quick succession, screaming out from behind the tree-line. The two guerrillas crumpled to the floor, almost on top of their dead colleague. There was a flurry of answering fire from up ahead, then silence. Reinforcements were coming up from behind, and two more guerrillas slipped out into the bush, trying to cut El Pishtaco off. Thirty seconds later, there was a loud, sustained burst of firing. The two guerrillas crashed back through the undergrowth, heedless of the noise now. They were dragging a body behind them. Jairo Paisa turned to Makepeace. His lean face was triumphant.

"You see your *pishtaco* now, *gringo*?" he said. "You see what has happened to him? Every monster can be killed in the end. *¡Viva La Nueva Raza!*"

Ben looked at the body. There was something horribly familiar about the posture of the dead man. But it wasn't El Pishtaco. He grabbed Jairo Paisa and dived back behind the shelter of a tree. The Colombian shouted out in fury as they tumbled down onto the muddy ground. Then they were both thrown into the undergrowth like rag dolls by the explosion from Geraldino's booby-trapped body. The blast ripped apart the two guerrillas carrying it, tearing limbs and organs asunder. Another guerrilla knelt, holding a shattered shoulder. She stared at Ben in shock, as the blood seeped into her T-shirt and through her fingers, then fell forward.

Makepeace struggled to his feet again, blinking through the grit and blood in his eyes. He hauled Jairo Paisa back upright.

"She's gone…" he said. "How many people do you have left?"

Paisa looked around them at the remaining guerrillas, shooting at ghosts in the forest. "Just Adriana and Nacho now," he said.

"Not enough," said Ben. "We have to get away from here. He's coming for us."

"Where to, *gringo*?" said Jairo Paisa.

"There's a helicopter coming back for me," said Ben. "It'll be in the clearing- where Río Guaviale and Río Mariana meet. One hour."

Paisa stared at him.

"Coming here?" he said. "Didn't you see what happened to the last one? Who's going to fly it in here? And why come back for you, if this is a suicide mission?"

"They're not done with me yet," said Ben. "It'll be here."

"And where do we run to, if we run?" said Jairo Paisa.

"To Cartagena de Indias. That's the only way out- the only way we can find out what happened here. And maybe even get a shot at revenge."

Jairo Paisa looked at the scared faces of the surviving guerrillas as they fumbled to change their magazines. Makepeace recognised the trauma in their eyes. They looked broken.

"Or we stay- and fight!" said Jairo Paisa. "Kill him here, and end this! Him- and you."

"Wasn't that Plan A?" said Ben. "Now you're running out of bodies- and body bags. Plan B is the chopper. You can take it if you want it. But I doubt it's going to land without seeing me first."

Paisa stared at him.

"Alright, *gringo*," he said. "Let's go to the river."

They were moving now, leaving the killing ground. Sometimes that's all that matters, Makepeace thought. Change the picture, change the odds. When you've lost that many soldiers, there's only one place you need to be- anywhere but the slaughterhouse you came from. He looked at his watch. Twenty minutes till rendezvous. The path was overgrown now, and one of the guerrillas began to cut through the dense foliage with a machete. She was working at an incredible pace in the humidity, but their pace was still slowing.

"How long will they wait for you, *mono*?" said Jairo Paisa.

"Christ, the flare!" said Ben. "I used it last night. We need a flare to signal the chopper down! Do you still have the antibiotics I brought?"

"The *gringo* medicine?" said Jairo Paisa. "Adriana has it in her pack. I was trying to figure out how to filter the thallium..."

"OK, let's get to this fucking clearing, it's ten minutes to RV!" said Ben.

Then Adriana stopped, cursing. Her machete had snapped on a wiry thorn-bush. "Five minutes to RV..." said Ben.

He heard the slightest of movements from a bush behind them, the sound trapped and cushioned in the thickening air.

"He's behind us," Makepeace whispered to Jairo Paisa.

Jairo Paisa nodded. He signalled to Adriana and Nacho to stop moving.

"Two minutes to RV."

Then the red dot appeared, on a huge green leaf just above Jairo Paisa's head.

"Shit!" said Ben. "Laser sight. Don't move. Don't fucking move! One minute till RV. We're going to miss it!"

Now Ben could hear a dull thumping sound, and then the roar of the twin General Electric turbine engines. That was when the noise should have intensified, as the helicopter got a visual on the flare, manoeuvred into position above the clearing and dropped down into it, whipping up the debris of the jungle floor into a maelstrom of dust and sound. Makepeace willed the miniature whirlwind, the man-made hell of rotor wash, to break loose all around them. But there was no flare. The helicopter made two passes of the clearing, arced back around and headed back to base. They were trapped in the green room.

"Fuck..." said Makepeace.

On the other side of the clearing, El Pishtaco smiled and changed his clip.

CHAPTER 57

GONZALO MEJÍA AIRPORT, TURBO, ANTIOQUIA DEPARTMENT, COLOMBIA

"How did you get in here, *mi amor*?" said the pilot, lounging back on the threadbare flight-room sofa in his mirrored Aviators, cigarette in hand. "This is a restricted area. That means not for the public. Even the beautiful female public, *señorita*! Don't believe all you hear about helicopter pilots. We're like a priesthood..."

"Isn't this Colombia?" said Laura. "There are ways and means, Javier. Mostly with American presidents printed on them."

The pilot laughed and put his feet up on the sofa.

"Well then?" he said. "Now that you are here- what do you want? And how do you know my name?"

"I want you to fly back out to Riosucio right now, and do the job you were paid to do," said Laura. "A contract is a contract."

The smile slipped from the pilot's face.

"It's time for you to leave, *señorita*. Now!" He stood up. "The joke was good while it lasted, but it's over. I don't know who you are, or what you think you know, but..."

"I know that you're a dead man if you don't go back," said Laura. "I'd say you have about..." She looked at her watch. "Ten minutes. Before Bezique realises what's happened. How much does it cost to call in a hit in Turbo? A hundred dollars? This is *sicario* country. Fifteen minutes here on the back of a motorbike. And then..." She held out one finger. "Bang! *Adiós*, Javier. You don't mean anything to him. And when you sell your soul to the Devil, you better deliver it."

"Don't talk about things you don't understand, *flaca*!" said the pilot.

"You took money from some very dangerous people, Javier," said Laura. "It's just a matter of time before they find out you bailed on the mission. If I can find you with a couple of hundred dollars and an iPhone, imagine what a criminal society with unlimited resources can do! They'll cut you up into little pieces."

"Who says we bailed?" said Javier. "It's hard to find one man in a big jungle, *no*?"

"Cartagena airport control had two passengers registered for landing. I've got a copy of the flight log right here," said Laura. "So where are they now?"

"Maybe they changed their minds about the trip..." said Javier.

"Save the sob-story for the *sicario* who comes to your house tonight," said Laura. "See if you can persuade him. Maybe he'll change his mind. Maybe he'll even knock on the door first, before he shoots your house up with an Uzi. You need to get with the fucking programme here, Javier! The last person who crossed these people ended up with the *corbata colombiana*. I saw it for myself, back in Panama City. Is that what you want for yourself- and your family? They couldn't even bury you in an open casket- believe me, it's horrible. You're disfigured- mutilated..."

"Don't bring my family into this..." said the pilot.

"It's too late for that," said Laura. "This sucks everyone into it. It's like a black hole. Do you think I wanted to get involved in this? But they killed my brother. They're trying to kill my friend. And I'm not losing anyone else. We're going back to Riosucio, and we're going to get him out of there."

"You want to go into MAC territory, *señorita*?" said the pilot, laughing. "The House that SAMs built? You know what happened to the last helicopter? To Geraldino? He was a brave man- and a powerful man, in this world. Now he's dead. And we will be too if we go back there, believe me. They have Stingers. RPGs. And these things are just little commercial helicopters, you know, they're not like your *gringo* Blackhawks or Apaches!" He pointed at the Bell helicopter outside. "If that gets hit by an RPG, it's going straight down… I've seen horrible things too- the wreckage of one of these babies, still smoking on the jungle floor. So if it's all the same to you, I'd rather take my chances with both my feet on the ground!"

"I'll pay you a hundred thousand dollars if you take me there," said Laura, opening the duffel-bag slung over her shoulder. "Cash down. Used hundred dollar bills. Take your chances, and you could get rich. Stay here, and you'll definitely get shot in the face. But either way, we have to leave right now."

The pilot rummaged in the bag with his hand.

"You always carry a hundred thousand dollars in your purse, lady?"

"I went to the bank specially," said Laura. "When you're dealing with donkeys, you better bring carrots."

Javier laughed, but he was still looking at the money.

"You have *cojones*, *señorita*! More than most men in this town. Maybe enough to get us all killed."

"So when do we leave?" said Laura. "There's only ten minutes in your flight window. It's now or never, Javier."

The pilot opened the door and whistled towards the ground crew. He stubbed his cigarette out in an overflowing ash-tray.

"I guess it's now, then," he said. "I always did have a weakness for a pretty face… But we need to be clear on one thing."

"*Cuéntame*," said Laura.

"We're not landing out there unless we get the signal- the flare," said Javier. "Not for all the money in Colombia. There's *cojones*- and then there's fucking suicide. *¿Me entiendes?*"

"Sometimes there's both..." said Laura. "We'll know which it is when we get there."

"Just keep the money where I can see it, *gringita*," said Javier. "It helps me fly straight!"

CHAPTER 58

RIOSUCIO, COLOMBIA

Makepeace and Jairo Paisa inched closer to the clearing again, crawling on their elbows now. Only the jungle knew where El Pishtaco was- which way death would come from. The red laser sight flitted in and out of the foliage like a demonic mosquito, constantly changing angle and vantage point, denying them a second's mental respite. They crouched down at the edge of the tree-line, taking cover behind fallen tree trunks. The guerrillas trained their guns around the clearing, as Ben gathered brushwood and kindling together.

"What makes you think the helicopter will come back, *gringo*?" said Jairo Paisa.

"It'll be back," said Ben.

Jairo Paisa shook his head.

"We can't wait here forever!" he said. "We'll be easy targets."

"We are already…" said Ben. "What is he waiting for?"

"What do you mean?"

"Come on, Jairo!" said Makepeace. "You have to assume that he could have killed us at any point in the last ten minutes. But for some reason he hasn't."

"Maybe he wants the helicopter too," said Jairo Paisa. "He's already taken one out, remember?"

"Let's call it double or quits..." said Ben. "But listen, Jairo- the burnings back there. You called it the Achilles Effect. Have you studied it?"

"Haven't you?" said Jairo Paisa. "You must know how the reaction occurs. The sonoluminescence. The reaction is normally instantaneous. But sometimes multiple bubbles of inert gases form in the heart. It's more likely to happen under extreme stress- when the subject is hyperventilating. A series of bubbles are cavitated by the mitral valve, causing a rapid build-up of heat inside the body that can kindle stomach gases, and then body fat. Once that ignition has taken place, it's almost impossible to stop. The fat creates a wick effect, soaking into the clothes and generating extreme heat. What you saw back there."

"Spontaneous human combustion!" said Ben. "That's why the Club is so obsessed with it. Bloody Charles Dickens..."

"What's that noise?" said Jairo Paisa.

"That's rotor chuff," said Ben. "The helicopter."

"How far away?" said Jairo Paisa.

Makepeace listened to the dull whir of the rotor blades, thumping through the damp, heavy air above the jungle.

"Close now..." he said.

The engine whine intensified, and then the helicopter swept down over the clearing. The two surviving guerrillas leaped up and started waving it down, signalling with their arms.

"Get down!" shouted Ben. But someone else had seen them first. Two high velocity rounds whistled through the clearing, and both guerrillas crumpled to the ground.

"No!" shouted Jairo Paisa. "Nacho! Adriana..."

Makepeace lit his signal fire, just outside the tree-line in the open clearing.

"Just fucking shoot me, already," he muttered, as he blew on the base of the fire. "Because I'm a sitting duck here..."

Then the kindling took, flames licking up the length of the drier branches and twigs.

Ben crawled back into cover and rummaged in Adriana's ruck-sack. He pulled out the packages of penicillin and amoxicillin and unwrapped them, careful to keep them off the damp ground.

"What the fuck are you doing, *carajo*?' hissed Jairo Paisa, reloading his rifle.

"I need the antibiotics," said Ben. "Or to be more precise, the thallium."

He swigged down the rest of his water, shook out the last drops and then poked a few holes into the bottle-top with his Swiss Army knife. Then he folded his map into a funnel and poured the powdered penicillin and amoxicillin into the empty plastic bottle. When the flames of the fire started to lick up to waist-height, Makepeace crouched down next to it.

"This had better work…" he said. "Because it's going to be extremely toxic."

Then a single shot rang out across the clearing.

CHAPTER 59

RIOSUCIO, COLOMBIA

"A gun-shot!" shouted Laura in the cockpit. "Did you see the muzzle-flash? It's them! It must be them!"

"Yeah!" said the pilot. "Getting shot at! I didn't see any flare, either…"

"Put the chopper down!" said Laura. "We have to get Makepeace out of there!"

"We had a deal, *señorita*!" said Javier. "Don't start fucking with me now! That could be anyone down there. And they have guns."

"Of course they have guns!" screamed Laura. "What did you think you were getting into? A fucking Sunday school outing?"

"No flare, no landing," said Javier. "I'll give it one more pass, and then we're out of here!"

Makepeace waited for the impact of the bullet that never came. Now assume you're alive until you hear otherwise, he told himself. Then there was a roar in his ear. The helicopter. It was making another pass. He pumped the Dasani bottle like a bellows, blasting the powdered antibiotics onto the flames of the fire. He pulled his head back as the thallium ignited and oxidised. The violence of the exothermic reaction on the dry powder sent a bright green chemical fireball billowing twenty metres up into the sky. But the chopper just kept on going. Ben sank down onto his knees. He wasn't going to get another chance.

"There!" said Laura. "You see the green flash?"

"That's not a rescue flare!" said Javier.

"What is it then?" screamed Laura.

"I don't know!" he said. "A frog fart? A camp-fire. But you said a flare. That's no flare!"

"Just put the fucking helicopter down!" shouted Laura. "They must have had to improvise something."

"You think that's a good sign?" said Javier.

"That's the best we're going to get!" shouted Laura. "Now do it! Do it! Or I'll hire the *sicario* myself!"

The helicopter completed a half-circle round the clearing and then dropped its nose before sinking down to the jungle floor.

"Ready?" said Ben.

"He's still out there!" yelled Jairo Paisa over the rotor wash. "We'll be completely exposed!"

"We are already!" said Ben. "We'll just have to risk it. Because they won't come back a third time. Not for me, or anyone!"

They watched the helicopter bump and then settle on the forest floor, side door sliding open.

"*¡Vámonos ya!*" screamed Ben, running hell for leather in a swerving line to the helicopter. "Let's go!"

Jairo Paisa sprinted after him, spraying rounds back into the bush as he ran.

"Go! Go! Go!" shouted Laura, as she pulled Makepeace and Jairo Paisa into the helicopter and slammed the door shut behind them.

"Don't worry, *flaca*, I'm going!" said the helicopter pilot, lifting them painstakingly up over the tree line. "I'm fucking going! We're in the hands of

God now! God and Javier! Now we fly fast, and pray they're out of RPGs…"

"Look," said Ben, taking Laura's arm.

A lone figure stood below, hugging the fringe of the clearing. He was barely visible in his camouflage netting, but they could just make out the sniper rifle cradled in his arms.

"El Pishtaco?" said Laura.

Makepeace nodded. The helicopter straightened up and then accelerated forward over the jungle roof.

"But why did he let us go?" he said.

"Let us go? He just massacred my people!" said Jairo Paisa. "We were lucky to survive."

"We saw a shot," said Laura. "The muzzle flash."

"That's just it," said Ben. "His weapon had a flash suppressor. I saw it- too close up for comfort. He must have taken it off to fire that shot."

"Why?" said Laura.

"Because he wanted you to find us," said Ben. "Which reminds me- thanks for doing that. What on earth are you doing here?"

"It's a long story…" said Laura. "But first there's something you need to see. You remember Andrew Fairley?"

"The guy the Club targeted in Edinburgh?" said Ben. "The cardiovascular researcher?"

"Yeah," said Laura. "They got him, Ben."

"I'm sorry…" said Makepeace, putting his arm around her.

"Thank you," said Laura. "But I'm locking all this grief in a box for now. Because this is important. It turns out that the day after Laurence Pearce died, the Club killed one of Andrew's main funders: Professor Malcolm Carmichael. At an oil industry dinner in Edinburgh. The murderer was a so-called ecoterrorist- Hector Strontian. He died too, of course."

"The Strontium Dog!" said Ben. "The Robin Hood of the North Sea. The guy was a fucking lunatic. They had to shut in a whole string of offshore oil installations because of his stunts. It cost Lloyd's a fortune in insurance claims by the oil companies- which by some coincidence always seemed to happen when the oil price was low anyway."

"The police couldn't find any other connection between Anarchy Scotland and the attack on Andrew," said Laura. "And that's because there wasn't one. But I found this. Meet the Chairman Emeritus of the North Sea Oil Club."

She held up her phone. Ben stared at the photograph.

"Trevor Braithwaite!" he said. "Yeah, that sounds like the kind of pie he would have a finger in."

"Another bloody club! But that's not all," said Laura. "When I went to meet Ian Simms in Abu Dhabi, he identified your boss by a different name."

"Well?"

"He knows him as Bartholomew Malthus," said Laura. "The one man in the Club you've still never met. And I guess now we know why."

"Jesus Christ!" said Makepeace, smashing his fist into the helicopter door. "Brother Number One was under my nose the whole time! Braithwaite is the Suicide King."

CHAPTER 60

CARTAGENA DE INDIAS, COLOMBIA

"Where are we going, *gringo*?" said Jairo Paisa, as the cab bustled along Avenida Santander. "I told you I don't like the city."

"The old town," said Ben. "El Centro. To the Club. With Geraldino gone, this could be the best chance we ever get to find out what they're doing."

"But they must know he's dead by now," said Laura. "Won't they have flown a new Geraldino out, to tie up the loose ends?"

"I'm counting on it," said Ben. "But it's still a hell of a lot easier to crack *La Heroica* than St James's, believe me."

As they passed the Monumento a la India Catalina and turned onto Avenida Venezuela, there was a sudden roar of traffic noise. A motor-cycle accelerated level with the cab.

"Shit!" said Ben, just as the pillion passenger shot out the taxi's tyres with a raking burst of MAC-11 rounds. He rolled down onto the floor of the cab, pulling Laura with him. The taxi skidded forward and smashed into the back of the car in front of it. Makepeace looked between the seats into the front of the cab. Jairo Paisa and the driver were both slumped forward on the dashboard.

"Jairo..." said Ben, shaking the Colombian's shoulder. Nothing. He rolled back over the shattered perspex to the pavement-side of the cab, jerking open the passenger door and slipping out onto the street. He crouched low as he pulled Laura out after him.

"Are you alright?" he said.

She nodded.

"Let's go for those shops," he said. "On three…"

"Three!" said Laura.

They sprinted for the first door, burst through it and found themselves jostling through a busy *comedor,* packed with workers eating heaped plates of rice and beans, fried chicken and roasted plantain. The air was thick with grease and cheap cigarettes.

"They're coming after us!" said Laura.

Makepeace opened his sports bag, pulled the flip-top carton of Marlboros out and ripped the top off. The diners looked up at him with greedy eyes as he tore open the first soft-pack and started to hand them out amongst the forest of clutching hands.

"*¡Cigarillos gringos! ¡Gratis!*"

The diner rang with the sound of dropping knives and forks as the eaters rushed to grab handfuls of free, white-filtered cigarettes. Beyond the mob, Makepeace could see two *sicarios* lurking outside the glass door of the diner, waiting for the crowd to disperse before they made their move. He looked around the *comedor* for another way out. The carton was nearly empty now. He tossed the last packet into the throng and shoved past a perspiring waiter, through saloon doors and into the kitchen. The cooks looked at them in amazement as they ran straight through the open door at the back of the kitchen and out into the yard.

"*¡Puta madre!*" swore Makepeace. The back wall loomed above them, surrounded by teetering crates of empty soda bottles for recycling. It was topped with a jagged perimeter of broken glass. "We'll never get over that…."

"Ben- we've got company…" said Laura.

There was shouting from inside the *comedor,* and then the back door swung slowly open. Makepeace crouched behind a tower of soft-drink crates, sweat beading up on his forehead. Then the gun came into view, the wrist following, the forearm of a biker jacket behind it. The gun turned again, muzzle sniffing them out, hunting them down. Now the only sound was the thud of the rusty extractor fan, chopping through the muggy, rice-water laden air behind the kitchen. Then the first *sicario* burst out into the yard, and Ben threw all his weight at the Coca-Cola skyscraper next to the door. For a moment the crates stayed up, swaying back against him, and then they broke like a rolling wave over the *sicario*. As the tumbling bottles crushed the gun-man to the ground, Ben made for the door back to the kitchen, and caught the butt of a Colt .45 straight to the head. He sprawled on his back, broken glass tearing at his clothes and skin. The pillion passenger was pointing the gun straight into Ben's face now. He stood up straight and Makepeace closed his eyes. When he opened them, he saw a slim figure in an elegant suit standing over him. He smiled around the polarised lenses of his sun-glasses and put out a hand to pull him up to his feet.

"Follow me, Makepeace. And you please, Señorita Newman. You both have a long journey ahead of you."

He led them back through the *comedor*, tossed one small bundle of *pesos* to the owner of the café and another to the *sicarios*, and then stepped into the back of the black Chevy Blazer waiting outside. Ben and Laura clambered in beside him, brushing broken glass off their clothes. That was when Makepeace saw the man sitting in the front passenger seat.

"*¿Qué más, parces?*" said Jairo Paisa.

"This is a miraculous recovery, Doctor…" said Makepeace. "I see that the rumours of your death were greatly exaggerated."

"It looks like the tables have turned a little," said Jairo Paisa, passing each of Ben and Laura a black silk scarf. "We prefer to be in control of the situation. So put these over your eyes."

"Why?" said Ben.

"There is another way to preserve our secrets," said Commissioner Herrera next to him, taking his sun-glasses off.

"What's that, *Señor Comisionado*?" said Ben. "We pinkie promise not to tell anyone?"

"You're still asking the wrong questions, Makepeace," said Herrera. "Take my word for it, for once- you'll prefer this one. You owe me some information. And you better be a lot further from Panama than this before you forget your debt to me."

CHAPTER 61

ST JAMES'S, LONDON, UNITED KINGDOM

"This wild card of yours is wreaking havoc with my Game…" whispered Bezique to Malthus, sat next to him as usual as he presided over the *salle de jeux*. "He's erratic- unpredictable. I'm starting to wonder if Makepeace is a fool or a knave."

"He's both," said Malthus. "That's the point. He's a problem child. And he's achieved more than a hundred other brothers could have. Look where he is!"

"Can't you recall him now?" said Bezique, sipping at his port.

"Oh, I don't think Torquemada will answer to Trevor Braithwaite anymore," said Malthus. "The time for bluffing is over. *La Nueva Raza* are preparing to make a hero call. Makepeace has his part to play in that too."

"Then we must make our own preparations," said Bezique. "Turn, Mr Whitby… The queen of clubs, the Flower Queen. Turn."

"It's possible to over-prepare," said Malthus. "Sometimes you just need to get to the showdown. I do hope you haven't lost your nerve after the Hong Kong affair, Bezique?"

"Mr Stamp, the two of hearts- Love Match. Turn!" called Bezique, and then leaned closer to Malthus. "You heard Sands for yourself- how many of them there were! He was as brave a man as I ever met, but I could hear the fear in his voice. Mr Baldwin, the queen of spades- the Old Maid."

"I prefer to call her Black Maria…" said Malthus.

"Turn!" said Bezique. "How many more of them must be out there, Malthus? Gathering… For all our plans, they will soon overrun us."

"But not yet!" said Malthus. "We have made decisive strikes in Africa, and now in Asia. If we can crush the Latin American social cell with young Benjamin's unwitting assistance, we will have dealt them a fatal blow! It will be the beginning of the end for *La Nueva Raza*…"

"If!" said Bezique. "We are running short of brothers with the skills to execute such deep operations. Mr Pettigrew, the jack of diamonds- Laughing Boy. Turn!"

"And yet the well is not quite dry…" said Malthus. "If it comes to that, we will all have our parts to play, Bezique. I think you understand me?"

Bezique nodded.

"Good," said Malthus. "And here comes Old Frizzle, right on time."

"Mr de Mestre, the ace of spades- the Death Card!" said Bezique. "Champagne, Florizel!"

"Bravo, de Mestre!" said Malthus. "Now can I interest you in some life insurance, my dear fellow? The Club has connections with the most exclusive Lloyd's syndicates…"

CHAPTER 62

CARTAGENA DE INDIAS, COLOMBIA

Makepeace tried to memorise the turns of the Chevy as it bullied its way through the traffic, but it was impossible to stay oriented, sightless on the side-streets of Getsemaní. Then he heard a growing roar, the discordant shouts of ten thousand voices, filtering into the car over the noise of the traffic. The noise intensified, hoarse individual yells coming through the cacophony of the crowd. Now Ben knew where they were- near Estadio Olímpico Jaime Morón León, the Real Cartagena football stadium. That put them on Avenida Quinango or Avenida Quinta- heading out of town. The chants of the Real crowd died away as the car continued its winding journey through the dusty, clinker-board outer *barrios* of Cartagena. Vision blacked out by his blind-fold, Ben kept slipping into fitful sleep and then waking with a start as he slumped forward against the seat-belt. He had no idea how many hours- or days- had passed, when Jairo Paisa lifted Laura's head off his shoulder and shook him awake.

"You can take the blindfold off now, Makepeace. And you, Señorita Newman," said Herrera. "We are a long way off the grid. This is Magdalena Province. Even a wild rover like Makepeace doesn't know his way around out here."

Ben looked out of the window. The village dogs watched without curiosity as the Blazer rumbled past them. The car blew dust onto numberless ramshackle roadside houses, in nameless one-whore *pueblecitos*. Palm fronds overhead dappled the rough road with soft shadows as the evening sun gave way to twilight, a gentle breeze driving out the stifling heat of the day.

"Who is we?" said Ben. "Who are you working for now, Herrera? Panama? Colombia? I'm guessing not the Club, from the company you're keeping. But I've never seen you in civilian clothes before. It's very disconcerting."

"Who do you think, Makepeace?" said Herrera. "Surely you know us by now? We are *La Nueva Raza*. We have no nation but our own."

"*¡Por La Nueva Raza- todo!*" said Jairo Paisa.

"So you were protecting de la Peña in Panama," said Laura. "Just not very well."

"Just not to the exclusion of our long-term survival," said Herrera. "Be reasonable, *señorita*! How well have you- or Makepeace- looked after those around you?" Ben took Laura's hand in his, and she squeezed his fingers. "Of course de la Peña worked for us- he was good to Caridad, and she managed him perfectly. By the end, he even saw himself as one of us. But you don't make an omelette without breaking some eggs. Besides, I told you the money was moving for a reason, didn't I, Makepeace? At that time I thought you were working for British Intelligence. I didn't realise how subtly Malthus was playing you."

Smiling children in replica soccer kits stared and waved at the Blazer as it bumped down pot-holed tracks. Laura waved back though the open window of the car.

"But if you knew about the Club already- why did you let de la Peña go?" she said.

"We had to, once your homicidal friends had started to pursue him," said Herrera. "He could have dragged all of us down with him."

"What about his brother?" said Laura. "That was a loose end."

"That was a mistake," said Herrera. "We made two. First, we underestimated the strength of Gustavo de la Peña's brotherly sentiments."

"You thought he would just keep his mouth shut?" said Laura.

"Of course!" said Herrera. "But then I'm an only child. He had to know that as soon as he talked, he made himself a liability to both sides. And you saw what that led to. This man was no saint, Señorita Newman. He chose the wrong moment to come to God."

"And second?" said Laura.

"Second, we overestimated his ability to look after himself. I thought he would be safe enough in Panama."

"Enter El Pishtaco…" said Ben.

Herrera shrugged.

"You saw him?" he asked Jairo Paisa. The guerrilla nodded. "Inca Túpac Amaru! Malthus took me by surprise- raising the stakes like that. That was a big dog to bring to a backyard fight."

"Where did he come from?" said Laura.

"Who can say what lost mountain-top he was lurking on?" said Herrera. "A man whose life, whose whole past is just rumours- legends."

"No one has no past," said Ben. "Some people just bury it deeper down than others."

"You learned that in the army?" said Herrera.

"In the insurance business," said Makepeace.

Herrera smiled.

"Here there are still places that can keep secrets. Secrets that don't make sense in a world of spy satellites and super-computers. During *La Violencia*, I went down to Tingo María to dig out his secrets. On a lead from Interpol. We were prepared to dig deep, to spend as long as it took there. In the end, we were in Huánuco for two whole months. Peruvians, Bolivians, Colombians- me. There isn't a country in Latin America where *El Pishtaco* isn't a wanted man. Dead or alive. Here in Colombia more than anywhere."

"A cop-killer?" said Ben.

"Cops, commissioners- presidents," said Herrera. "He has enemies in high places."

"So what did you find?"

"We found clues lost in the past- paths that tailed off into the mist," said Herrera. "We already knew that *El Pishtaco* had no living relatives, that he was brought up by two old *indígenas*. That was all part of the legend. How can you believe in a monster, if you can chat to his brother or sister in the local *bodega*? Finally we tracked his parents down. Neither of them spoke much Spanish, but in any case they had both been dead for ten years by the time we got there. Burned to death in their cottage. No one could explain what started the fire."

"Firestarter genes?" said Ben.

"Who can say!" said Herrera. "They took that- and the truth about their adopted son- with them to the grave. Another part of the legend."

"Why was it so personal?" said Ben. "Did he work for you? And then go rogue?"

"*El Pishtaco* could never be an asset for *La Nueva Raza*," said Herrera. "We always knew that he was connected to Malthus' organisation."

"The Club?" said Laura.

"If you want to call it that," said Herrera. "We call it *El Odio*."

"The Hate?" said Ben. "That seems apt enough."

"Like this *pishtaco*!" said Herrera. "He hates us. And he fears us, which is the other side of the same coin. That's what makes it personal. Even a killer like him has things that mean something to him- things that can be broken. He believes that *La Nueva Raza* are new *conquistadores*. Fresh persecutors to ravage indigenous America. So he has hunted us, wherever he has found us. And we can never ignore him- can never lose sight of him. We must keep our friends close, and our enemies closer still."

"I thought that was money-launderers?" said Ben.

"It seems that we must keep many bad men close to us, doesn't it, Makepeace?" said Herrera. "Even you."

"Until you can kill them."

"That would certainly be my preference," said Herrera. "At least for El

Pishtaco. But he is not an easy man to pin down. Many have tried- police, armies, guerrillas. Even you and Jairo here, *no*?"

"I wasn't actually trying to kill him," said Ben. "I just wanted to get out of there in one piece. It was Jairo who made such a hash of that."

"Fuck you, *mono*!" said Jairo Paisa. "It was my people getting killed out there!"

"Enough!" said Herrera. "There are almost as many questions about you, Makepeace. Now we find you in the Billionaire Suicide Club. So what are you? Soldier, spy, insurance salesman- or a suicidal maniac with a death wish?"

"Is that why we're here?" said Ben. "To answer that question?"

"You're here because you're the only lead on the Club that we have," said Herrera. "You and Señorita Newman. Somehow you two have become part of the end-game."

"We're also the Club's only link to you," said Makepeace. "Stuck in the middle. I'm starting to think it must be the death wish that brought us here."

"You should be careful what you wish for, Ben," said Herrera. "But do you even know what that is anymore?"

"Well, I'd like a drink, *Señor Comisionado*," said Makepeace.

Herrera laughed.

"Not long now," he said. "We're running out of road."

The Blazer battled down the dirt track for another kilometre, then halted in front of a huge fallen tree, blocking their way.

"Dead end…" said Jairo Paisa.

Makepeace looked at it. The wood at the bottom of the trunk was scorched and splintered, shorn away from the tangle of roots left behind in the ground. The tree had been dynamited, precision-blasted to throw it across the track.

"It looks more like a road-block," he said.

"We don't like surprise visitors here, either," said Jairo Paisa. "This is where we get out."

CHAPTER 63

MAGDALENA PROVINCE, COLOMBIA

Jairo Paisa led them on foot along the track and past a discreet gate-post, bearing a faded paint sign.

"Welcome to the Hacienda de La Luz, *gringos*!" said Jairo Paisa. "This is the Big House! *Ay*, it's good to be back here after all this time."

He lit the way ahead with a flash-light as they walked up a steep track, leading up and over a ridge. In the natural basin below it a brackish-looking pool swallowed up the light, the water limpid like oil. Jairo Paisa swept the torch over it and twin answering flashes glimmered back, reflected in the crocodilian eyes of a caiman submerged in the water. It rolled over and moved back into the shadows.

"We call him Malthus!" said Jairo Paisa. "Because he doesn't like the other *caimanes* swimming in his pond..."

On the higher ground beyond the basin, a huge clay and bamboo hacienda rose up out of the vegetation. It was surrounded by a wall topped with razor-wire, the front gates dominated by two fortified gatehouses. Ben's legs were getting heavy by the time they reached the top of the path leading up to the gate. An armed guard greeted Herrera and Jairo Paisa as they entered the compound.

"*¡Buenas tardes, señores! ¡Por La Nueva Raza- todo!*"

They stepped up onto the veranda of the hacienda, enjoying the cool of the evening.

Jairo Paisa disappeared inside and then returned carrying a brimming jug of orange liquid, topped with white froth, and four glasses.

"The true taste of Magdalena!" he said, filling the glasses. "Aguardiente Sour! Orange juice, sugar, egg whites, a slice of lime- and aguardiente. Everything a man needs to survive!"

"*¡Salud y amor!*" said Ben, drinking deep.

"Cheers..." said Laura.

"So what is this place?" said Makepeace. "A country house- or a fortress?"

"No, no- first we drink, *mono*!" said Jairo Paisa. "Then we'll show you everything we have built here- the school for the children, the new hospital. The medical research lab. What we have fought for so long. I thought it about every day I was out there in the jungle. There we did some terrible things, for a great good. But this- this is home!"

"*Amén*," said Herrera, clinking glasses with him. "The dark days are nearly over. We must win this final battle with *El Odio*, and then we can put the ugliness behind us forever."

CHAPTER 64

ST JAMES'S, LONDON, UNITED KINGDOM

"Two officers from the Metropolitan Police have asked to see you, Mr Malthus," said Noel. "They say it's a private matter. Should I show them through?"

"By all means," said Malthus. "I have nothing to hide! We'll speak here, in Bezique's office."

"Very well, sir," said Noel. "Commissioner McDonald and DC Spencer!"

"What can I do for you, officers?" said Malthus, as Noel showed them in. "Will you have a seat? Bezique has some rather fine Hepplewhite pieces, as you can see."

"We'll stand, thank you, sir," said McDonald, taking off her hat. "And I'll come straight to the point, if you don't mind. The fact is that some rather disturbing accusations have been made about you."

"Really?" said Malthus.

"About you and this Club. And Mr Bezique. Accusations linking the Bohemian Sports Club to a number of murders in the United Kingdom, and beyond."

"That is disturbing!" said Malthus. "And we have Miss Newman to thank for this, I suppose?"

The Commissioner looked at DC Spencer.

"That's one of the names, yes, sir."

"The poor thing!" said Malthus. "She's been through an awful lot lately, as you have probably heard. Her brother Julian- one of our valued members- was involved in a terrible incident in Laos. But the Government of the People's Democratic Republic of Laos have made it perfectly clear where they stand. It was a tragic accident, that's just been waiting to happen at one of these 'Boun Bang Fai' rocket festivals of theirs for years. The whole event is literally sat on a powder-keg! Young English tourist, prominent local politician and several by-standers regrettably injured in a sacred annual ritual. Which, of course, people do need to respect in its full cultural and religious context. All of which I'm reliably informed is the Laotian for: 'When you're in a hole, stop digging'!"

"And what about this Hugo Capstick?" said McDonald. "Now also deceased. Erasing a very long history of narcotics offences. Was he another member of the Club?"

"Miss Newman's ex-boyfriend, I believe…" said Malthus. "She was besotted with him, poor girl. He was rather less keen. Young blood, and all that. The long and the short of it was that he took himself off to California, no doubt in pursuit of some new young lady, where some months later he was caught up in the ghastly forest fires that they've been having in those parts. I'm sure you've heard all about it on the news. For the rest you would have speak to the police over there, who concluded that it was an accidental death. No arrests were ever made."

"Thank you, sir," said McDonald. "And Mr Andrew Fairley?"

Malthus screwed up his face in concentration.

"I don't recall ever meeting a member of that name here, Commissioner," he said. "Although doubtless Noel could consult the membership register for you, if you like?"

"No, he wasn't a member of the Club," said McDonald. "He was another friend of Miss Newman though. And another one who seems to have died in tragic circumstances recently. She says that he was shot and killed by Mr Capstick in her flat in Bayswater last week, shortly before it was destroyed in a gas explosion. Mr Capstick had apparently been holding her against her will with the same fire-arm. When he tried to attack her, Mr Fairley intervened and was fatally wounded. He hasn't been seen since, although there is an on-going fire investigation."

"Quite a catalogue of woes!" said Malthus. "But I'm afraid my knowledge of Miss Newman's hyper-active love life only extends to the members of this Club! From everything you say, she does appear to be rather a troubled girl… So sad for Lord and Lady Newman, on top of poor Julian's accident. And you say that this Mr Fairley was killed at her flat?"

"By Capstick, she says," said DC Spencer.

"Yes- she says…" said Malthus. "That's rather convenient from her perspective, is it not- given that poor Capstick himself can now tell no tales?"

"Are you suggesting that Miss Newman herself might be implicated in his death?" said DC Spencer.

"Far be it from me to speculate," said Malthus. "Given that I wouldn't know either of them from Adam! But by her own account she was there, and we have no way of establishing whether or not Hugo was too. We can hardly ask him now, can we? Would it not seem more likely that such a disturbed young lady might be capable of anything, if she were disappointed in love yet again? Particularly when she was reeling from the death of a beloved brother? What if this young Fairley, like Capstick before him, simply did not requite her feelings- and she took it amiss?"

"Did you get all that down, Spencer?" said Commissioner McDonald. "Rather charmless stuff, but I think it ought to do the trick."

"Do you want anything on Pearce and Horrocks?" said Malthus.

"Let's leave it for now," said McDonald. "We've got all the Horrocks driving convictions. Clearly a reckless young idiot, with a good deal more money than sense! It would have been more surprising if he hadn't died on the road. It's the Capstick-Fairley connection that would give us the biggest headache, if anyone else looked at it."

"Which I trust they will not..." said Malthus.

"With Fairley having been killed here in Britain, that is," said Spencer. "We can't see anyone in law enforcement wanting to dispute the coroners' findings in Panama or Uganda."

Malthus glared at him.

"There is no need to labour the point, Spencer," he said. "But of rather more importance than Miss Newman's accusations are her present whereabouts. Have you managed to track her down yet?"

"Of course, sir," said Spencer. "She's travelling on a British passport- under her own name. She's in Colombia now."

Malthus cracked his knuckles.

"Like rats in a trap!" he said. "This could hardly have worked out better..."

"Sir?" said Spencer.

"That will be all for now- thank you, officers. File your report as I have outlined, and I will be in touch if I require anything more."

"Is Bezique here, sir?" said McDonald. "I'd like a word with him too, if I may. We're going to need a little extra contribution from the Club this month, to cover all these incidentals."

"I'm afraid Bezique is travelling on business," said Malthus. "With Florizel. I'm minding the shop now. They may be gone for quite some time."

CHAPTER 65

MAGDALENA PROVINCE, COLOMBIA

"Peace does not last long in this world," said Herrera, staring out into the perfect darkness through night-vision goggles. "That is why we cherish it. Days like today. The times we can remind ourselves what life is really about. Why it's worth fighting for."

"You seem to have found peace here, Commissioner," said Ben. "But who are you expecting now?"

"Sixteen men," said Herrera. "Moving in single file. The hacienda is designed to allow them only one approach. Or rather, no approach at all. Jairo Paisa is out there to make sure of that."

"The Club?" said Laura.

"It must be," said Herrera. "We knew this day would come. I suspect your adventure in the jungle has merely hastened it."

"Is *El Pishtaco* with them?" said Ben.

"Does that make a difference?" Herrera said.

"It changes the odds a bit, doesn't it?"

"We always knew we would be fighting for our lives. For survival," said Herrera. "So are you in, Makepeace?"

"Why not?" said Ben. "Let's just get tooled up and do this."

"You see?" said Herrera. "This is why I worry that you really are as bad as they are, Ben. That you actually want to die. There's a fine line between going undercover in a suicide club, and joining it for real, you know?"

"I'm tired of running away," said Makepeace. "From everything. If they're going to take me out, it may as well be here."

Herrera passed him an M4 assault carbine.

"Here! The Bushmaster is the impatient man's friend," he said. "Time to make yourself useful for once, Makepeace. Let's see if you can fight as well as you write insurance policies."

Ben checked and cocked the rifle.

"Do you know how to use one of these, Señorita Newman?" said Herrera. "This is not your quarrel, but you too have great losses to avenge."

"Give me a pistol," said Laura. "I'm all in. I'm not leaving till it's done."

Herrera nodded and handed her a side-arm.

"This is a SIG Sauer P226. The professional's weapon," he said. "You get twelve rounds per clip."

"Am I going to need them?" said Laura.

"Malthus is a formidable foe," said Herrera. "He has got the better of me at every turn so far, and we know that his men will fight to the death. But so will we, this time. There is nowhere left to retreat to."

"Where do you want us?" said Makepeace.

"Jairo Paisa and our best men are out in the bush already," said Herrera. "We will stay here to defend the Big House. As you have seen, our children are in there. Two hundred and twenty-four innocent souls. You know how much mercy we can expect from *El Odio* if they get in. Any of us."

"You said sixteen men?" said Ben.

"You don't like the odds?" said Herrera.

"It's not that," said Makepeace. "It's just that the Club normally favours smaller assault teams. One or two operators. Even for big jobs like the West African social cell. Killing with explosives, not fire-arms. It makes it easier to run the operation remotely, from London."

"So what are you trying to tell me, Ben?" said Herrera.

"I'm not sure," said Makepeace. "It just feels strange. Ops guys don't usually depart from what they know. And if you're not trained to fight as a platoon, it's a hell of a thing to learn on the job. In the dark."

"Keep thinking, soldier," said Herrera. "But in the meantime, get into the left-hand gatehouse with Señorita Newman. It's made of reinforced concrete, lined with Kevlar mesh. So unless they have some very big guns and SLAP ammunition, you should be fine. As long as you don't let anyone in."

"We won't open the door to strangers," said Laura.

"They're not really strangers though, are they?" said Herrera.

"Where will you be, *Señor Comisionado*?" said Ben.

"I'll be in the right-hand gatehouse," said Herrera. "There's a comms link between them, and out to Jairo Paisa's team in the field. I want to be there when you finally get taken out, Makepeace."

"Despair is power!" said Ben.

Herrera waved and stepped into his gatehouse.

"You two have quite a complex dynamic," said Laura. "I'd say locker room, but I think it's actually more prison yard."

"Get inside the Kevlar mesh, Newman," said Ben. "Let's give them hell. SIG Sauer means never having to say you're sorry."

"Aren't you going to tell me to save the last bullet for myself?" said Laura.

"No way," said Makepeace. "You fight for every last breath you get. What else is there?"

CHAPTER 66

ST JAMES'S, LONDON, UNITED KINGDOM / MAGDALENA PROVINCE, COLOMBIA

"Suicide Station, we have a visual on the target," said Bezique. "Preparing to make first contact."

"Roger that, Brother One," said Malthus, pulling on his Havana as he watched the thermal imaging camera feed on the monitor display. The control centre was already fogged with cigar smoke. "You know what to do. No gods, no masters! And more importantly, no survivors. No witnesses."

"None?" said Bezique.

"Do you think the Colombians will let any of you leave the country, after the massacre we're about to inflict on these Firestarter dogs?" said Malthus. "You would be hopelessly compromised. I would not do you, of all people, the dishonour of leaving you there to rot in a Medellín prison cell, my friend. You have earned a far more glorious death! To die with your boots on. Despair is power..."

Bezique lowered his head.

"They're coming..." said Herrera over the comms link. "The Hate is coming. Still moving in Indian file. Is everyone in position?"

"*Chévere*," said Jairo Paisa. "We're going silent. We'll see you on the other side, *parces… ¡Por La Nueva Raza- todo!*"

Ben and Laura watched the monitors on the wall of the gatehouse. Blackness.

"What are you thinking?" said Laura.

"The same thing I've thought every time I've been in this situation," said Makepeace.

"What's that?"

"Is it too late to run away?"

Laura laughed.

"And is it?"

"Yeah, far too late," said Ben. "It's O.K. Corral time right here… Ask me again in five minutes."

"Can I ask you something else?" said Laura.

"There's literally nowhere I can go."

"What happened to you in Central America?" she said. "What is that burden you carry everywhere with you?"

"Is it too late to run away now?" said Ben. He paused. "It happened after I left the Marines. I had spent a lot of time training up there, spoke the language. And so Lloyd's sent me back there- on an insurance job. Or so it seemed, back in London. Things got out of hand, quicker than I would have believed possible. The way they can do in Central America. Before I knew it, I was out of my depth, in a fucking warzone. And I guess I forgot that I wasn't in the Marines anymore. I tried to help some people, and in the end I just couldn't."

"And that hurt you?"

"It hurt them more, that's for sure," said Ben. "That's how it always seems to happen. The strong should protect the weak, but somehow they end up hurting them instead."

"And so is Herrera right?" she said. "Do you secretly hope for a way out? To leave those memories behind? The survivor's guilt?"

"Sometimes," he said. "But it doesn't feel that way right now."

"No," said Laura, resting her head on his shoulder. "Nor for me."

"Here they come…" said Herrera. "One last battle, Jairo. Now- bring the light!"

Suddenly the thermal imaging screen in the gatehouse went bright white.

"Look outside…" said Makepeace, peering through the arrow-slit window of the gatehouse. The night had exploded into brilliant, blinding colour.

"Flares launched," said Herrera. "The night of the fireflies… And now there's nowhere to hide, Señor Bezique. Everything is finally out in the open."

The bursting flares illuminated the natural bowl of lower ground in front of the hacienda, and the straggling line of gunmen stranded on the track in the depths of the basin. Then the silence was broken by the rasp and bark of automatic weapons fire. Jairo Paisa and his men spread out in a ring around the top of the depression, pouring rounds into the Club's men from above.

"Three brothers down…" said Bezique. "Johnson is hit! Make that four brothers. Repeat, four brothers down..."

"Just return fire, you fools!" said Malthus, relighting his Cuban cigar. "Live, die, but whatever you do, don't stop shooting! We must root them all out. Guns hot, Bezique!"

"Graham down…" said Bezique. "Wood is hit."

The startled Club men reeled around, dazzled by the blinding phosphorus light scrambling their night-vision devices. They poured rounds indiscriminately into the undergrowth, as Jairo Paisa's men picked out their targets from the rim of the basin.

"Now, Jairo!" said Herrera. "It's time for Ma Deuce to make her grand entrance."

"What's that?" said Laura.

"That's the big gun," said Makepeace. "Browning M2. This is going to be like shooting fish in a barrel…"

The night was torn apart as the heavy machine gun opened up from the cover of an outcrop of rocks above, following the bursts of fire from the Club men, scything them down with tracer rounds and then huge armour-piercing slugs, wherever they stood or fell.

"Sixteen lives. Just like that," said Laura. "When does it all end?"

A lone rifle spat resistance back towards the M2 nest. Now all of *La Nueva Raza*'s fire was concentrated on the muzzle flash from it.

"No gods, no masters!" shouted the last gunman, struggling to his feet and emptying his rifle into the void. Then the M2 caught him, the .50 Cal rounds literally ripping him apart. His body crumpled in the fading light of the flare and splashed into the pond. The blackness swallowed everything once more.

"They're all gone…" said Jairo Paisa. "Caiman bait. *¡Por La Nueva Raza- todo!*"

CHAPTER 67

MAGDALENA PROVINCE, COLOMBIA

Ben watched the insects dance around the light outside the gatehouse.

"They did it!" said Laura. "I can't believe they did it!" She put her arms around Ben's neck and kissed him. "We won! *¡Viva La Nueva Raza!*"

But Makepeace was looking over her shoulder.

"Look at the moths..." he said. "They're not flying straight. Why is that?"

Laura watched the plump white insects wobble through the air, fluttering in crazy detours towards the light.

"The wind?" she said.

"Something like that..." said Makepeace. "Listen!"

There was a roar of twin gas turbine engines, and then a wall of sound hit them, blasting the moths away in the blade-wash.

"Jesus Christ!" he said. "I recognise that rotor signature. But it can't be..."

"What is that, Makepeace?" said Herrera through the comms link.

"A Mil Mi-24 Hind..." said Ben. "The Devil's Chariot. But what the fuck is it doing here? Where could the Club get hold of kit like that?"

The Russian-built helicopter gunship arced back towards the hacienda, held its position for a moment, and then erupted into light as it launched a volley of white magnesium illumination flares from the flare dispensers mounted on its fuselage.

"That isn't good…" said Makepeace.

Then the YakB-12 rotary cannon mounted in the chin turret of the helicopter started to stitch its own tracer fire into the black satin of the night. The luminous trail of 12.7x108mm shells hunted out the M2 nest and its occupants, rounds the size of milk bottles throwing them up into the air, tearing them into pieces.

"They're going to be slaughtered out there!" said Laura.

The Hind banked and the four-barrelled cannon spewed another arc of fire down into *La Nueva Raza*'s positions. There was a scream, and then silence.

"Yeah…" said Ben. "And so will we, inside here. Those Yak rounds will open this place up like a fucking sardine can! Let's get out of here…"

They grabbed their weapons and scrambled out of the door of the gatehouse. Herrera stood at the gate of the hacienda, watching in silence as the helicopter picked off the *Nueva Raza* troopers outside.

Then there was a bellow of a rage from the ridge, and Makepeace saw Jairo Paisa in the dying light of the flares, levelling an RPG-7 launcher at the huge gunship.

"You know what to do, Jairo," whispered Makepeace. "Take it to the house…"

Now the helicopter pilot had spotted him too, and the murderous rotary cannon swivelled towards the doctor. But before it could open fire, Jairo Paisa launched the rocket-propelled grenade straight at the Hind. The warhead fizzed towards its target, bucking and rearing as the rocket motor powered it through the turbulent air around the helicopter, and hit it head-on, crashing into its right flank.

"Direct hit!" shouted Herrera.

Then the rocket glanced off the thick troop compartment armour and careered harmlessly past, exploding in the dead air beyond the gunship. The four barrels of the cannon rotated again, and the heavy rounds pitched Jairo Paisa up into the air and then sent him tumbling down into the basin.

"He's gone…" said Ben. "Come on, Herrera- we've got to evacuate the hacienda! We can't defend it now. They can level it, floor by floor, with those rocket launchers."

"It's too late for that, Makepeace," said Herrera. "It's coming back. He's trumped me again."

The three of them stood in silence as the helicopter wheeled back towards the hacienda and loomed over them. The under-nose turret lowered the gun towards them, like a spider poised to inject venom into its prey.

"Are you still ready to meet the Reaper?" said Herrera.

"He's a bit bigger than I expected," said Makepeace.

CHAPTER 68

MAGDALENA PROVINCE, COLOMBIA

There was a scream of feedback as the helicopter's PA system was turned up, the speakers wailing over the blade slap.

"People of *La Nueva Raza*!" said Bezique. "Firestarters. Open the gates and put down your weapons! Put down your weapons, or we will destroy the whole building. I repeat, open the gates and put down your weapons. I will not ask you again."

"Do it, Makepeace," said Herrera, laying down his rifle and activating the gate release mechanism on the side of the gatehouse. Ben looked at him.

"Are you sure, *Comisionado*?" he said. "This might be the last chance we get to fight it out..."

"Do it!" shouted Herrera.

Ben and Laura followed his lead, laying down their guns. They linked hands in silence as the Hind landed on the turning circle outside the gates, its external lighting system bathing the hacienda in an ethereal glow. The downwash buffeted them, blasting grit into their faces. At close range the Russian helicopter gunship was even more intimidating, the bullet-proof glass of the pilot canopies bulging like grotesque insect eyes.

"So what do we do now?" said Ben.

"We negotiate," said Herrera. "What else can we do? We promise anything and everything we can. At all costs, the Hacienda de La Luz must survive. That is the only thing that matters now. There's money in the gatehouse- a suitcase full of dollars. If they kill me, offer it to them. Improvise, Ben. Never stop trying! Stay alive for every last moment you can. And tell the world about us!"

"This is madness..." said Laura.

"Then at least it is our madness," said Herrera. "Our own way. Not the way of *El Odio*."

The cabin door of the rear troop-utility compartment dropped open, and four armed men stepped out. The last pair carried a huge metal ammunition case between them.

"I'm not sure they want to negotiate..." said Ben.

The first man walked straight towards them. He produced a cigar from his jacket pocket, and Florizel hurried up behind him to light it, the flame of the lighter dancing in the rotor wash.

"It cost me a small fortune to persuade the Peruvian Air Force to lend me this little toy!" Bezique said, gesturing back at the helicopter. "I had to bring it all the way from La Joya air base, in Arequipa. And then pay another fortune to the Colombian Army, to bring it across the border. But I think you'll agree that it was worth every *peso*? The Hind is a natural born killer. Once it scourged the *mujahideen* of Afghanistan- and now it has scourged *La Nueva Raza*!"

"Do they know how you look after your assets?" said Ben. "I hope they took a deposit."

Bezique ground the cigar out in front of Makepeace.

"The Club always pays its debts, Brother," he said. "And it always pays off its scores."

"Good to see you too, Bezique," said Ben. "You know *Comisionado* Herrera already, I believe?"

"Only by reputation," said Bezique, bowing to Herrera. "And I fully expect that it will be a short acquaintance."

Herrera inclined his head.

"We are all living on borrowed time now," he said. "So what is it you want, Señor Bezique?" he said. "There must be a way for us to coexist. There is always a way. We too have influence- information about Project Light International. Money..."

Bezique nodded.

"Florizel?" he said.

In one fluid movement, Florizel drew his Beretta, levelled it at Herrera and sent two 9mm bullets through his head. Ben caught Herrera's body as he slumped lifeless to the ground. He lowered him down and closed his eyelids.

"*Descansa en paz, Señor Comisionado...*" Makepeace whispered. "Rest in peace."

"That is how we can coexist!" said Bezique, spitting on Herrera's body. "We and all of your kind. And as for you, Makepeace... You seem to have gone native out here distressingly fast."

"We're a long way from St James's now, Dorothy," said Ben.

"Malthus will be most disappointed in his protégé," said Bezique. "But you know what they say in Colombia? Raise crows, and they'll peck your eyes out."

"Oh, I don't think Trevor will be too surprised," said Ben. "He wanted a crow. Doves are not much use in the Club's line of work. Besides, he's played us all, hasn't he? I'm not even sure which club is the real one anymore. I guess there's a fine line between an oil club and a doomsday cult."

"He has played you!" said Bezique. "He has used you to infiltrate this nest of vipers. To lead us into the heart of *La Nueva Raza*. The genius of the man! But that is you. Me, he has saved!"

"It seems to me that all he's saved here is the fossil fuel industry," said Ben. "Everyone else is dead- or dying."

"And made billions of dollars for himself!" said Laura. "Did you know about the North Sea Oil Club, Bezique?"

"Of course I did!" said Bezique. "Who do you think recruited that naïve fool, Strontian? And ran the operation in Scotland? It was all orchestrated from Suicide Station. Malthus was just my eyes on the ground, following my directions."

"But did you never wonder how Malthus had come to be Chairman of the Oil Club?" said Ben. "What he did there in Lloyd's all day, before he came to drink fine wine and watch the Game in the evening? The Billionaire Suicide Club was just a tool to protect his empire. A private army that paid for itself! He couldn't believe his luck when he stumbled upon it. In his world, the real billionaires don't die. The Game is rigged, Bezique."

"They're bluffing!" said Malthus through Bezique's earpiece. "It's pathetic. Kill them!"

"Why did you come here, Makepeace?" said Bezique. "You must have known that you would never leave alive."

"Because I wanted to know the truth," said Ben. "And now that I've seen it, it's too late to go back into the darkness. That's what Project Light is about! The *Nueva Raza* are building a better future for everyone. There's no conspiracy to overthrow humanity- there never was! Just new people, who can help to fix the world for the rest of us."

Florizel stared at him.

"But that doesn't suit everyone!" said Laura. "The system works just fine for Malthus and his billionaire friends. What do they care if there's a better way? They won't be here, and they want to take as much as they can with them when they go."

Bezique laughed.

"You've chosen the wrong audience for the Greta Thunberg routine, my dear!" he said. "Do you think you can dazzle me with a utopian future? I am already dead! I have been since Malthus first found me. I don't care why he led me to Death's private door- so long as it opens for me now."

"Bravo, Bezique," said Malthus. "Well said! Truly, nothing in life has become you like the leaving of it. But now the time for talk is over. No gods, no masters! You too must play your part."

Bezique turned to the two brothers behind him.

"De Mestre- O'Connor!" he said. "Set your charges."

Then he opened his own jacket to reveal the bandolier of explosives beneath.

"No gods, no masters!" he said. "*Vive la mort...*"

CHAPTER 69

MAGDALENA PROVINCE, COLOMBIA

De Mestre and O'Connor worked fast, laying wire-linked explosive charges all around the hacienda.

"Herrera's life's work will be destroyed, before his body is even cold…" said Bezique. "The exploding bridge-wire detonator set is really a little elaborate for a non-nuclear device. But then this is my life's work too, is it not?"

"An expanding plasma system would be more appropriate, don't you think?" said Ben.

"Bravo, Makepeace!" said Bezique. "At the end, I can see what Malthus saw in you. Do you have any last words?"

"Yeah- always keep a song in your heart," said Ben. "It's like karaoke for the voices in your head."

"Do you really think we're mad?" said Bezique. "After everything you've seen? What you learned out there in the jungle? In the darkness…"

"The *Nueva Raza* are right," said Ben. "The Club really is *El Odio*- your hate blinds you to what must come. You can never win! Even if you killed every last man, woman and child, more of them will be born. Evolution will find a way. Nature's best designs all win out in the end, Bezique. You're just King Canute, trying to hold back the tide."

"Florizel…" said Bezique. "I'm starting to weary of Mr Makepeace."

The steward was still staring at Ben.

"You believe that these people can survive?" Florizel said. "That they have a place in the world? Hateful freaks that they are?"

"They are how we will all be one day!" said Laura. "People who will not be struck down in their prime by heart disease. Who can harness the most powerful forces in nature. Who will find the way to save our planet from destroying itself! That's what Andrew Fairley taught me. We should celebrate them! Protect them."

"You really believe that?" said Florizel, then reeled back as Bezique struck him across the face, sending him tumbling down to the ground.

"I did not order you to speak, you dog!" said Bezique. "You forget yourself, steward. Compose yourself for death, and do not come between the dragon and his prey."

He held up the wires suspended from each side of his bandolier. "Now, at last, my work is done!"

"No!" shouted Florizel. He grabbed Bezique's hands by the wrists and prised them apart.

"You fool!" shouted Bezique, lashing out. "You can't stop me! De Mestre! O'Connor!"

The two Club men jumped down off the low roof of the hacienda's generator room and made back for the gates. But Makepeace was already moving, picking up Florizel's discarded Beretta and sending pistol rounds snapping into the thick adobe walls of the hacienda above their heads.

"Ben!" said Laura. "Look!"

As Bezique and Florizel wrestled with each other, a wisp of vapour crept out of the steward's shirt. The Bolivian's face was etched with pain, but he clung on to Bezique, twisting his arms around the bandolier as he strained to keep the wires in the president's hands apart. Now smoke was pouring off him, blinding Bezique.

"You!" hissed Bezique. "You're one of them! A Firestarter! A traitor in our midst…"

"That's why Herrera wanted to surrender!" said Laura. "He knew there was a chance of turning Florizel! He must have traced his genetic history… And he couldn't risk the helicopter firing on the hacienda."

"He never was a trusting man…" said Ben. "Lean back!" he shouted to Florizel, training the gun towards Bezique. "I can't get a clean shot away."

Florizel was writhing in agony as the flames took hold of his body, his clothes forming a burning shroud around him, but still he seized Bezique and held to him his chest.

"Let go of me!" said Bezique. "I command you! I'm burning! It can't end like this… Not like this!"

"Go!" shouted Florizel to Makepeace, his face streaked with tears. "Secure the explosives! Save the hacienda! I have him now! It's over for us…"

"No!" screamed Bezique. "This isn't over!" He was wreathed in flame now, the intense heat from Florizel's burning body incinerating him alive, the fat kindling up into an all-consuming torch. "It can't be!"

"Ben!" said Laura.

Makepeace looked round. De Mestre and O'Connor were standing behind them, but their weapons hung loose in their slings. They watched in shock as Bezique and Florizel burned together, the charges left unconnected.

"It is over…" said Ben, tossing his own gun away. "Bezique has finally found his peace."

"*¡Por La Nueva Raza- todo!*" shrieked Florizel, as he slumped down to the ground, arms still locked around his master.

"Suicide Station?" said De Mestre. "What do we do now? Bezique's gone…"

"This mission is blown," said Ben. "I'd suggest you get as far from here as you can, and try and forget any of this ever happened. You guys have somehow got a free pass. It's up to you what you do with it- just don't waste it this time."

"Who's in charge now, Makepeace?" said O'Connor. "Of the Club?"

"The same person who always was," said Ben. "Malthus. The Suicide King."

CHAPTER 70

EL DORADO INTERNATIONAL AIRPORT, SANTA FE DE BOGOTÁ, COLOMBIA

Laura leaned back in the plush leather seat of the Bombardier 500 private jet and sipped at her bourbon.

"We have to leave in the next fifteen minutes, *señorita*," said the pilot. "Or we'll lose the slot. No exceptions. This is a busy airport these days..."

"We're not leaving without him," Laura said. "I don't care what it costs me. We've been through far too much for that!"

The pilot shook her head and stepped back into the cockpit.

"Don't fail me now, Makepeace..." said Laura. "Don't fucking fail me now."

Then she felt a tap on her shoulder.

"Ben?" she said, wheeling round. She looked back, and straight down the barrel of an automatic pistol. El Pishtaco touched his finger to his lips.

The steps outside rattled and Makepeace climbed into the cabin, carrying a bottle of champagne.

"I got the passports," he said. "So let's get out of Dodge!"

El Pishtaco just touched the muzzle of the gun against the side of Laura's head by way of reply.

"It's a bit early for whisky, isn't it, Newman?" said Ben, sitting down at the table opposite Laura, careful not to make any sudden movements. "But then I see that you have a guest."

"I won't be staying long," said El Pishtaco.

"So you got some new contact lenses?" said Ben. "I preferred the old ones."

Without the piercing green eyes, lean face somehow padded out, El Pishtaco was almost unrecognisable. Only the sense of imminent danger surrounding him was the same.

"It seems that people have been looking for me," he said. "And I think that may have something to do with you two."

"So you came looking for us?" said Ben.

"You know why I'm here."

"I also know that Bezique is dead."

El Pishtaco shrugged his shoulders.

"Come on! *El presidente* is gone," said Ben. "The Club is out of business in Colombia."

"For now," said El Pishtaco. "No one knows what happened to Bezique, *blanco*. The Colombian Army is still digging. If they find him alive, there's a bounty on your head like *El Dorado*. I don't plan on leaving Colombia without it."

"If they could find him alive, how would we still be breathing?" said Laura. "His own man took him out- Florizel. He was one of *La Nueva Raza*! A Bolivian. We saw them burn together."

El Pishtaco inclined his head.

"So. Let's assume that's true," he said. "Bezique is dead. What does that change? I've come a long way to kill you. And I don't like Bogotá."

"I can understand that," said Ben. "Because this airport is crawling with DNI agents, and they're all looking for you."

"The DNI..." said El Pishtaco. "The famous Colombian secret police!

Just as effective as the DAS were before them- and no more honest. You know they used to stamp the passports too? That's what I love about this country."

"These guys must be from a different department then, *choche*," said Ben. "They didn't look like they had any stamps. Or an arrest warrant. Look at the roof of the terminal..."

A pair of DNI snipers were scanning the airport concourse through telescopic sights. At ground level, a Colombian police assault team fanned out around the private jet terminal. Makepeace whistled.

"*Compañía Jungla Antinarcóticos*," he said. "Crack troops. Headhunters! And I don't see any handcuffs..."

El Pishtaco smiled.

"No, I don't think they will want to arrest me," he said. "They are killers too- and they will kill me, if they can. But what about you? Your precious DNI aren't looking after you too well, are they, *gringo*? What did they promise you- passports, and a safe passage out of Colombia? You're going to get a bullet in the head, whoever wins."

"We're just the bait." Ben had already said it before he realised that it was true. "But it worked. So now there are two good reasons for keeping us alive."

"Human shields?" said El Pishtaco. "That's just the same reason twice. And it only works if the pigs want you alive."

"No," said Ben. "The first is that we have this plane, flying down to Uruguay and out of all this mess in five minutes."

"And the second is this..." said Laura.

She opened Herrera's suitcase from the Hacienda de La Luz. It was packed with neat bundles of used US currency. El Pishtaco picked one up and flicked through it.

"I could kill you and take it anyway," he said.

"Of course you could," said Makepeace. "You could make any gangster move you wanted. But what about the smart move? Where would you take it? It's time to make up your mind now. Any second now, those *Junglas* will burst in here, loaded for bear. And I'm guessing none of us will make it out alive."

El Pishtaco smiled again.

"Then you better get off my plane, *gringo*. Because I travel alone."

"Now wait just a minute," said Laura. "I chartered this plane, and I'm taking it out of here! This is our only way out too! The Club isn't just going to forget about us… We're dead if we stay here."

CHAPTER 71

AMAZON BASIN, BRAZIL

The Bombardier glided over the equatorial cloud line, a ghost plane in the realm of spirits. Now and again fleeting glimpses of green opened up below, windows into alternate realities, verdant possibilities left behind. The thread of life can be stronger than we could ever imagine, resilient enough to bend before it breaks, anchored to some primal refusal to let it go. But in the high places it can become taut and brittle, until it just- snaps.

The slender jet was ripped in two by the force of the explosion, tail sheering off and cabin fragmenting and splintering into shards as it tumbled down, down, down into the enveloping canopy of the jungle below. For a second the wreckage marred the perfect green carpet, and then it was swallowed up by it, a fly ingested by a great carnivorous plant and forgotten forever. The baggage it carried would never reach its destination now, doomed to roam the lines of history like a restless *Flying Dutchman*. Legends that would never be understood, penance that would never be done- demons that would never be exorcised.

CHAPTER 72

ST JAMES'S, LONDON, UNITED KINGDOM

"The ace of spades!" said Malthus. "The Black Spot... Old Frizzle didn't keep us waiting long tonight. And whatever setbacks we have endured, we are reborn each time we see him!"

Allan Whitby felt the world fall away from under his feet. It was too soon- whatever it was, it was too soon. He wondered again if this was really the only way out. Whether after all the opportunities he had been born with, all the inheritance he had squandered, all the second chances he had been given, this was the only road left to him. But now another million was gone- a million and a half, with the buy-ins for the Game- and he had to cut his losses at some point, for the family's sake. Perhaps for some, death really was the only stop-loss. The Death Card.

"I think Blue Curaçao is called for in the circumstances, Noel!" said Malthus.

"My name is Florizel, now, sir," said the steward.

"Of course!" said Malthus. "Legends never die."

"I took the liberty of decanting some earlier," said Florizel, offering round a tray of tulip-shaped glasses. "I fancied you might call for it, when I was typing up the mission dossier. Bols, of course."

"*Crème de Ciel*, we used to call it, in my old Monte Carlo days..." said Malthus. "Cream of the sky! And Mr Whitby just has time to toast the Club, before he leaves for his flight. Ian Simms will meet him at Biggin Hill. The Prodigal Son of the Club is returning to us. He came to realise that his position in Abu Dhabi had become- untenable, for his family's sake. For this thy brother Simms was dead, and is alive again; and was lost, and now is found!"

Allan seized a glass and tipped the Curaçao down his throat. The shock of the bitter orange liqueur somehow helped him collect his wits. He took another and held it upright.

"The Club!" he said.

"The Club forever!" said Malthus, draining his own tulip. "And its latest icon..."

He made a gesture to Florizel, who was standing beside a new portrait on the wall of the *salle de jeux*, covered with a red velvet curtain.

"Florizel's face may have changed, but his office remains the same," said Malthus, recharging his glass. "Death is the eternal, and the Club does not look back- or mourn. But we have lost another who is not so easy to replace. He was cut from a different cloth. He was my son, though he did not know it- for I sent him into the world with nothing, to learn despair for himself. And through that, he has become something more than that. Something greater. Where once he stood by my side, now he stands by the Reaper's! And those who undid him will be our blood offerings to both of them. If anyone tries to tell you that this Club is about money, remember this sacrifice! It is personal- it could not be more personal. And so now let us toast Charles Edward Malthus: Bezique! The Most Corrupt Rogue In Christendom!"

The new Florizel pulled back the red curtain, and Bezique's intense gaze seemed to bore out of the oil painting, deep into each member's soul, even from beyond the grave.

"Bezique!" the members toasted. "Together, we greet the Reaper!"

"As I have slain my own son, so I will slay each of you- and the seed of the Firestarters, one by one!" cried Malthus. "No gods, no masters! The Club forever!"

"The Suicide King!" chanted the Billionaire Suicide Club.

CHAPTER 73

CURAÇAO, NETHERLANDS ANTILLES, CARIBBEAN SEA

"When did you first know?" said Laura, pushing an unruly lock of hair out of reach of the evening breeze.

"I don't think you ever quite know, do you?" said Ben. "It's like a jumble of facts that finally start to form a pattern in your head, once they've rattled around there long enough. It was kind of strange that the DNI didn't even take a statement from us in Bogotá, don't you think? As though they weren't intending to investigate what happened at the hacienda…"

"I thought that," said Laura. "But then none of it seemed exactly- by the book."

"The DNI never cared about the Club- or *La Nueva Raza*," said Ben. "Herrera made sure of that. They wanted El Pishtaco badly though, dead or alive. And they got him. Colombia still has plenty of scar tissue from *La Violencia*. The scary thing is that the Club must be protected at a level far beyond anyone we've spoken to. Which is why…"

"This isn't over?" said Laura.

"Yes and no," said Ben. "The war is just getting started. But it's over for us. It has to be."

He handed her an envelope.

"What's this?" Laura said.

"Your new identity. Courtesy of the *Clan de La Nueva Raza*. The Colombians won't come looking for you now. It's the Club we have to worry about."

"And where do we go?" said Laura.

"It seems nice here!" said Ben. "Curaçao. And I always liked Aruba. St Maarten… Maybe mainland South America. It might be best to keep moving. Stay one step ahead of them. But don't tell me what you're planning."

"Why not?" said Laura.

"If I knew, I might be tempted to try and find you," he said. "And that can't happen."

"You mean?"

"You know I do," he said. "Nowhere is safe for us now- not together."

"Together…" said Laura. "Suddenly that seems the only thing that matters."

"You've lost a lot of people," said Ben. "More than anyone should lose in a lifetime. Your brother. Pearce, Walker, Horrocks. Even Capstick, I suppose. And then poor Andrew Fairley. I'm sorry. I could feel that you two had a- connection."

"We did!" said Laura. "I think he was the sweetest man I've ever met. But it was different from what we have- you and I. I wanted to protect him, his innocence- his naivety. It reminded me of Jules. And in spite of everything, I couldn't keep him safe either, I put him in danger. So I let him down too. It's like you said in Magdalena, Ben- the strong should protect the weak. And look at you, you're strong, you're a dog of war- like me! You don't need me to protect you from that. The problem for you is the peace. You need to find that inside you. So stay. Find it here."

"There is no peace," said Makepeace. "There's just waiting."

She kissed him long and hard, and then he set off along the Willemstad waterfront, a dark shadow against the brightly-painted colonial houses. In a few minutes he was lost in the milling tourists.

"Here's looking at you, kid," said Laura.

Then the peppery wind blew her hair across her face again, and she turned to walk back to the hotel.

Printed in Great Britain
by Amazon

42644441R00192